They Who Linger

Book One: The Everlight Saga

By Robert W Ling

They Who Linger

ISBN 978-1-7383118-0-4 (P.b.)
ISBN 978-1-7383118-2-8 (HC)
ISBN 978-1-7383118-1-1 (E-book)

First Edition: April 2024
10 9 8 7 6 5 4 3 2 1

https://robertlingauthor.wordpress.com

Books By Robert W Ling

The Everlight Saga

They Who Linger - Book One
In The Shadows - Book Two (coming soon)

To those who keep the dream alive,
And to those who wander but are not lost.
Keep going, don't ever stop.

They Who Linger

Book One: The Everlight Saga

By Robert W Ling

Chapter One

Vargus stood on the balcony of his stone carved dwelling overlooking the valley of Moonshadow. Dusk's last light sparkled off the surface of the river that snaked its way across the valley floor. Pine trees of a dark purple hue lined both sides of the river almost its entire length, starting at the base of the sheer stone face that marked the northern border of this shrouded place he had called home for many centuries. He knew it had not truly been so long, but time passed differently in this place than the world he had left behind so long ago to take up his current stead.

He ran his hands over his face and through his braided beard, the bronze rings decorating it clinking together lightly as his arms dropped to his sides and drew in a large breath of the fresh evening air. He exhaled with a loud sigh.

It was time to make his rounds.

He slapped one hand against the stone and metal railing, spun on his heels with exuberance and walked back inside. His sword hung in an ornate carved wood weapon rack on the wall next to the main door leading into the rest of the stone carved fortress. Not many of his fellow vigil men had come in from their guard yet, and he took advantage of the prolonged quiet to take in a simple meal of roasted chicken, potatoes and leeks in the mess hall. There was a hint of fresh citrus herbs in the meat, and he blessed the chef under his breath as he bowed his head momentarily.

The hall started to fill up halfway through his meal, his friends greeting him as they passed by on their way to the food line. It was a simple life, and not one of the men or women here would choose differently if they had the chance to do so again. It was an honor to serve the Vigil, and not entirely without its perks. Their families, if they had any when they joined, were well cared for after their departures. There was one catch, with the exception of a select few whom would recruit new soldiers when necessary, none could ever return to the world proper. It was a lifelong agreement to join the servitude of the Night Vigil.

Their charge was to stand guard against the darkness that remained sealed away in this place. Shadow touched creatures and beings of all kinds, powerful enough to destroy the world of Ierolden could be held in balance here, their power subdued. No one in the Night Vigil knew exactly how it worked, just that it did. It is a place wholly shaped by the Ancients themselves. A gift to the world of Ierolden after the war against the tides of darkness almost tore it apart completely. Soon after its construction, the forming of the Night Vigil, and the subsequent eternal imprisonment of all things dark and foul, the Ancients all but disappeared from the world, leaving the young races to live out their lives with free will and a bright future.

Vargus finished the last bite of his meal, set his wooden plate and mug in the wash bucket at the end of his table, and then unclipped a gold and leather bound book from the chain that secured it to his belt. He flipped the clasp open on the cover, set the book down on the table and began to read from the Vigil Texts that were routine to guard them from the darkness. It contained various daily prayers to start each watch or the day itself, recounting past deeds, and scriptures to guide them in their duties. If ever they felt the encroachment of darkness on their mind, or fear threatening to take root, they were to read from the book. The text of the day was short and simple, yet a stark reminder of the importance of alertness.

Pray not for deliverance from this watch,
Be strong in your duty,
Hold your light firm in grasp,
And tarry not in the night.
Be ever vigilant,
Lest you crumble to ash and ruin.

He followed it up by flipping a number of pages ahead to another entry. It was one of his own, from a life long ago.

Dusk is when darkness begins to creep out of the cracks of the earth, spilling the unseen across the land and through the air. All good things take to shelter and begin to slumber. Only those who must, brave the darkness with meager light sources, and never tarry long before seeking shelter and light again. The watchers have it the worst of all, for they are given no light to ward against the darkness, so that they can better see the things that move through the night, and if need be, warn of coming danger. Their tension does not ease until the break of dawn, when the sun begins to rise over the horizon once more, and its light burns the darkness away. The darkness recedes once more from whence it came, biding its time until the sun ends its watch, allowing darkness to return to the realm of men. Dare you stand guard against the encroachment of darkness? Have you no

fear? Do you carry the Everlight? We wait for the one who does, for we have feared the darkness far too long. Step out into the darkness and stand your vigil if it is so. Save us!
    ~Vargus the Old
    ~Head Watch of the Night Vigil - Ashen Bow Stronghold

It was a reminder that despite all the ages that had come and gone since the Vigil had sealed themselves away within the valley of Moonshadow, the threat to the realm of men was still very real. The Everlight remained hidden, extinguished for all he knew. If the beasts of the vale ever broke through the seal, Ierolden would be plunged into darkness beyond measure. It would be worse than the First Shadowfall.

He gently closed the book and clasped it shut, then clipped it to his belt on his right hip. He gave a nod to the men and women who had come in from their watch that now filled most of the seats in the mess hall, turned and exited toward the stairs down to the main entrance hall.

Many stone carved statues representing various founding members of their order festooned the empty spaces between the giant pillars of the long hall. A freshly polished granite floor reflected the candlelight from the hanging chandeliers, the light danced off the walls and the arched ceiling. Despite living within the heart of a mountain for the past thousand years or more, he couldn't rightly recall at the moment, the fortress was cozy and quaint. He would not go so far as to call it home, but it would suffice until his vigil came to an end.

Vargus walked along the hall toward the large stone carved doors that led out to the upper landing of Moonshadow Keep. As he approached, two of the guards standing watch pulled a series of levers in sequence and the hidden gears that swung the doors ajar clicked and clanged somewhere within the thick stone walls. A marvel of Dwarven engineering. The moon's light shone through the widening crack between the doors, and the view of the valley was revealed. He gave the guards a nod and silently stepped out into the night.

Silver light danced off the water of the river that wound through the middle of the valley. It still amazed him that a place that was a prison for such evil things as were held within the various enchanted prison networks of the mountains along either side of the valley, could have such a beautiful view. It was only betrayed by the hundreds of carved stone arches that lined the base of the mountain ranges, and the watchtowers that stood all along the valley's length next to the river. Dozens of stone bridges spanned the waters, and a network of paths wove between the trees connecting to each other. Vargus could see a number of patrols walking the paths between the watchtowers and over the bridges from one prison entrance to another as they routinely did.

The sun never directly shone in Moonshadow, and for that matter, they never saw anything but a darkened sky with the exception of the moon. It was a unique place. Both connected and disconnected from Ierolden itself.

He stood at the railing of the upper landing while the doors closed behind him, waiting for the seals to click back into place before he began the descent into the valley where he would begin his inspection of every purity seal that was in place on each of the prison networks.

It was his duty as one of the few Ancients within the valley, to maintain the purity seals, and make new ones as the evil inevitably grew in strength as they slumbered in their stone prisons.

Lately he had been erecting new seals at an increased rate, and he knew that the Second Shadowfall was soon coming. There was no stopping it without the Everlight. It had been foretold, and in some way he welcomed it. The Volskaia would be forced into action, and whatever world remained after the carving would bring with it a new way of life, something fresh. Many would die, and that saddened him, but there would be no sense in dwelling on it without the ability to prevent it. All he could do was maintain the seals for as long as possible, and hope that somehow the Everlight would be found.

The first twenty or so prison networks were as they always were, silent and intact. Unchanged. He was crossing one of the stone bridges to the opposite side of the valley when he noticed that the watchtowers in front of the next prison were silent and without motion. As he got closer, he could see a dark spot on one side of the entrance. A hole in the stone. Cracks spider-webbed out from it in all directions across the stone door. He rushed forward and planted his hand on the stone's surface, and quickly muttered a prayer. His hand lit up with a white glow, and when he looked again at its surface, the seal was revealed to him. It was failing. The hairs on the back of his neck stood on end as he realized that something had already escaped from the prison. He looked up at the watchtower to his left, just as a shadowy figure rose from within and turned its attention to him. It held a dead guardsman by the neck, where it had been feeding. Calmly, the figure discarded the body over the side of the watchtower. Red eyes glowed in the night, and a deep, chalky voice filled his mind.

"Hello Vargus, I've been waiting for you," greeted the figure.

"Shem," replied Vargus, instantly recognizing the voice. "How-"

"You became complacent. Your routine, predictable. You didn't even notice the slow spread of corruption from within, weakening your seals."

"You are alone, and you face a Light Master. What do you think will come of this?"

Shem tilted his head to the left slowly and cackled. He crouched and leapt from the tower, landing on the ground in front of Vargus. Shem stood up, and began to grow in size. His slender figure became a behemoth, and shadowy horns grew from his forehead. A tail quickly grew from his backside, much like that of a scorpion, and a fog of darkness slithered off his skin. He stretched and sighed. When he looked down at Vargus, his eyes flared with hate.

"You, too, are alone. And you forget, I am not merely another demon of the dark. I am Shem, father of the Shadow Touched, and as I said, I have been waiting for you. For a long time indeed. You see-"

Vargus reacted, his mind racing to retrace every time he had visited this prison. He uttered a scripture and a shield of light burst into existence in each of his hands. His body became enveloped in golden armor, his red cape billowing out behind him as a glimmering field of light shot out from him.

Shem reeled back from the burst of light, raising his arms to ward it off.

Vargus leaped forward and began slamming both shields into Shem's legs and torso, wailing on him relentlessly.

Shem screamed as the shields burned gashes in his flesh, sizzling with each impact. He braced himself with his new tail and kicked out with his left leg. His foot, now the same size as Vargus, sent the Ancient sailing through the dark toward the river.

"Not this time," bellowed Shem. He jumped into the night sky, trailing after Vargus. Dark leathery wings erupted from his jagged spine, and he flapped them twice to gain more height, then dove after Vargus.

Vargus, unable to change his trajectory, raised both shields in front of him as he flew backward through the air. He hit the surface of the river, and the cold, frigged water stole his breath away. Before he could breach the surface, a giant shadow filled his vision, and Shem collided with him, driving him to the bottom of the river.

A giant hand gripped his body, pinning him in the mud. He could feel himself being pushed deeper and deeper into the silty bottom. His shields prevented Shem from doing much more than pushing him, but if he could not fight free, he would drown. He closed his eyes and calmed himself, then recited the prayer of Everlight.

Be gone the night,
Make darkness take flight,
And all its dark children with it.

Bathe me in light,
Give me sight,
And purity to combat against it.

Lift me from the shadows,
Protect me from despair,
And give me the strength to endure.

He felt his skin tingle, and felt Shem's grip lift. His body was aglow, his armor emanating bright light. He righted himself and kicked hard off the muddy bottom of the river. He shot out of the water up into the night sky, arching toward the shore. He landed and rolled across the ground, gulping in air.

Shem was floating above the river, groaning in pain. His hand burned with golden light, tendrils spreading through his veins up his arm. Before it could spread too far, he whisked his tail around in front of him and brought its sharp tip down on his forearm, severing it in one clean blow. He bared his teeth and roared.

"You'll pay for that Light Bringer," bellowed Shem. He leaned forward, wings flapping, and shot toward Vargus.

Vargus got to his feet, his back to Shem, and as he turned, felt a sharp stabbing pain rip through his side. His shields fell from his hands, bounced once off the ground and dissipated into golden mist.

Shem's face filled his vision, one giant red eye inches from his own, filled with delight.

"Welcome to the family Vargus," said Shem and quietly chuckled. He lifted Vargus up in front of him with his tail as he stood up to his full height, now towering fifty feet off the ground. He tilted his head to the night sky, stretched out his wings and let out a bellow that shook the valley. Torches lit the night, and bells rang out their warnings, but it was far too late.

Vargus could feel the light bleeding out of him, and the darkness infecting his veins. His mind became filled with rage and hate as dark thoughts took root, replacing an eternity of pure life. He could also feel the seals he had held vigil over for so long, breaking one by one.

With his victory over Vargus complete, Shem lowered him to the ground and let his tail spike slide free of his side. He spit on the wound and watched it sizzle as it sealed the corrupted flesh.

He then turned his attention toward the fortress that was now the only thing in his way to freedom from the eternal prison.

Chapter Two

How many times had he attempted to put ink to paper in the past year?

'Many,' he thought as he tried to settle on a number. None seemed to do the enormity of his plight as a writer any justice.

Festus stared blankly at the blank sheet of hand pressed paper in front of him, nestled comfortably in the holding groove of his writing desk. He grew increasingly agitated by his own thunderous silence.

After what seemed like an eternity, he fluttered his quill between his fingers rapidly, before slamming it back into the inkwell's mouth. It made a *clinking* noise as it struck against the clay stem, and the desk shook, threatening to topple the inkwell over onto the blank paper.

"At least something would make it to the page," he blurted defiantly as he reached out to steady the inkwell.

The iron banded, wooden door to his private study creaked open on neglected hinges behind him and a soft voice greeted him before he had turned around to see who was breaking the most sacred rule in all the library.

"Is everything alright in here? Do you need me to bring you a fresh cup of Javium to calm your nerves," asked the young attendant? She folded her hands in front of her, a calm expression on her face.

"No, I'm fine. That's entirely unnecessary-" he cut himself off and changed his mind. "Actually, yes, do that. Would you?"

"Certainly," replied the girl. She bowed respectfully, turned and exited as quickly as she had appeared.

This would be his third cup of the bitter drink, but he enjoyed the flavor, and the warmth of it as it worked through his body, delivering a surge of energy while calming nerves and muscles alike.

He usually drank his with a healthy portion of boiled milk if there was enough to go around. The library didn't have a lot of livestock in its stables and fields, but they tried to keep some chickens and dairy cows when they could.

The girl returned a short time later, a metal serving tray in her hands, preceded by the delightful aroma of Javium.

To his delight, more so than he had realized it would be, the kitchen had extra milk that day, and the steward, remembering his preference, had them prepare a small cup to mix in with his Javium.

Festus thanked her profusely and took a long sip, holding the brown glazed porcelain mug by its handle and resting the other side of its rim against his index finger of the opposite hand.

He closed his eyes as he sipped, and breathed in its sweet and sour aroma. It had a lovely hint of nuts and fresh turned soil, and a hint of cinnamon. He sighed with delight and opened his eyes, feeling his body relax already. He hadn't realized how strained his neck muscles had become.

The steward was smiling at him as he made eye contact with her, and she had a glow in her cheeks.

"Better," she asked genuinely?

"Much, thank you my dear."

He lowered himself into a cushioned reading chair nestled in one of the corners between two bookshelves, and a side table with a glow orb stand on it. He set his mug on the table and began sifting through one of many stacks of books piled along the back edge of the table, up against the wall; the spines facing out toward the room.

It wasn't until he had picked a book to read and opened its cover that he realized the steward was still standing in the middle of the room near the large, intricately carved wooden table where she had put down her serving tray. She was still smiling as she watched him. He gently closed the book's cover and set it in his lap as he began to ask her what he could do for her, slightly irritated. It was at that moment that he realized he didn't know her name.

Festus flushed slightly at his own ignorance. This nice young woman had been aiding him for almost eight seasons and he couldn't recall a full conversation with her.

"My deepest apologies young lady, but I fear my mind has neglected the normal courtesies of regular interaction. What is your name," he asked and folded his hands together, resting them atop the book in his lap.

"Maddi, with an 'I'," she replied with a look of surprise. "At least that's what they have called me since I arrived here at the Library."

Festus wondered at that for a moment. He knew some stewards were brought to the library from orphanages and the like, but he had an inkling her story was much different.

"It's evident to me that productivity is fleeting at best today, and I could do with some conversation. Would you care to join me for a spell," he asked? He hoped she would politely decline and be on her way.

Maddi's smile melted into hysterics as she gave him a toothy grin and replied very excitedly, "Yes! Absolutely, I would love to!"

Festus couldn't help but smile and chuckle. "How old are you Maddi, if you don't mind my asking?"

"Oh, I don't mind at all. I'm fourteen, or so I'm told. I don't know exactly. The Steward Mother says that's her best guess."

"You don't recall your birthday?"

"No."

"I'm sorry for that."

"It's okay. It's just another day anyways."

Festus laughed raucously. "If only more people had your outlook child. Alright, pour yourself a cup of Javium and pull up a seat."

Maddi did just that, a toothy grin on her face all the while.

"What would you like to talk about Maddi," asked Festus?

"Well," she said and thought for a moment. "I've always been curious how I could become a renowned chronicler like you."

"Oh," exclaimed Festus, surprised! "Well, I assure you, I did not set out to be renowned. I merely had a lucky turn of fate when I stumbled into the chance to record the events that took place during the Dark Wash."

"Yeah, but, you could teach me right?"

Festus sat in stunned silence for a while.

"I suppose. I've never really thought about taking on an apprentice. It's been done in the past by others, and surely makes sense. I've just, well, never had the time or the right pupil."

"What's a pupil," asked Maddi, scrunching up her face?

"Oh dear. We have a ways to go then. A pupil is a student of a sort," replied Festus with a smile.

"That's me!"

"Indeed."

"So you will teach me then?"

"Well, I'll have to talk to the Steward Mother and work out the details but I don't see any harm in it. Perhaps it will do us both some good."

Maddi jumped out of her seat and danced excitedly, then quickly hugged Festus.

Festus hugged her in return then asked her to take her seat again.

"Don't thank me just now, she hasn't said yes yet," said Festus.

"Even if she says no, I'll still want to learn. Is there anything I can do to start right now," asked Maddi? She vibrated in her chair with uncontrollable excitement.

"Well, first thing is first, do you know how to read and write?"

"I do," she exclaimed!

"Good. That's good."

"Next, you'll need some paper, a quill, and some ink. Oh, and a place to sit and write."

"I don't have any of those things."

"Hmm, maybe we can solve that here. I don't seem to be getting much use of mine lately, so, let's start by setting a time each day that you can sit at the big table in the middle of the room there, and practice chronicling the tales I read for you. At the end of it, you will have learned the art of listening and recording, and I will have another copy of a book that we can send off to one of the other libraries. How does that sound?"

"FANTASTIC," shouted Maddi, unable to control her excitement anymore!

Festus laughed heartily.

"Ok then, let's say just after breakfast until just before lunch each day until the tale is told in full. Deal?"

"Deal!"

"Alright then, apprentice Maddi, I will work out the details with the Steward Mother before tomorrow."

"Yay," she shouted as she jumped from her chair, gathered up the now empty cups and her tray and made for the door.

"And Maddi," called Festus after her.

She stopped at the door.

"Thank you for the warm milk to go with the Javium."

She smiled and giggled then left the room, closing the door behind her with a dull thud.

Festus shook his head, smiled, and began digging through his books to pick out the right volume to begin with for Maddi's first lesson. He ran his fingers along the engraved spines as he read them aloud.

"The Formation, no. The First Age, no. The First Shadowfall. That could be fun, but no. Descent of the Light Bearers. Tempting. War of Shadows, too dark for one of her age."

This continued for some time before he decided. He pried the dusty tome free from the stack, blew the grime from its cover and gently set it on the table in the center of the room. He opened the cover gingerly and caressed his fingers across the first few pages as he recalled his time with the narrators. It felt like so long ago, another world even. He missed them all dearly.

"Ahh, The Fourth Age. Yes, you will do just right for this task," he said absently, then sat and began to read, not to refresh his memory, but out of respect and reverence. It had been a long time since he had thought about the events laid down in the tome, and he wished at that moment, he could see his old friends once again.

Chapter Three

It had taken little convincing for the Steward Mother to agree to Maddi's apprenticeship, and as it turned out, she was glad to have some help with her. It seemed she was not so good at any of her other tasks, choosing to spend as much time in the study wing of the library as she could.

Festus was not at all surprised to see Maddi waiting in the hall outside his study with a tray containing a pot of Javium and two cups when he arrived from his breakfast the next morning. She was aglow with joy, and it was infectious.

"Good morning Maddi, I hope you slept well," greeted Festus.

"I didn't sleep much actually, I was too excited. At least that's what the steward mother said," she replied.

"I suppose that's to be expected at your age. Shall we begin? Here, let me take that," said Festus, taking the tray from Maddi.

He set the tray down on the table and ushered her to take a seat at the end of the table near the door. He had placed a small stack of paper, an ink well, and a quill there in preparation. He took his own seat near the middle where he had opened The Fourth Age the day before. He poured some Javium into each of the two cups, passed one to Maddi, then picked up his own and took a sip.

"Are you ready to begin," asked Festus with a glance over at Maddi?

"Oh yes, Mr. Festus, definitely," she replied.

"Alright then. Let's start with The Fourth Age. Have you read or heard the chronicle told before?"

"No. My parents never owned any books, and there was no library in or near my village."

"Not even from a traveling bard?"

"Never seen a bard."

"Truly?"

She shook her head.

Festus shook his head in surprise. "A shame that." He picked the book up off the table and set it in his lap, flipped to the first page, then looked up at Maddi.

"Let's go over a few things before we start. First, try to keep your questions to a minimum. The art of chronicling is about listening and transcribing the narrator's story, not prodding for details. That's not to say you should never ask questions to make the details clear. You'll understand better in time when the right time is to ask or not. Secondly, there are two things that every story has in common. They all have a beginning, and they all have an end. This story is no different in that respect, but where it differs, is the truth of it. It seems like it should be purely out of a story book, but I assure you it is not. Everything I chronicled within this book really happened," said Festus as he patted the book in his lap.

Maddi nodded.

"Lastly, we will go until either our time is up or your hand becomes cramped, or your mind wanders. Writing takes effort. Many people forget that. Clear?"

Maddi nodded again.

"Well, then let us begin. Remember to dip your quill when the ink starts to run thin, and hold up your hand if I'm going too fast. It will be slow at first, but that's okay. You'll get faster in time, and before you know it, you won't even be looking at the page as you write anymore."

"Really," asked Maddi excitedly? "People can do that?"

"Not everyone. It takes a lot of practice," replied Festus with a smile. "Okay, dip your quill and let's begin."

Maddi did as she was instructed and Festus took another sip of his Javium to wet his throat.

Chapter Four

Standing more than two thousand feet high, the Great Tree has been a marvel to all those that set eyes on it for centuries. It has stood against a sheer rock face that juts many hundreds of feet into the sky for as long as anyone can remember. The oldest texts in the oldest library in the entirety of the O'Marah kingdom even make reference to it.

All who wander here want to see it. It is sacred; precious. Not a single other tree like it exists in the known world, and it is widely regarded as the father of all trees. Its leaves are plentiful. Composed of all shapes, sizes and colors. Its bark is all shades of brown mixing together. Its pitch shimmers and glows a golden hue beneath the bark's surface, this is only known because of the little bit of pitch that seeps from its leaves periodically during the turning of seasons, causing it to light up like a constellation of stars for one night at the start of each season.

It has never shed a leaf or a flake of bark.

No one knows where the tree comes from or how it came to be the towering nature sentinel against a sheer rock face that looks like it was once a mountain which was then cleaved in half at its highest point, the missing half then used to sculpt the landscape of the O'Marah kingdom itself.

It is impervious to blades of all kinds and fire alike. It has survived numerous wildfires without so much as a scorch mark on its bark.

During rainstorms, the Great Tree hums as if singing, and provides branches aplenty for shelter from the storms and nesting space for all breeds of birds from across all of Ireolden. It's as if the Great Tree's humming is a sort of siren's call to them, beckoning them to the safety of its bows. The lower branches are so thick and rich with leaves that it is impossible to climb any further than the first of its branches which are more than a hundred feet off the ground and the span of a house.

The ground around the tree is pristine. Lush with a plethora of foliage and is as impervious to destructive intent as the tree itself.

One legend claims that there is a tomb deep beneath the tree, in the tangle of its roots, and within lies the remains of the First Watcher. Encased in a tomb woven from the roots of the tree itself. Etched on the stones embedded in the hardened earth walls, is the Watcher's recorded history of Ierolden and the events that led to the planting of the first Great Tree, or so it is said. Some say the legend is just that. Others claim it as truth, the verbal history of a world lost to the sands of time, before the realm of men. Those that believe the tales, also believe that the First Watcher is not truly dead, but rather dormant. That he or she will rise again, during Ierolden's darkest hour. When we need the Watcher most.

Another story of the Great Tree, is that the First Watcher's knowledge flows through the pitch of the Great Tree, and that if one is to be present during a turning of the seasons and is blessed with the droppings from the leaves, that they will be blessed with the Watcher's wisdom and memories.

Lastly, and most far-fetched, is that if one is open minded and listens closely, they will hear the First Watcher speak through the Great Tree as it hums during rain storms.

Ingvar recalled the legends and theories about the Great Tree every time he made the long walk from Melar. There was plenty of time to let his mind wander as it was a multi-day journey and his favorite escape destination. He rarely saw other people on his trips, which was part of the appeal. He passed into the clearing surrounding the Great Tree, paused and breathed in deep. The air was always so fresh and crisp in the clearing around the tree. All the chaos in his mind dissipated like voices on a dying wind when he crossed that barrier between his realm and this place. It was a realm unto itself. The clearing never ceased to make him dumbfounded, no matter how many times he saw it.

He hated his job. He was conscripted into the militia against his will when he was in his early teens. Looking back he knew there really was no other option, being an orphan of simple farming folk that worked the King's farmlands. He had nowhere else to go when they passed on. He learned quickly as he trained and rose through the ranks. It appeared he had a natural talent for the work, despite his hatred of it. He often dreamed of what he would do if he ever had the chance to abscond from his duties for good, but nothing ever seemed to stick long enough in his mind to drive him to finally sneak off in the middle of the night.

Ingvar drew one hand across the top of the long grass lining the path as he walked into the clearing, the moss beneath his feet seemed to recede as opposed to squishing beneath his weight as he passed over it on his way to the base of the tree. This was his favorite place to visit. It eased his mind to lay beneath the bows of the Great Tree and dream of other places. He was sure it was the only thing that really kept him where he was. The sun was out and the many birds above flitted and sang their songs as he lay down on the soft earth at the base of the tree. He yelped and dug what he expected to be a large pebble out of the moss beneath him, but what he pulled from the moss instead, surprised him. It was a ball of translucent amber the color of sunlight and half the size of his palm. He gently rolled it around in his hand as he held it up to catch the sun. He was in awe. Smiling from ear to ear, he put the amber orb in his pack and laid back against the trunk of the tree. It had been a long, non-stop journey from Melar to make the most of his time off duty and his eyelids were heavy.

The meadow glowed with a rainbow of colors as the sunlight bathed its entirety. Before long, he had dozed off.

~*~

The peace and tranquility did not last. It was shattered by an echoing boom, followed by a shrill howl similar to a gust of wind racing down a chimney only much, much louder. He covered his ears as he jolted awake and jumped to his feet. He looked all around the clearing. It was dark. Was it night time already? Had he really slept all day? The sound reverberated in his chest as he looked around the base of the tree, but could see nothing. He raced around the trunk of the tree for a while but still couldn't find the source of the agonizing sound. Hindered by darkness and a growing sense of unease, Ingvar retrieved his pack and made to leave the clearing. Another wave of sound doubled him over in agony. He clasped his hands over his ears, to no avail. He screamed until his jaw felt like it would part from his face, and his throat was raw. As quickly as it began, it was over. Silence and calm once again filled the clearing. He caught a glimmer in the bark of the Great Tree out of the corner of his eye as he retrieved his bag and turned to run to the tree line. He blinked and it was gone. A quick, dim flash of light cut through his vision as he stared at the trunk of the tree where he thought he had seen the glimmer, and suddenly there it was again, only this time it was bigger. It vanished as quickly as it appeared, then again a flash of light, this time brighter, and the glimmer bigger yet again. He thought himself entirely mad until gusting wind slammed into the meadow like it had somehow come to life and had come to wage war. His feeling of peace and tranquility were replaced with sheer terror. He turned and ran as fast as he could, his arms falling to swing at his sides as he sprinted for the tree line, not caring about the sound deafening him.

His head began to pound painfully, and nausea threatened to double him over. He was halfway across the clearing when his whole body began to ache. Every bone felt like it was vibrating, every muscle like it was tearing from his body. Fifty feet to go. Ingvar's vision blurred and he screamed in pain. He knew he was racing against certain death, so he pushed his body to the brink. He all but leaped over the fringe of the clearing onto the worn dirt path leading back to town through the forest. As soon as he crossed the threshold between his world and the Great Tree's domain he collapsed, completely exhausted. The pain was gone instantly, like it had never been. If not for the sweat soaking his clothing and the severity of his exhaustion he would not have believed what he had just experienced was real. He looked back into the meadow as he sat on the dirt path recovering, and what he saw horrified him more than anything ever had in his whole life. Dark, smoky, clouds billowed around the base of the Great Tree and lightning flickered and danced from the center of a vortex that now swirled where he had seen the glimmer, and as he looked on, a single giant leaf fell to the ground, shriveled.

The Great Tree was dying.

Chapter Five

Ingvar ran all night through the forest back to Melar, pausing no longer than to drink from his water skin when his body threatened to give up on him if he did not. He hadn't looked back. He couldn't believe what he saw was real. He wouldn't believe it. He thought there had to be an explanation. Perhaps he was coming down with a fever, or some sickness. He needed to see the healer immediately. Maybe even a priest.

He was delirious with fright when he crested the mountain path that led to Melar's main gate. The guards recognized him immediately and shouted greetings to their friend and started hurling joking insults his way at his apparent state of exhaustion when they realized something was wrong. Ingvar barely acknowledged they were there. He stumbled past them through the gate. Without so much as a look back, he raced up the snow covered street toward the healer's house, shouting the old man's name at the top of his lungs.

Fahstad swung his door open, his salt and pepper hair and long beard in disarray. He wrapped a wool cloak tightly around his lanky body and stepped out into the street to see what all the commotion was about. He barely got the door ajar when Ingvar rushed into his home and shouted for him to close the door and follow. The healer waved off the guards from the front gate who had arrived hot on Ingvar's heels to see what had gotten into their friend.

"I will tend to your friend, return to your watch," said Fahstad. He watched them go before retreating through the door, latching it behind him.

Ingvar had wrapped himself in a blanket and taken perch by the fire which was now crackling and popping, having been fed fresh logs. The healer sat slowly in his chair across from the fireplace near the one window in the tiny home that looked out into the street. He glanced once out the window to ensure the guards had returned to their duties before turning his full attention to his patient.

"Tell me, Ingvar, what has you troubled so?"

Ingvar explained all that had transpired. Fahstad made some tea from various herbs and encouraged Ingvar to drink until the cup was empty.

Fahstad scribbled in his journal throughout the day as he kept watch over Ingvar, his wrinkled face distorted with worry.

~*~

Ingvar's dreams rocked him violently in his sleep. Giant beasts made of shadow chased him relentlessly through the forest, shattering trees in their wake. They howled with rage and tore up the ground between them and their prey.

The beasts chortled with anticipation as they rapidly closed the distance between them and their quarry. They were gaining on him quickly and were right on his heels within seconds of the chase beginning, although it felt like a lifetime of running.

Every hair on his neck stood on end, and his heart pounded in his throat. He was chilled to the bone by the icy grip of fear. Darkness washed over everything around him and he pushed himself even harder. His muscles screamed for release from the burning agony of relentless abuse. The darkness devoured the light like a tidal wave would a boat that failed to sail clear of its path.

Small stones rose off the path and spun out of his way as he ran through them, gravity seeming to lose its control over the world. His footfalls became lighter and lighter, until his feet no longer touched the ground and he spun forward, tumbling through the air as he began to float away into nothingness.

He wailed in agony as something slammed into his back, stopping his spinning and holding him in place. He tore at his chest with his hands as he frantically tried to stop the black clawed appendage that was now present there from pushing any further through his torso. The creature grabbed hold of his hands and squeezed hard, the joints popped and bones cracked.

The last thing that he remembered before he gave in to pure darkness, was a chorus of guttural, maniacal laughter that left a chill in his soul even after he bolted awake gasping for air. He screamed and clawed at the air in front the fireplace before realizing it was a dream, then, exhausted, fell back into a deep slumber.

Chapter Six

Ingvar shifted his weight and paced around in a small circle in his watchtower, rubbing his hands together to warm them up. It had been half a moon cycle since his ordeal at the Great Tree, and he did not yet feel himself. He still wasn't sure if what he experienced was real or a dream of some sort. A cold wind blew over the wall, causing him to pull the long collar of his jerkin tight around his neck. He hated the night watch during the warm seasons, let alone having to do it during the height of the cold season. The brazier at the back of the perch along the log wall that looked out over the mountain village did little to fend off winter's cold bite. Over the years he had learned a few tricks to help keep the blood flowing, and the cold out of his bones, but despite his pacing and wolf skin lined armor, boots and gloves, failed to do so this night. The cold air made him cough, the condensation from his breath collected and froze in clumps on the whiskers of his mustache. The end of his watch could not come soon enough.

While he contemplated his plight, a screech echoed over the rooftops of the city below, loud and shrill. It had come from off in the distance to the south. *What fool has gotten himself into trouble this time* he thought. He retrieved his poleax from the weapon rack. He looked out over the edge of the watch tower, straining to see anything in the moonlit darkness. Nothing but shadows, cast across the snow covered streets. Not even a patrolling guard. That was odd.

Ingvar grunted to himself and furled his brow. Why were none of the torches or lanterns lit? Melar was never this dark.

"Lazy sodding buggers, probably ducked into the Inn for a drink near the fire while I'm stuck up here," he lamented to himself. He dismissed the situation with a forward wave of his free hand and turned back towards his vigilant watch of the north. "Probably just some drunkard slipping on the ice again anyways."

The landscape dropped sharply not more than ten feet from the north wall all the way to the coastline a few hundred feet or more below. It was littered with tall fir, pine, and jagged rocks. On a good night like this one, visibility allowed him to see hundreds of meters out into the open waters of the bay. The water was relatively calm, and the only boats in sight were those moored at the fishing docks. A single lantern hung from the harbor master's cabin, and was lit, indicating that he was in for the night.

All was as it should be. There at least.

Moments later, a series of even shriller and louder screams echoed across the night behind him, causing the hairs on the back of his neck to stand on end, and a shiver to race the length of his spine. He gritted his teeth and narrowed his gaze as he rushed to look out over the village once more.

Flames poured from the windows of the inn, and the smoke billowed up in a large, dark pillar slowly wafting out to the west with the light breeze.

"FIRE," he shouted as he reached for the warning bell rope and tugged hard, repeatedly. "FIRE AT THE INN!"

His shout was echoed by the west and east towers, and soon the streets were filled with people racing towards the inn. Ingvar leaped from the ladder half way through his descent from the watchtower, landing in a run. He barely noticed the impact in his aging bones. He kicked up snow behind him as he raced through the streets, rapping each door he passed with the butt of his poleax and shouted his warning.

He rounded the corner of a longhouse near the street the Inn was on and heard the distinctive clang of metal on metal off to his right in one of the alleys across from the Inn. It was quickly followed by a groan and a shout of defiance.

Ingvar immediately redirected to assess the situation.

Dark shadows washed over him as he entered the secluded, narrow alley between two shops, working his way around the back side of them, where the commotion continued. A dozen curses flitted through his mind as he edged up to the corner of the wall on his left, and peaked around the corner. He was ready to deal with any number of types of miscreant the coastal mountain village had drawn in over the past few years due to favorable fishing seasons, and open trade with the colonies further to the south, but what he saw froze him in place. He felt his legs buckle slightly as he shrunk back towards the safety of his cover.

A giant bear faced behemoth was squared off against two guardsmen, swinging a massive two handed hammer over its head. They were barely able to fend off the heavy blow with their shields. One of the guards lost his footing, the weight of the impact knocking him off balance. He hit the ground awkwardly and hard. The sound of snapping bone was audible across the distance. The injured guard wailed in pain, dropped his axe, rolled to the side and reached for his broken arm with his shield hand. The only thing that saved his life was the metal reinforced, wooden shield still strapped to his left arm. It caught a downswing which followed the initial blow. Before the beast could attempt another swing, Ingvar collected himself and raced out of the darkness, poleax lowered in front of him as he charged forward. The giant spike on the tip connected with the creature, but only scraped along the side of its ribs. It snarled and roared at him with such ferocity that he could feel his blood run cold in his veins. The beast bared its teeth and roared. Drool hung between its jaws. The beast was huge. It towered over Ingvar and the remaining guard that stood yelling at it, flailing wildly with his own axe. None of the strikes seemed to penetrate its thick hide.

Ingvar circled the creature, trying to find an opening while the beast was distracted.

The guard with the broken arm scrambled back from the encounter through the snow, moaning.

Ingvar heard a soft thump behind him, but before he could fully turn to see what the cause of the noise was, brilliant stars filled his vision and the ground came up to meet him, then darkness.

Ingvar's eyes opened as pain shot through his head. He slowly brought his arms up from his side where he lay in the snow, and held his head in both hands. Snow fell from his armor as he righted himself, and a wave of nausea rushed through his body. He looked about for his helmet as he realized it was not on his head, and he was freezing. Snow and ice matted his hair. He spotted his helmet sitting awkwardly and half buried in the snow a few feet away. There was a large dent in the top of it.

He attempted to stand up so he could retrieve his helmet, but a fresh wave of nausea hit him. He retched into the snow at his feet before falling back on his rump. The top of his head felt like it had been hit with a splitting maul and he struggled to recall what had happened. He leaned back and propped himself up with his arms. His right hand brushed against the haft of his poleax, which lay covered in the snow. He gripped the haft, pulled it to himself and used the poleax to steady himself as he attempted to stand again. This time he managed to stay on his feet, although with a slight wobble in his knees. He sighed heavily, standing there for a moment before he reached to pick up his helmet with his left hand. A fresh wave of pounding pain filled his head as he retrieved the dented helmet.

Ingvar moved to lean against the wall of the nearby building, brushed the snow out of the helmet as best he could, then placed it on his head. It didn't sit quite right anymore, but it would hopefully help keep the cold out for now. He remained against the wall for a few moments longer while he gathered his bearings. The smell of smoke was heavy on the air, and he now noticed that warm light lit the night sky. He could not see the sky for all the smoke. Then it hit him. He remembered the events all at once. He looked about for the guardsmen that had been battling the giant bear man, but there was no sign of them. Only drag marks in the snow towards the wall of the town. Claw marks and frozen blood marred the surface of the giant logs that formed the city wall. He had a sickening feeling that wasn't caused by his bump on the head. It made sense now. He must have been hit from behind by a second intruder. Not wanting to stick around to see if the creatures would return to drag him away as well, he wobbled on rubbery legs back through the dark alley towards the main street where he recalled the inn had been ablaze. There was no sign of anyone as he emerged into the street from the shadows. Multiple buildings beyond the inn on either side of the street were also engulfed in fire now. Debris from the shop interiors littered the street.

Ingvar's first thought was joyful delight at the prospect of not having to deal with the dullards and drunkards that frequented the Inn anymore, but was quickly replaced by hopelessness. He had not felt hopeless in many, many years. Not since he was a child. Firelight danced off his helmet as he leaned against his poleax and stared into the heart of chaos. Where was everyone, why were they not fighting the fires? These and a dozen other questions raced through his mind. An unnatural desire to flee the city beckoned him, and he listened. He backed away from the main street slowly at first, but within the span of a few heartbeats, had turned his back to the scene and ran towards the main gate. Luckily his home was on that side of the city, and he made a quick stop only long enough to grab the coin pouch he had stashed under the floorboards beneath his straw lined bed, and a small travel pack which he filled with a change of clothes, some dried meat, cheese, bread and his water skin. On his way out the door he grabbed an unlit torch from its sconce on a post in the street. He had no idea where he was headed, but he knew he couldn't stay inside the city walls. He was no hero, nor did he desire to be. There was no chasing after unearthly beings through the night to save people he cared little about, just the will to survive. The exertion melted away the cold in his bones, and the rushed intake of fresh winter air cleared the fuzziness from his groggy mind. He flew through the small heavy door built into the west gate house, out into the mountain farmlands beyond. The further he got from the burning city, the better he could see the stars in the sky, aiding in his navigation. Whether by instinct or by choice, he decided he would make for the outpost along the coastline a few days' journey north of Melar.

He had never wanted a life with the militia, and had tried to leave a few times in the past, but each time his captain had somehow talked him out of it. He had been a conscript during his youth, when raiding bands threatened the borders of their kingdom. Perhaps this was his chance to abscond from his duties for good without anyone being any the wiser. He had saved enough coin over the years to survive for many years without having to worry about employment. He had always wanted to find a chunk of land, build a house, and perhaps open a smithy or a workshop. Only time would tell how that would play out, but for now, he would be happy if he made it away from this place alive and unnoticed.

Chapter Seven

Corlag ran through the streets dodging people that were fleeing from burning buildings and screaming about dark creatures attacking. Fire danced all across the city, dark plumes of smoke rising into the sky. It was dusk, and the air carried a mixture of acrid smoke, and something else, something foul; fetid. Bodies lay strewn in the street like discarded bits of a meal. Some lay partly in the doorways of their homes or shops, some had been torn apart and flung into the air, the halves landing wherever gravity decided. Vacant stares from horrified faces both alive and deceased stuck in his mind as he raced through the streets towards whatever danger was drawing him.

He had no idea where he was going exactly, only that he felt compelled to head further south, deep into the city's core.

His sword, his constant companion, was in his right hand and shimmered with golden light, and swirling musical notes that circled the blade from hilt to tip. There was definitely a great evil nearby.

He rounded a cramped street that led into the city's central garden at its very heart. The sight was horrific. Every bit of the garden was charred black, embers danced into the sky from the still burning trees, the bodies of the city guardsmen and otherwise, were everywhere; torn and mutilated.

Standing in the midst of it all, facing down those few that still stood bravely attempting to defend against its onslaught, was the largest creature he had ever seen. Its breath wafted across the desecrated garden, sulfuric and rotten; Its eyes blazed with a bright red glow, and a mane of fire blazed down the back of its neck and between its shoulders. Huge leathery bat-like wings jutted from its shoulder blades, slick black claws at the elbows and tips of the wings glinted in the firelight that lit the city center. Its spine had giant black spikes, like polished obsidian, down its length; a tail flailed behind it, similarly spiked, ending in a giant pincer.

The beast was massive. It raised its serpentine head towards the sky, roared, and reared up on its hind legs. Its claws dug huge trenches in the earth as it shifted its weight and swiped at the group in front of it with one massive limb. It towered over the multi-story buildings nearby, and it was clear there was no chance the brave guards would be able to escape its reach.

Corlag called out a warning instinctively anyways.

Too late, the guards realized their fate. They dropped their weapons and shields, attempting to flee in all directions from the descending doom. The massive claw cleaved them all, sending their bodies flying in all directions.

Corlag stood stunned at the fringe of the garden, mouth agape.

How can this be? The Great Tree stands vigilant, an eternal guardian, holding all the darkest things at bay within Moonshadow, far from this world.

The beast slammed back down on all fours and tilted its head toward Corlag. Its fiery gaze boring into him hungrily.

Its maw fell open and a deep roiling laughter assaulted Corlag, shaking his entire body. Its hot, disgusting breath washed over him, making him gag.

Suddenly his surroundings changed.

He found himself standing in a giant clearing, the Great Tree towering in front of him, stark against the flat rock face where it had remained for centuries. The once magnificent tree was rent down the middle, its leaves wilted and mostly gone. Its bark was charcoal black, and the clearing surrounding it was but ash and dirt. A giant hole, darker than night, rested in the middle of the giant tree trunk's base. Clouds swirled overhead, blocking his view of the top of the rock face let alone the top of the Great Tree. Not that he would have been able to see the actual top of the thousands feet high nature sentinel on a good day.

He fell to his knees in disbelief at the site of the dead tree and wept.

The end of an age was coming.

~*~

Corlag burst awake, threw his covers away over the side of the bed as he bolted completely out of it. He spun around looking for a threat. It took him a few moments to realize he had unsheathed and activated his sword. The blade danced with golden light.

Seeing that there was no real threat, and no acrid stench of smoke on the night air wafting through his window, he spoke softly to the sword and wiped his hand across the flat of the blade. The light dimmed and flickered out. Moonlight filled the room.

He breathed a heavy sigh of relief, sat down on the edge of his bed and wiped cold sweat from his brow with the back of his hand.

Just a nightmare, he thought to himself.

Despite the reassuring thought, he knew deep down that there was more to it. He had not had any sort of dark dream since the Southern War long ago. He would have to ponder its meaning before speaking of it with his friend.

There was no point attempting to get back to sleep, his body was dancing with energy, so he got dressed and made his way out to his study to write. He paused at the hearth in his small kitchen long enough to stoke the fire and set a kettle to boil over the fire to make some Javium.

Chapter Eight

The city of Beorhtsige, meaning Bright Victory, was named so after the last war against the demon horde of the southern lands of Ael'andar, in memory of those that gave their lives to end the horrific slaughter that had gripped the continent in the Shadow War that ended the Fifth Age and heralded in a new age, that of man.

Fitting to its namesake, the sun shone on the city's tallest buildings and the mountain peak that stood sentinel over them from dawn until dusk, a beacon to all those seeking comfort and peace. That is not to say that it was without its share of problems. Where there are humans, there is squalor and strife. Here it was simply much less, and well tended to.

Corlag stared out over the beautiful cityscape from the balcony of his simple cliff side home, memories of the war flitting through his mind as they often did. Nothing would take them from his thoughts it seemed. It had been many, many years since the war, and despite the calm and beauty of his home within what is called the most beautiful city on all of Ierolden, he was constantly restless. The city was nestled in the mountains on the western fringes of the Upper Fel'Thain forest, at the base of the Western

Obodoon Mountains. The farmlands around the city were rich in soil, and the forest was full of wildlife. The Glimmering Falls backdropped the city, its waters cascaded down a jagged cliff and ran through the middle of the city into the forest where it wove its way west to the sea.

He was broken out of his trance by a knock at his door. He took a deep breath of the fresh air and turned from the glowing sunrise to step inside and make his way through the living room to the front door of his home.

"Morning Bran," he said before he had even opened the door fully.

"How do you always know it's me," his friend asked, holding out his hand which held a rolled piece of parchment?

"Simple, I don't get any other visitors, and I prefer it that way," replied Corlag and took the offered parchment.

"That's got to be the saddest thing I have ever heard."

"Why's that?"

"Because, life is long. Even longer when spent mostly alone in your home. When was the last time you got out and did something besides spin some tales?"

"I do get out, into the mountains and the forest, often as you well know."

"Aye, but it's not the same. You need to remind yourself of the good that has sprung up since the end of the old wars, instead of letting yourself be haunted by their memory. You need to allow yourself to connect with people."

Corlag sighed heavily. He knew his friend was right. He looked down at the parchment gripped in his right hand and picked at the wax seal for a moment.

"Is this what I think it is," he asked his friend and tapped the rolled parchment against the palm of his left hand?

"Aye, another request from the council to consider joining them."

Corlag flicked his wrist towards the fireplace and the unopened parchment sailed softly through the space between, landing on the slow burning logs.

Branick nodded and joined Corlag in the living room, taking a seat in one of the cushioned wooden chairs.

"Are we going this year," asked Branick?

"The Spring Festival? I suppose it's nearing that time again isn't it," replied Corlag.

"Aye."

"Honestly, I hunger for more than a stroll through the forest this year, old friend," said Corlag wearily as he sank back into his chair and sighed. "I miss it."

"Which part, the cold nights or the endless walking?"

"All of it, the adventure of the open road."

"Battle you mean," stated Branick knowingly.

"No, not battle so much, but hunting evil yes. Ireolden is far from free of darkness, despite the sealing of the valley all those years ago."

"It's been a long time since anything stirred worth hunting. Have you felt something I haven't?"

"No, not that I'm aware of. Maybe-" Corlag trailed off.

"Maybe?" Branick leaned forward in his seat and raised his eyebrows at Corlag. "Tell me."

"I don't know, it's just a feeling in my stomach, and I find myself getting more restless by the day. Maybe the festival will do me some good."

"Well, in that case, you best start warming up your skills. Not that they need honing or anything, but you should at least visit one of the taverns here and get back into the swing of things and shake off the dust so to speak."

"I suppose you're right. Again."

"Tonight then?"

"Aye, tonight."

"Now that we've settled that, hunting or sparring today?"

Corlag laughed heartily at his friend's easy going nature before replying with a glint in his eyes, "Sparring!"

With that they got to their feet and left Corlag's home.

Chapter Nine

Corlag sat by the hearth tuning his lute in preparation of the crowd for the evenings storytelling at one of the local taverns near his home. It had been a while since he had spun any tales at the establishment, but he knew it would be crowded. It always was, and he did not want to disappoint.

Daylight faded, the room filled, and before long, it was time to begin. He set down his cup of water on the mantle of the hearth and took a seat on a wooden stool to one side of the fire. He cleared his throat, then addressed his audience.

"Good evening friends, neighbors, and travelers alike. Thank you for joining me at this wonderful establishment for an evening of merriment and entertainment. Now, before we get into it, what would everyone like to hear?"

"Tell us something we ain't heard before," shouted a woman from the back of the room.

"Yeah, somethin' new," answered another voice from the crowd.

"An' not nothin' from this side o' the ocean," added a third.

Corlag smiled and held up a hand to halt any further requests.

"Very well, a bit of history from beyond our lands then. Let's see now," he said and thought for a moment, "Ah yes, I have the perfect thing for this occasion. Have any of you heard the history of the Kingdom of O'Marah?"

Silence was his answer.

"Oh excellent, you're in for a treat then. There will be two parts to this telling. First, a poem, then the history. I won't go back as far as I would like, but far enough to give you all something to think on."

Corlag paused, plucked a string on his lute to find the right tone for the poem, then began.

Something old and forgotten,
This way lingers.
Always there,
But never spake of.
Legends rose and fell,
Now truth be told.
To life they come,
Returned from whence they departed.
Seeking retribution,
Atonement.
Fear them, hear them, respect them,
But most of all,
Do not anger them.

The audience clapped softly for a moment as he reached up, grabbed his cup and took a drink of water.

"Alright, on to the next bit."

Corlag once again plucked a string and began his tale.

"There's one thing every story has in common. They all have a beginning. This story is no different. Before

Ierolden, before the realm of men was born, there was the Volskaia. Always the Volskaia."

"Who the heck are they," called an onlooker.

"Let me explain," replied Corlag with a stern, yet warm look at the stranger.

Kelvos stood taller than the tallest of men. A mane of golden hair adorned his head, and his features were strong. He was like a pristinely chiseled statue hewn from the strongest of stones by a masterful artisan.

He had wings of golden feathers that shone like sunlight during the day and shimmered like stars at night. They spanned half again his height and shook both earth and sky alike when he took flight. His mother was a giantess of great renown amongst the Vendrin nation of giants. They were the third strongest of all the tribes. His father was of the Volskaia, unknown in name and did not remain in the realms beneath the sky which was their domain.

Few have ever laid eyes upon those who dwell in the sky, and even fewer still have lain with them. A perversion of the highest order it is said, and those birthed from such unions are twisted, violent, and lustful beyond end; But for a few.

None of the halfbreed Volskaia offspring grew up like normal children, all of them sprung from seed to grown form within the length of a single turning of the seasons. Such unions were not only between the women beneath the skies and the male cast of the Volskaia, but also between the matriarchs of the skies and men beneath them.

Kelvos, like his sky father, was a born leader. He was not content to live life among men as a demigod in their eyes. He knew it was a wrongness of the natural order, and feared the repercussions of embracing the untruth. He knew there were others of his kind that felt as he did, and sought them out with great purpose.

He loved his earthly mother and knew it would tear her apart, and knowing this, shared his thoughts with her and sought her guidance. She agreed in whole, but with one condition, he was to take her with him. She would help persuade the other parents to see as she did, and to build a safe kingdom far away from the realms of men, where they could be free and uncorrupting of the realm of mankind. Many agreed, but there were those who opposed, those that loved their unnatural power and the control it gave them over others; Those that were twisted in mind from impure unions, wild and vengeful of their skyward parents.

The Volskaia responsible for all the unions with mankind were gathered together by the Father of the Heavens, and shown the chaos that was about to unfold across the surface of Ierolden.

War, death, and famine unlike anything ever before imagined. A world brought to ruin at the hands of their offspring.

They pleaded with him, claiming only a desire to create new things, not to ruin. In their blind love for their children they could not see the truth.

They were banished then, to live among the realms of men as they had so desired, doomed for eternity to roam the land of their giving, but no further; Even if it too, came to ruin. Thus was born the greatest of earthly kingdoms, O'Marah. Ruled by O'ahmog, The Fallen King, Son of the Heavenly Father. He was also known as The Eternal King. His reign would be more than a thousand years, before being brought down by one of his own Blade Mystics.

Its people, stripped of their wings and rights to the heavens, were given laws to bind them to their fate. The laws would be enforced by the Father's legion of loyal Volskaia.

They Who Linger

He alone would judge them and the rest of the realms of men, watching day by day forever more for signs of their further corruption. Those offspring that had survived the unearthly war were rounded up by the Father of the Heavens and imprisoned beyond the realms of men, encased behind stone and shadow, living only in the space within the gap between them. The door was sealed by a great tree planted by the father himself and fed by the waters of his loins. It grew and grew, up into the sky beyond Ierolden. Life giving fruit and nursery roosts for all manner of sky creatures, it remains to this day, the Great Tree that eternally guards the entrance to the Valley of Moonshadow.

Corlag finished his tale about Kelvos of the Volskaia, stood from his stool, stretched and bowed to the applauding crowd. The people went on howling, cheering and clapping for some time despite his protests between many thank yous.

Chapter Ten

"Bard, tell us of the Weeping Willows," called a haggard man over the rim of his carved drinking horn at the back of the room.

"Do you know the tales," asked another?

The bard looked at them in surprise. Not many folk knew about the wars in the south from ages long past, let alone the myths that came with them. He smiled and turned away from the crowd to stretch against the stone hearth. He lowered his head and closed his eyes to reflect on the tales that remained archived in the recesses of his mind, the firelight dancing across his face. The room was deathly quiet but for the wind squeaking through the cracks between the wooden slats of the latched windows and the large front door.

"Aye, this is a tale I know."

The Grove of Weeping Willows formed when the Sons and Daughters of the Volskaia gave themselves to Ierolden to stop the armies of the south from marching any further into the realm of men whom the Sons and Daughters had become smitten with. They sang to life a great forest to entomb the army and in so doing, crumbled to dust themselves as they gave all of their lives to stop the destruction being sown in the army's wake.

In that place, where they stood atop a stony hill in the midst of a great valley where the army had come to pass into the north, jutting into the sky forever more at the tip of the hill's precipice, a grove of Weeping Willows stands taller than the hill itself. Each of the willows grown from the ashen pile where the Sons and Daughters fell, has a face in its trunk. A tribute to those that gave them life.

It is said that when great sorrow fills the world, their eyes close, and they weep. The wind carries their eternal song across the valley, quelling the darkness that threatens to rise again and again. The great forest moans and roils, constantly at war with the thousands and thousands of souls it now entombs.

When the end of our world comes, darkness shall break free and sweep into the north once again. Then, and only then, will the Weeping Willows be set free.

The bard raised his head once more and turned to face the awestruck crowd. A glint of light still danced in his eyes, but he no longer faced the fire.

"Well, that was one way of doing it," exclaimed the haggard man who had requested the telling.

~*~

Corlag and Branick made their way through the streets of Beorhtsige towards their homes on the northern edge, up on the hillsides that rose toward the base of the mountains. They spoke of their journey and decided that they would depart the next morning. Plans agreed upon, they parted for the evening.

That night Corlag had the same dream. This time he did not see the Great Tree, withered and dead, but instead startled awake just before the Beast's massive paw could crush him into the ground. Again he found his sword in hand, lit and swallowing the darkness in his room. He doused the blade, got dressed and went to his study. He needed to start chronicling the dreams, his other writing forgotten for the time being.

Chapter Eleven

Corlag yelped and cursed angrily under his breath as he grabbed his foot in both hands, hopping about like a one legged rabbit. He fumbled his way to a nearby log and quickly sat down. He rubbed at his foot agitatedly, his face contorted in pain.

"What did you do," Branick asked through stifled laughter.

"Stubbed my foot on something," Corlag replied through gritted teeth and waved one arm in the direction of a dirt caked object jutting from the middle of the path.

Branick, failing to contain himself any longer, smirked and burst out laughing. When he managed to regain his composure, he flashed Corlag a smile full of teeth and shook his head. He turned and walked back to inspect the would-be culprit.

"I keep telling you to buy thicker leathers for your feet, like them ones the cobbler had back in town before we set out this morn-" Branick's voice caught in his throat abruptly. He stood to full height, taking on the resemblance of a bear standing on its hind legs. He looked at Corlag, who was now resting his hands on his knees shaking his injured foot around.

Sensing the pause in his friend's voice more than hearing it, Corlag stopped shaking his foot and looked up to see what had caught Branick's tongue.

"What," he asked with a shrug?

"You'll not believe me if'n I tell yeh, just come have a look," replied Branick, pointing at the object in the dirt.

The odd rock speckled the path, giving it a well worn yet not rough and tumble look. Roots from the nearby trees threatened to reclaim the precious patch of earth that had been worn bare by travelers and wildlife alike.

Corlag let go of his foot, and forgetting the pained limb, made his way to Branick's side.

"No need to mock my clumsiness Bran-" he gasped suddenly as he spotted the glimmer of gold jutting out of the dirt.

They both stood there dumbfounded for a short while. A bird chirped off in the distance, breaking the silence between them.

"Think we should unearth it," asked Branick as he stared at the object?

"Well there's no sense leaving it here for the next person to break their foot on now is there? What good would that do anyone? We're doing everyone a favor by removing it from the path don't you think," he replied with a grin.

"Hah, you speak the truth."

The rest of the afternoon passed in a blur of digging, and joking amongst themselves. The golden treasure came free as the last bit of dirt holding it in place cleared away, causing a roar of victory between the two travelers, startling a couple of birds who had been resting in the nearby trees. They held their trophy aloft, sunlight danced across its bejeweled, golden surface, sending dancing waves of color out in all directions around them.

"Now that's a beauty," exclaimed Branick.

"Truly," replied Corlag as he measured the size of the half circle shaped treasure with hand spans.

It was two full hand spans across, from the etched outer edge to the jagged edge that would have been the middle if it were a complete disk.

"What do you figure it is," asked Branick?

"No idea, but it looks valuable. It also looks as though it has been here a long while."

Corlag examined the disk absently. He rubbed some dirt off of it with his thumb, his mind working to recollect an ancient memory. Some part of his subconscious recognized the etchings on the outer edge, but he could not fully place their meaning or recall where he recognized them from.

"And these gems... I've not seen the likes of them in many years, not since our time spent on Thayrium. I think it may be an artifact of some sort from there."

"We best set camp for the night. Not much traveling to be done in the dark of the forest now is there," replied Branick. He clamped a meaty hand on his friend's shoulder, "and we certainly wouldn't want you breaking your other foot stumbling over another treasure because you couldn't see would we?"

"Just for that, you can fetch the firewood," Corlag fired back with a chuckle and shrugged off Branick's hand.

"Aww come now, I was just jesting."

"Aye, but I was not," Corlag laughed.

Smirking to himself, Corlag turned from Branick and headed off the path to find a suitable place out of the rising winds. He set his pack against the trunk of a large tree on a moss covered knoll next to a large rock outcropping on the down slope. Without realizing it, he still held the artifact in his left hand. His fingers ran over its surface again, his mind lost in thought for a time.

He shook free of his daydream, stowed the disk away in his pack, and set about making a fire pit with what stones he could find laying about. Next he gathered up a few clumps of dried grass, twigs and bark to aid in starting the fire. The flames began to lick hungrily at the tinder. Branick returned with an armful of logs a short time later.

"Plenty of old wood in these parts, I didn't have to chop a single piece," he said as he gently dropped his burden into a pile off to one side.

"Did you see a stream down the hill anywhere," Corlag asked?

"Aye, there be a small stream not too far past the tree line there," replied Branick, pointing down the grassy hill from their camp.

"Excellent, we can make some stew then. I've got a bit of dried meat left, a few carrots, and a potato or two. I'll search for some wild onions and herbs if you want to get the water."

"Fine by me. I'd be more likely to squash the things beneath my feet then I would to spot them as you do."

Branick retrieved a cooking pot and both of their water skins, then headed down towards the stream.

Corlag went about searching the grassy hillside for his herbs and onions. It was not long before he had what he needed and was back in camp preparing the ingredients. The wind whistled through the tree bows overhead, and with it came the scent of a storm.

His preparations complete, he laid back against the trunk of a giant tree nearby and took in the scenery while he waited for Branick to return with the water.

Chapter Twelve

Branick pushed aside some jutting branches from a wild berry bush as he reached a small clearing near the side of the trickling stream. He bent down to fill the cooking pot, the setting sun glinting off the water. When it was full he set it off to the side, uncapped the waterskins and plunged them both into the cool water, air gurgled up to the surface as they filled. He looked up at the trees across the water, the wind howled through their bows, and took in the full serenity of the area. He soaked it in for a moment, before recapping the waterskins. He set them aside and bent closer to the water, splashed his face a few times to wash away grime from the day's journeying, and scooped up a few mouthfuls of the cool water with his hand.

On his third scoop, an audible crack broke through the small clearing near the stream. The water trickled through his fingers, escaping back to the stream. He looked about for the source of the sound.

Another crack sounded, followed by some rustling of dry leaves on the forest floor across the water, this time downstream and up a small hill from him. The hair on the back of his neck raised. He flicked what little water remained in his hand back into the stream and gathered the cooking pot and waterskins.

Branick was not easily unsettled, but something felt off. He made his way back through the berry bushes, daring only to pause long enough to pick one handful of the ripe berries, which he placed in a shirt pocket, before continuing back to the camp.

He heard more rustling off in the distance from a few directions. Again he looked around, but saw nothing.

"Bah, yer letting the wind get the better of you Bran," he uttered in frustration, more with himself for letting such things get to him.

He broke through the tree line and increased his pace up the hill towards camp, sloshing a bit of the water from the pot as he climbed. Thinking of the coming meal made his stomach growl. He hadn't realized how hungry he was after all of the day's excitement.

Corlag met him as he crested the knoll and took the cooking pot from him and set to prepping the stew.

"I thought maybe you fell in or something," said Corlag. He dropped the ingredients into the pot and placed it on the fire.

"I found some wild berry bushes near the stream," replied Branick as he looked over his shoulder down the hill.

He took the handful of berries out of his pocket and handed half to Corlag, who promptly tossed one in his mouth.

"Not too many berries on them then I take it," inquired Corlag?

"Aye," replied Branick, still looking down the hill, "not many."

"That's too bad."

They Who Linger

They ate their dinner once it had cooled enough to be tolerable, and then rolled out their bedrolls near the fire.

Branick propped himself against a log that lay near the base of the rock outcropping, affording himself a clear view of the tree line down the hill. He did not fall asleep right away, and the sense of unease in him grew. Something had disturbed him greatly while he was at the stream, and he couldn't figure out what it was. He was certain something lurked in the darkness beyond their fire. When exhaustion won the battle, he fell asleep still propped against the log.

Chapter Thirteen

The sun licked the tips of the Obodoon Mountains to the north and east, caressing the snow covered peaks on its daily journey across the sky. Corlag rustled awake as the first rays of light bathed the mossy knoll on which they had made camp. Birds chirped in the branches above them, creating an echoing orchestra of nature.

He stoked the warm coals that remained in the fire pit, adding small bits of wood, bringing the flames hidden within dancing to life.

"Up you get, you big oaf," he said and prodded Branick with his foot.

Branick groaned and rolled over away from the log he had slumped against.

"Is it that time already?"

"Indeed it is, a new day, another adventure."

"With no broken toes let's hope," Branick jested groggily and struggled to crawl out of his bedroll. "What's for breakfast," he added with a stretch?

"Bread, cheese before it goes bad on us, and a bit of Javium if you can fetch some water," replied Corlag. He rummaged in his pack and produced a small bundle of the brewing beans.

"Ah, nothing like a bit of Javium to wash down breakfast and put an extra spring in our steps eh?"

"I find it soothing."

"You're a strange fellow sometimes Cor."

Branick grabbed the cooking pot and water skins and headed for the stream once again. Halfway to the trees from camp, his uneasiness from the evening before returned. He scanned the area as he approached. Nothing seemed out of the ordinary, but he couldn't shake the feeling that someone, or some*THING*, was watching him.

He quickly filled the pot and water skins, plucked two pocketfuls of berries from the bushes, and returned to camp. He was almost back when a shriek erupted from behind him where he had been in the trees. He spun around quickly enough that he spilled part of the water from the pot again.

Instinctively, his free hand drew his sword from its sheath. He watched the trees for movement, still as a stone statue.

"What was that," called Corlag, while he ran down to meet Branick?

"I have no idea. I grow uneasy with this place. Let's be gone sooner than later shall we," replied Branick.

"If it's enough to make you uneasy, I don't much care to find out what it is. Let's be going then. We'll take the Javium on the road with us."

Branick remained fixated for a few moments longer before slowly backing his way up the hill, watching for any movement in the trees below.

Corlag took the pot from him and quickly made his way up the hill. He added the Javium to the pot and set it in the coals to boil while they packed up their things.

Chapter Fourteen

Corlag and Branick sipped at their freshly brewed cups of Javium while they walked down the dirt path winding through the greater part of Fel'Thain forest towards the pass into Thain's Reach. Steam rose from their wooden cups as they held the hot liquid not far from their faces, breathing in its delicious aroma. They traveled throughout the morning without a word between them, soaking in the warming rays of sunlight.

Branick spared only a handful of glances over his shoulder during their journey away from where they had made camp, one hand never far from the hilt of his weapon.

A light fog wafted up from the forest floor as the soil was warmed and dissipated on a light breeze. The air was crisp, laden with the smell of pine and fir. Dew glistened on vegetation to either side of the path. The tranquility of the forest aided in melting away their worries, some. Their past and their burdens forgotten for the moment.

The path led downward for a time, bringing them close to the center of the Upper Fel'Thain. Trees towered above them on all sides now, blocking out all but the strongest rays of light. Their surroundings took on a greenish tint as the light reflected off of the large variety of vegetation that filled the woods, and the path was encroached upon by moss, ferns and other plants that made their homes on the forest floor.

Corlag felt that he could dwell within the depths of the Fel'Thain forever, without a care in the world, if not for the rising hairs on the back of his neck.

"Do you feel that," asked Corlag, holding up a hand to signal Branick to stop.

Branick cocked his head to one side, slowly reaching for his shield on his back, and the hilt of his sword at his side.

Corlag also reached for his sword and began humming a deep throaty tune. As he did so, tendrils of golden energy danced behind the movement of his hands, enveloping the hilt of his blade like a wild vine swallowing stone. A string of golden musical notes swirled around his forearm, over his hands, and up along the etched blade of the sword.

"I don't hear anything Cor, but something definitely feels-" Branick paused, his jaw tensing slightly as he continued to scan the forest around them, "Off."

"We'll keep moving, but be on your guard."

"That I shall," he replied and gripped the leather holding strap of his shield tighter.

The path widened a short stint later, meandering through the center of a small clearing. Tall grass and weeds swayed like undulating waves in the ocean. A few stumps, fallen logs and large rocks littered the area.

They were halfway across the clearing when the first creature attacked, lunging from the grass, seemingly from the ground itself. It let out a high pitched screech that sounded part avian and part wild beast.

Branick was quick to react.

"Watch out," he yelled and hurled his shield through the air at the creature, striking it fully in the chest. The impact knocked it out of the air in mid-leap.

Corlag instinctively dropped into a roll away from the creature and came up in a crouch facing the crumpled beast, weapon at the ready. It flailed on its back, attempting to right itself.

Branick let out a bellow that echoed across the clearing, the vegetation bending as the wave of sound traveled. He lunged at the fallen creature before it could recover and buried his blade halfway to the hilt in its mouth.

The creature shrieked and wailed, chortled and clicked angrily as it swiped at Branick with glistening, black claws.

Branick dodged the beast's frantic attempts, ripped his sword free through the side of its face and dashed to retrieve his shield. Four more creatures leapt from the grass on all sides, one landed on a rock to the right of the path, perched above them, another on the path behind Corlag, and the remaining two just out of reach to Branick's left and back. The creatures looked like something out of a nightmare, with blackened skin covered in quills that had a damp sheen to them, and four gangly limbs that ended in what looked like half human hands with bird-like talons jutting from each finger. Their elongated skulls were inset with black orbs that seemed to pierce the viewer's very soul, and were attached to stubby necks that connected to a bonny carapace-like abdomen. Every part of the creature was black, and writhing, like shadows and ink. There wasn't a hint of any other color anywhere on the creatures. They appeared as though they were formed from darkness itself. The quills rustled like the tail of a rattlesnake. They screeched in unison, their mouths agape, revealing dark fangs dripping with even darker ichor and forked tongues. They lunged to attack.

Corlag leaped into the air from his crouching position, spun on the creature behind him and swung his sword. The blade whistled and hummed as it arced toward the creature, golden tendrils trailing behind the sword as it carved through the air. The beast attempted to reverse course at the last moment, but failed. It squealed in surprise when the blade cleaved it in half diagonally. The beast landed in two parts, one to either side of Corlag as he landed on the path again. He spun on his heels to face the second creature that now skittered down the side of the rock to his right.

Corlag's humming became more audible, enveloping the clearing. The creature halted its advance. It moved side to side, searching for an opening in the defenses of its prey, chortling and shaking its head erratically. They circled each other in a standoff.

Branick turned his shield upward to fend off the creature that was raining blows down upon him like a thunderstorm, throwing all his weight behind it as the creature collided with him. He rolled with the momentum, lifting the creature up and over his left shoulder and away from him. He brought his blade to bear in the same motion against the second creature that was advancing low to the ground, like a prowling wolf in front of him. Ichor dripped from the creature's fangs when it snarled. Black clouds wafted from two slits in its snout, like smoke plumes from a couple of chimneys. The creature to his left had not yet recovered from the stunning shield slam that had sent it sliding across the ground, but Branick kept his shield focused in that direction anyways, his blade focused fully on the advancing creature.

"To me," he bellowed.

Corlag circled toward Branick, keeping the creature he was facing off against in front of his blade as he did so, until he was back to back with his friend.

"Don't let them circle us in, there may be more," said Branick.

Corlag raised his hymn to a deafening crescendo and golden tendrils enveloped the duo.

The creatures shied away from them as the hymn increased in intensity, unsure of their prey.

"They don't seem to like that Cor, keep it up," said Branick.

Corlag increased the tempo further and the creatures shied further away, this time hissing and snarling, dipping and diving agitatedly.

The creature to his left had regained its footing and posed the most threat, but had not yet turned to face them. Seeing an opening, Branick struck at it with practiced precision. He slammed the edge of his shield into its jaw, knocking it silly once again, and then stepped to the side and brought his blade down with full force, severing the beast's head from its neck. The creature's body convulsed, flailing its claws through the air as it rolled on the ground. The remaining creature facing him chose that moment to leap at his back. It slammed into him, claws first. His armor absorbed most of the blow, and the claws scraped along the metal plates of his breastplate. Branick pitched forward in an attempt to shed the beast and rolled with the impact. He came to bare on one knee, facing his attacker with his shield ready for its next attack.

Corlag swirled the tip of his sword in the air in front of him as he changed the pitch of the hymn. The creature in front of him lolled its head to one side, confused. It stared at the intensifying golden glow that enveloped the blade, dancing like fire. Without pause, Corlag flung the sword towards the creature, with barely a flick of the wrist. It shot towards the beast like an arrow from a taut bow and slammed into its skull, between its dark eyes. The creature let out a low, short moan and slumped to the side. The glow from the blade washed over it briefly before dissipating. Corlag turned to face the creature that was now assaulting Branick with full force. He maintained the hymn as he approached the beast from behind.

Deep gouges had been rent in Branick's shield, and it oozed with dark ichor where the creature had been biting at it, attempting to pull it free. Branick had his blade crossed behind his shield, propping himself behind it with both hands. The beast hammered against him repeatedly. It chortled and lunged again, this time getting a firm grip on the shield with its teeth. Branick released his grip on the leather strap, pulling his left arm free so as not to have it broken as the shield was wrenched away, and brought his blade to bear in both hands.

Corlag leapt at the creature with his fists raised like a mallet over his head, now emanating a radiant light. A mist-like cloud drifted from his eyes. He let out a bellow as he soared through the air at the creature. His fists connected with a thunderous force against the creature's carapace, cracking it in several places and sending it crashing into the ground, wailing in agony. It sunk into the soil a few inches under the force, dust scattering out around them. Golden flames burned the creature where Corlag's fists had impacted, spreading rapidly across its entire body.

Taking no chances, Branick swung his blade at the downed creature, burying his blade in its chest. His blade bit into the dirt path and pinned it in place.

Corlag and Branick straightened, searched the clearing for any more signs of trouble, both of them poised for battle. None came.

They slumped against the side of the boulder to catch their breath. Corlag ceased his hymn and sprawled out in the sun, his eyes closed.

"I need to re-energize for a moment," said Corlag.

"Aye, do your thing," replied Branick as he too sprawled out on the ground in the sun.

After a brief respite, they retrieved their weapons, and knelt down next to the last of their attackers for a moment, inspecting it curiously.

"I've never seen the likes of those before, how about you," asked Corlag?

"Nae, they're not natural, of that I'm certain," replied Branick.

"Right then, let's get out of here before more of them decide to show up."

Sheathing their weapons, they began to sprint down the path without a backward glance, exiting the clearing on the far side.

A gust of wind swept across the clearing as they ran, and if they had looked back, they would have seen the creatures bodies begin to break apart and blow away in the breeze as a cloud of black smoke and grit.

Chapter Fifteen

Syndara trudged through the fresh snow towards Garomvol with her best friend, Aileesha, not far behind. They had been very successful on their hunting expedition for Mammoth. Two sleds worth of meat, hide and tusks from just one giant beast. It never ceased to amaze her just how large the Mammoth could get, yet how fragile they could be if someone or something knew where to strike them. She could tell the day was short as the drop in temperature made their breath visible in front of them.

She paused to catch her breath, setting the sled reigns down on top of the covered meat, and adjusted the bow and quiver slung across her back. She basked in the sunshine glimmering on the snow as she stretched. Snow covered trees and rocky outcroppings pillared the landscape around them. The creek that normally bubbled and gurgled over the rocks in the small gully to their left was frozen over and buried between a tomb of fluffy white powder, not to be seen or heard again until spring thaw.

Syndara breathed deeply and let out a relaxed sigh and shifted her gaze further down the valley toward their home. She stretched her muscles out, raised her arms overhead and twisted her body left and right, leaning to each side as she did. A bright light caught her eye causing her to pause in mid stretch. She stood upright and drew her vision along the path her eyes had wandered a second time in hopes of catching a glimpse of it again. She was rewarded with a glinting of something in the distance.

"Aileesha look," said Syndara in surprise, pointing towards a jagged chunk of ice jutting from a cluster of snow-covered rocks.

Sunlight was dancing off of something encased within it.

"What do you suppose it is," replied Aileesha?

"I have no idea. Let's go see!"

They secured the sleds and made their way through the snow to the jutting ice. Small rays of color were visible depending on the angle of approach, serving only to heighten their curiosity. Examining the object embedded in the ice proved challenging, and not much could be made of it other than it was much larger than the little bit that was showing.

"What do you think it is," asked Aileesha?

"Not a clue," replied Syndara, eyes fixed on the ice-entombed object.

"Should we break it out of there," asked Aileesha grinning excitedly?

Syndara nodded, her own smile spreading across her face as she pulled out one of her axes.

"Maybe it's something of value we can trade for supplies when the traveling merchants come north in the spring."

Aileesha began digging the snow away from the ice, and Syndara set to chiseling away the ice with her axe blade. It wasn't long before they had the object uncovered, and as they broke it free from the last bit of its icy prison, they gasped in awe at the relic they had discovered.

It was made of gold, and seemed to be one half of a larger disk shaped object, with gemstones of various colors embedded into its surface. There were etchings around its outside edge, unreadable symbols neither of them had ever seen. There were odd rectangular protrusions on the back of the object that didn't seem to fit with the regal nature of the artifact.

"It's magnificent," said Syndara, running her hand across the surface of the half disk.

Her fingers paused on each gem, rubbing away whatever filament had gathered on them over the years.

"I've never seen anything like it," replied Aileesha.

"Nor have I. Where do you think it's from, and what do you think it's for?"

"Better question is, how in the nine realms did it end up here? Maybe it's a crest from a shield of some long dead knight," Aileesha chuckled.

"You and your tales of adventure," Syndara smiled and shoved Aileesha playfully with one hand.

Aileesha laughed, scooped some snow into her gloved hands and threw it at Syndara in retaliation.

They both looked at the broken ice that had held the treasure, pondering.

"Do you think there are more beneath our feet," asked Aileesha?

"It's entirely possible, but that's an adventure for another day and warmer weather," replied Syndara, rubbing her arms for emphasis.

The sun had begun its descent, the shadows of night were creeping along the ground and light was fleeting fast.

"It's getting dark, we should find shelter," she said as she stood and offered a hand to Aileesha who had returned to inspect their new found treasure.

"There's a rocky overhang not far from here that should provide us with enough shelter. Let's make camp there for the evening. We'll continue on to the village in the morning, and we can ask the chieftain about this," Aileesha replied, holding up the disk to catch the retreating sunlight. "After we deliver the meat to Jarmus for curing that is."

"A good plan," agreed Syndara, brushing the remaining snow away that clung to her fur lined clothes.

She patted Aileesha on the shoulder and headed off to find some wood. Not long after, a small fire was crackling away with a bit of Mammoth meat roasting on a makeshift spit.

Syndara rubbed the meat with some spices and Aileesha unraveled their bedrolls over a layer of green bows freshly cut from a nearby fir tree. They ate in relative quiet, each pondering what they had discovered in silence.

"I'll take the first watch," offered Syndara after they had finished with their meal.

"Fine with me, I'm exhausted," replied Aileesha. She crawled into her bedroll by the fire and was soon snoring lightly.

Syndara let the fire die down to coals, stoking it just often enough to keep them warm, but giving little light. The Obodoon Mountains were no place to sleep in the wild without a watch. Snow leopards, mountain bears, and many other dangers hunted for food at night, looking for unsuspecting prey, even in the winter months; perhaps more so than the warmer months. She found her mind wandering with thoughts of the relic they had found, and inspected it in the dim light of the fire. Her fingers traced absently across its surface while her mind wandered in thought as to its origins.

They Who Linger

Her gaze drifted out past the overhanging rock where icicles had begun to form where the warmth of their fire attempted to creep past the threshold. The valley was bathed in moonlight, casting dark shadows out from trees and rock outcroppings alike. It was one of the most serene sights she had ever seen, and as she watched the snow catch the moonlight, like a thousand stars floating on the wind through the darkness as it blew about in a soft breeze. A rhythmic humming crept into her mind and she began to slip into a deep sleep; the relic still in her grasp.

Chapter Sixteen

Aileesha was awoken by a howling screech that echoed through the valley. She rubbed sleep from her eyes and scanned the moon lit night for the source of the sound. A gentle breeze was blowing steadily through the trees, drifting snow in the direction of Garomvol down the valley. Seeing no sign of a culprit did little to comfort her.

Syndara was passed out on her bed roll with the relic in one hand and the grip of her bow in the other.

Aileesha grabbed her own bow and tapped Syndara on the head with her free hand to wake her. Aileesha held a finger to her lips to signal for silence and point out into the night.

Syndara nodded, a look of shame clear on her face for having fallen asleep on her watch. She silently mouthed her apology, thrust the relic into her pack and followed Aileesha to the mouth of the overhang.

Another screech echoed through the valley as they scanned the night again.

Syndara tapped Aileesha and pointed north up the valley in the direction they had traveled from the day before. She put a finger to her lips, signaling silence, as she looked her friend in the eyes. There was a dark figure near a clump of trees not far from where they had dug out the relic. Its head was raised to the night sky, sniffing the air.

"I see something near the trees where we found the relic, can you see it," whispered Syndara?

"I see it. I don't think it's very friendly looking. What do we do," asked Aileesha?

"Defend ourselves," replied Syndara, planting a handful of arrows tip first into the snow beside her.

"Is it wolves," asked Aileesha as she did the same.

"Unlikely, it looks too big to be a wolf and it sure didn't sound like any wolf I've ever heard."

Aileesha looked around anxiously. A second screech echoed through the valley, this one much closer, and seemed to come from above and behind their shelter. She leaned out slowly from the mouth of the overhang, her bow taut and ready to strike.

"What are you doing," whispered Syndara sternly?

"Seeing if I can spot whatever it is," replied Aileesha, glancing back at Syndara over her shoulder.

Aileesha was returning her attention to the opening, when a creature jumped down just in front of the overhang, barely missing her with a giant, clawed appendage. It immediately skittered to the side from where it landed with unnatural speed.

Reflexively, Syndara nocked and fired an arrow at the beast in one quick motion, striking it in the neck. The creature reeled back through the air with the impact. It gurgled and squealed as it swiped at the air in front of it in a desperate attempt to assail its prey before it fell limp in the snow.

Before she could focus on the first figure she had spotted further up the valley, another creature lunged from the shadows, growling hideously. Still surprised, Syndara realized she had no arrow ready. Without thinking, she quickly threw herself backwards, grabbed an arrow as she rolled and notched it in the same motion. She came up on one knee with her bow raised ready to fire. Her mind was racing but her body was focused and calm, like she was two people. What were these nightmare creatures and how had she fallen asleep? She had never passed out on watch before. How had she just performed the action that she had?

Aileesha, shouted at Syndara to snap out of her daze, let out a bellow and loosed an arrow of her own. The arrow struck the new creature in one of its shoulders, but failed to halt its forward momentum. It scrambled and failed to keep its balance, landed on all fours and slid out of control towards her. The collision knocked them both to the ground in a tangled heap at the back of the overhang.

Syndara snapped out of her momentary self reflection and back to the unfolding events. Still crouching, she kicked out with a bent leg to spin herself around on her other knee, following the pair as they tumbled out of control. She stretched her bow as taught as she dared and let her second arrow fly when she spotted an opportunity.

The creature had recovered quickly and was hovering over Aileesha with a clawed appendage raised to strike at her exposed throat. Aileesha heard the bow string stretch and kicked out with both feet as hard as she could, catching the beast in its stomach, forcing it back on its hind legs with its back to her friend.

Syndara's arrow pierced the base of its skull and exited through its snout. It lolled back and forth momentarily before releasing its final breath in a whimpering chuff, falling to the ground like a felled tree.

"Get away from it Aileesha," called Syndara as she rushed over and shot another arrow into the creature's chest without hesitating, giving it no chance to strike out again in its death throes.

It convulsed a few more times, the final remnants of life fading from it.

"What are these things," shouted Aileesha in a shaky voice. She crawled quickly away from the beast, her hand searching through the darkness for her bow.

"I don't know, but we can't stay here, it's not safe," replied Syndara.

"Do you think they're drawn by the meat?"

"Probably."

"What if it's the thing we found?"

"Don't be silly, this isn't one of your stories."

"Stories come from somewhere," retorted Aileesha defensively.

"Yeah, the imagination of troubled bards and chroniclers," said Syndara with a slight eye roll.

Breathing heavily, Syndara shouldered her bow, kicked at the creature once to make sure it wasn't moving anymore, and then retrieved the remaining arrows she had planted in the snow at the mouth of the overhang.

"Get your things together as fast as you can."

They checked to make sure there were no more creatures lurking in the shadows, waiting for them to come out of their shelter. The only creature they saw was the one near their dig site, and it slowly slunk into the shadows between some trees and disappeared into the night. They secured their belongings to the sleds and started off down the valley towards Garomvol as quickly as they could, looking over their shoulders the whole way. Daybreak was beginning to creep over the mountains around them, bringing some comfort that perhaps if there were any more of the creatures pursuing them, they would think twice about approaching in the coming daylight.

They Who Linger

Out of sight behind them, the bodies of the beasts melted to smoky ash where they lay in the snow-strewn area of the overhang and drifted on the light breeze, leaving no trace of their existence, not even a stain in the snow.

Chapter Seventeen

Syndara and Aileesha staggered into the village, ready to collapse in exhaustion as they pulled the sleds in front of the butcher's longhouse. Most of the villagers were still indoors, most likely still asleep or eating breakfast. The few who were moving around in the early morning quickly gathered around them and relieved them of their burdens.

"Get some water boy, hurry," Jarmus ordered, waving a hand at his young assistant. "What brings you back to us in such a state, and at such an early hour at that? You must have traveled all night."

Devlin hurried off to get water, having been all but shoved away.

Jarmus, a monster of a man, dragged the sleds out of the way one by one and secured them. Satisfied that they would not run away down a hill, he returned his attention to the women who were still catching their breath. He folded his arms and waited for a reply.

Devlin returned a short while later with the water and both women drank greedily. Water trailed down their chins and dripped off their furs.

Syndara wiped the excess water off her face with the back of one gloved hand and thanked Devlin. Having caught her breath, she looked at Jarmus and shook her head in disbelief as she explained the events that transpired.

"We were attacked by some dark skinned creatures just before dawn, not far up the valley. I think they might have been after the meat," said Syndara.

"I still think they wanted our treasure," said Aileesha.

Syndara rolled her eyes and shushed her friend.

Jarmus raised an eyebrow, "Treasure?"

"It's nothing," replied Syndara.

Aileesha shrugged and turned away, playing with the string of her bow which was still slung over her shoulder across her chest.

Jarmus eyed them both for a moment but let it be.

"They woke us from our sleep, screeching like no beast I've ever heard. Nor did they look like any I've ever seen. Their feet were nothing but claws, no, more like taloned fingers. And quills, they were covered in black quills I think," added Aileesha furrowing her brow.

Jarmus unfolded his arms and helped them to their feet.

"Are either of you hurt? Do you need the healer," he asked with concern?

"No, we're fine. We managed to fend them off without any serious injuries to anything other than our pride. We slew two creatures before grabbing our things and making for home," replied Syndara.

Jarmus looked them over once more anyways. Seeing that they were fine, he nodded and turned his attention to Devlin and the sleds of meat.

"Right then, Devlin, take this meat to the smokehouse," he instructed his assistant, throwing two of the meat sacks from the sleds at him.

"But I-" Devlin grunted as he caught the sacks in both arms and slung one over each shoulder, "Fine, I didn't want to know anymore anyways."

The young lad trudged off toward the smokehouse around the back of the butcher's home, kicking at snow drifts along the way, grumbling under his breath all the while.

Aileesha chuckled as they watched Devlin leave.

"What was that about," asked Syndara?

"Boys will be boys," replied Jarmus, "He's always afraid of missing something. He means well, but he's too quick to grow up."

Jarmus snorted.

"Takes after his old man here I suppose," he added and slung a couple of meat sacks over each shoulder, "Should we be worried about wolves or something else then?"

"No, not wolves, and I don't think there were any more of whatever they were. We watched for any sign of them as we made our way here," answered Syndara.

"Very well then, I should get this meat to the smokehouse and start getting it ready for curing."

"Ok, I need to speak to the chieftain. Thank Devlin again for the water please."

"I shall."

"Talk to you soon Jarmus," said Aileesha.

Syndara turned her attention to Aileesha as Jarmus strode off towards the smokehouse.

"I'll catch up with you after OK," asked Syndara?

"Ok, I'm going to check the baker's supplies," replied Aileesha. Her tummy grumbled.

"It's good to be back isn't it," added Syndara with a smile?

"Very, and I think I smell fresh spiced bread," replied Aileesha, licking her lips hungrily.

They Who Linger

They laughed heartily and went their separate ways.

Chapter Eighteen

Festus set a strip of felt cloth between the pages to mark his spot and closed the book, its pages making a dull *thwump* as they clapped together.

"Why did you stop Mr. Festus," inquired Maddi?

"It's time for lunch, and that means the end of your first lesson. I'll review your work, and we will go over it tomorrow," replied Festus.

"Wow, that went fast. I didn't even notice how hungry I was."

"That's a sign that you have writing in your blood," said Festus with a chuckle.

"How does one get writing in their blood? Does it come out," asked Maddi with a worried look? Before Festus could explain further, her face contorted into horror. "Am I going to die Mr. Festus? How is that good?!" Her face went red, emotions threatening to break free of the damn.

"Oh, my dear, no. You misunderstand. I apologize," replied Festus. He scrunched up his face as he fought to find the right words to stave off Maddi's tears. "I should be more careful with my words. I will be more mindful in the future, and be sure to explain things better. I simply meant you have a natural talent for this kind of thing. You are blessed."

Maddi sniffed, catching a sob in her throat before it could escape. Her lip quivered, but soon stilled as she won the battle against her emotions.

"Oh," she said simply. After a short pause she smiled, jumped out of her chair and ran over to hug Festus. "Thank you, Mr. Festus."

"No thanks needed child. I'm sorry I upset you. I forget you are young and unlearned in many things. Please, be sure to let me know if you don't understand what I say sometimes."

"I will."

"Ok then. How about a book to read in the evenings as the second part of your studies? You can pick a new one when you are finished."

"REALLY," exclaimed Maddi?

"Yes, really. But, you mustn't lose it, or damage it in any way. Deal?"

"Deal!"

"Alright. I know you said you can read and write, but I need a way to gauge how advanced your reading and comprehension skills are, so how about we start you with one of the simpler fable compilations?"

"What's a fable?"

"A fable is a short story, usually with animals as characters, conveying a moral."

"What's a moral?"

Festus looked dumbfounded momentarily then explained as best he could. "Morals are the principles of right and wrong behavior and the goodness or badness of actions.

"Oh. That sounds fun!"

"Very well. Look for the title 'Adventures of Anarik Finabarin Volume One' on the shelf next to my reading chair," said Festus and pointed towards the corner.

Maddi hurried over to the book shelf and began reading out the titles while she looked.

While she was busy hunting for the book, Festus gathered up the papers that Maddi had written on while he read and stacked them next to his book in the center of the table.

"Got it," shouted Maddi and held up the book in triumph!

"That was quick. Let's see, child," said Festus.

Maddi rushed back to the table and handed the book to Festus.

"That's the one. Ok, remember what we agreed upon, keep it safe from the other children."

"I will Mr. Festus, I super duper promise," replied Maddi with a toothy grin.

"Let's go get some lunch," said Festus and ushered her out of the study, closing and locking the door behind him.

~*~

The next morning was much the same. Maddi was waiting for Festus in the hall outside of his study with a tray. This time it had some pastries as well as the Javium and cups. Fresh baked hazelnut buns if the smell wafting down the hall to greet him as he approached was any indication. His stomach growled at the smell.

"Good morning Maddi," greeted Festus.

"I brought pastries. They're fresh from the oven. The Steward Mother sends her regards," replied Maddi.

"Thank you, I could smell them all the way down the hall."

93

Festus unlocked the door, opened it and stepped into his study. He held the door for Maddi, then closed it.

"How did you find the fables in Anarik's first volume," asked Festus curiously?

"Delightful. I read them all," replied Maddi.

"Already? That's... amazing. How did you manage to read them all already?"

"I don't sleep much most nights. I sure did after I finished the book though."

"Oh child," exclaimed Festus! "You need your rest if you are to put your mind to the creative task of putting ink to paper. That will be the first lesson for the day, and an amendment to our book deal. You must get proper sleep each night."

Maddi sighed. "Ok. But what if I just can't fall asleep?"

"Have you spoken to the Steward Mother about your troubles sleeping? I'm sure she has some tea that could help."

"I have, and she's tried that."

"Well, maybe another tactic is needed. I find that journaling helps me. We will get you an extra quill and inkwell, and a journal of your own to write in. You can read for a little while each night, but then you must journal until your eyes grow heavy. How does that sound?"

"Like fun!"

"It can be quite enjoyable indeed, but the object of the exercise is to get all your thoughts out of your head and onto paper so that your mind is empty and ready to rest."

"Ok. Do I still get to pick another book," asked Maddi? She pulled the book from a giant pocket at the waist of her steward gown, walked over to the book shelf in the corner and placed it back where she had found it the day before.

"Yes, you can pick another. Perhaps something a little more challenging this time?"

"Sure."

"Let's go with a history book this time. Look for 'The Formation'."

Maddi went about her search and Festus poured himself some Javium. He opened his own book on the table and then took one of the pastries from the tray, savoring the first bite before following it with a sip of the Javium.

"Got it," said Maddi, sliding the book from the shelf. She walked back to the table, set the book down and took her seat, eager to start.

Festus finished his pastry, wiped his hand on his robe and moved the felt cloth marker off the page.

"You did a fantastic job yesterday Maddi. Your spelling is very good, and your attention to detail is on par with many of the chroniclers that have been doing this for many years. If you don't mind my asking, who taught you," asked Festus?

"My mother and father both," replied Maddi. A haunting look passed over her face and Festus quickly changed the subject, not wanting to upset her.

"Masters in their own right no doubt. Today we will meet Corlag the Wanderer and Branick the Indomitable," said Festus. "Any questions before we start?"

Maddi shook her head, grabbed her quill and uncorked her inkwell.

With that, Festus began to read of spring time in the Fel'Thain Forest.

Chapter Nineteen

The soft scratching of the quill against the rough paper came to a pause as Maddi finished the last sentence and looked up at Festus. "Is it time," she asked?

"It is," replied Festus. He replaced the cloth marker between the pages and set it on the table, stood and stretched. There was still one pastry on the tray, and his stomach growled audibly. "Are you going to eat that," he asked, nodding at the tray?

"No, that's okay Mr. Festus, you have it."

"Thank you."

Maddi cleaned up her writing space at the end of the table, doing her best not to get any of the ink from her fingers on her gown or on the freshly scribed pages.

Festus retrieved one of the rags he used to wipe ink on from his own writing desk and handed it to her.

"It's amazing how the ink finds a way to get on the fingers no matter how hard you try to avoid it. It still happens to me even now. A hazard of the trade I'm afraid."

Maddi laughed as she accepted the rag and wiped her hands.

"Let's go find some lunch. I'll walk with you to the kitchen," said Festus. He picked up the tray, placed the cups on it and walked toward the door.

Maddi grabbed her new book and followed.

Once Festus had locked the door to the study with his free hand, they walked down the long hall toward the front of the library. They passed from the hall into the book stacks where a few people were browsing the shelves, and a few more were looking over open books on long wooden tables in the reading area in the center of the library's first floor. It was well lit with reflected natural light that came from windows recessed in the walls of raised channels that ran the length of the ceiling. The design was perfect, allowing for ample natural light during the day without the threat of direct sunlight to fade and age the plethora of manuscripts, books, and scrolls that were kept in the stacks.

It was an enchanting place, and despite not having spent much time within the stacks himself in recent times, Festus felt the same level of elation as he did the first time he visited before his tenure as an apprentice scribe. That thought made him nostalgic.

"Did you know I was once an apprentice scribe here at the library myself, Maddi," he asked with a glance down at her? She was smiling from ear to ear, looking all around at the stacks of books and scrolls.

"Really," she blurted?

"Shh, not so loud please," came a voice from behind a nearby stack.

"Sorry," replied Maddi in a loud whisper instantly. She continued in a loud whisper "When did you first come to the Library Mr. Festus?"

"I was not much older than you I think. Twelve in fact. My father wanted me to be a wood carver like himself and his father before that, but my hands had other plans. I did not have the same skill for carving wood as they did. Luckily, my mother loved to read, and she taught me when I was quite young. It stuck, and I never wanted to do anything besides study written words and learn to write my own."

"I don't remember much of my parents at all. The bits I can remember are," Maddi paused for a moment trying to find the right word while they walked through a door into another hall leading to the Library Residence wing, "foggy, I guess."

"Do you remember anything at all about where you were before the Library," asked Festus?

"No. I mean, I see images when I sleep, of a small farm near a small village in the mountains, but I don't know if it's real or just another dream."

"Well, I hope the fog clears in time."

"Thanks."

They continued the rest of the way to the kitchen in silence. The Steward Mother greeted them when they entered the kitchen. She was in the midst of ushering some of the other stewards out into the serving hall with trays full of sandwiches and vegetables fresh from the gardens.

"Maddi dearest, would you take this tray out with the others please," said the Steward Mother without skipping a beat.

Maddi nodded, rushed over to pick up the tray, and exited through the door into the serving hall.

Festus set the tray down on the counter next to a large wash basin near a window that looked out over a large hedged lawn.

"I see some of the vegetables are ready," said Festus.

"Nothing better than some fresh from the soil vegetables is there Fes," replied the Steward Mother.

"Especially them carrots. Good for the eyes you know."

She smiled at him, leaned against the counter and wiped her hands on a cloth. "Thank you for taking an interest in teaching Maddi, Fes. It really means a lot. She's had a rough time adjusting since she arrived, and honestly, this is the first time I've seen her happy."

"Honestly, she's given me something to do for the first time in a long while. I have had a horrible time putting down words on the page lately. It's helping to unclog my mind, and distracting me from brooding on the fact that I haven't done anything. It feels good to teach again."

"So she's really dedicated to this then," she asked with genuine curiosity?

"I don't think I've seen a more naturally talented child in all my years here at the Library. Whoever her parents were, they taught her well. She read through the entire first volume of Anarik Finabarin's adventures in a single evening, and she's kept up with my reading pace while scribing. It's beyond remarkable. Her spelling and writing competency are advanced beyond her years."

"Wow, I had no idea. Wait, did she even sleep a wink? Oh, that girl!"

"Don't worry, I already spoke with her about proper rest and pacing herself. We made a deal that she would only read for a short bit each night, and after that she is to write in her journal. She did say that she has trouble sleeping though, and that you've given her sleeping tea but it didn't really help, is that so?"

"Yes, yes. I really don't know what to do for her."

"Hmm. Perhaps the healer in town would have something that could help?"

"That stubborn old coot wouldn't know how to treat a pimple."

"I take it you don't like his methods?"

"Pah! To call what he does 'healing' would be like me saying I'm the Empress of Ael'Andar."

It was Festus' turn to smile.

"If it's all the same, I'll write a letter and see if there's something we can try."

"Do as you will. You always do," she frowned and sighed. "Sorry, I don't mean anything by it."

"It's quite alright, Elania. I know how you feel. Though he may be a bit crazy, Zev does do some good now and then.

"I know it," she replied. Elania bowed her head and slapped her hands against her thighs.

Festus recognized her trademark look of embarrassment and quickly stepped over to wrap her in a hug. "Don't worry about it. I'll look into it and let you know. Now, I'm going to go grab a sandwich before they are all gone."

Elania smirked and waved him on with her hands as she would to usher one of her stewards away on a task. "Off with you then, and thanks again Fes, really, I mean it."

Festus waved over his shoulder and walked out into the serving hall.

Chapter Twenty

Maddi found the door to the study ajar the next morning, and Festus standing at his writing desk near the window that looked out over the valley. He was so intent on whatever he was writing that he did not hear her enter or set down the tray on the table.

"Good morning," she said.

Festus startled slightly, turned and greeted her in return. "Hello Maddi, I hope you got some sleep last night." He had a quill in his right hand, and she caught a glimpse of freshly inked paper.

"What are you writing," she asked, avoiding the question.

"Oh, this? Just a letter to an old friend. I'll be with you in a moment, you go ahead and get all set up. Did you use your journal last night," asked Festus as he returned his attention to writing his letter?

"I did."

"Good, that's good. I hope it helps."

Maddi said nothing more, silently laid out her paper and quill, and then sat in the reading chair in the corner and picked up a book at random from the stack on the small table next to it. She was half way through a short story about the exploits of an old farmer searching for his lost sheep and an unruly mountain giant when Festus cleared his throat and set his quill in its stand. He corked the ink well on his desk, folded up the paper and tucked it away in a pocket on the inside of his robe. "Okay Maddi, are you ready to begin?"

Maddi closed the book and nodded, then scooted over to her writing spot at the end of the table.

"Once again I commend your abilities Maddi. You're a natural. I reviewed yesterday's work and only have a few minor things to cover with you before we start today." Festus slid a piece of paper across the table toward Maddi with a small list of things on it. He went over each thing on the list and she read the instructions as he did so. "Any questions," asked Festus?

"No, I think I got it," replied Maddi with a smile.

"Alright. If you have questions about the techniques later, don't hesitate to ask." Festus flipped open his book to his cloth marker and placed it in his lap.

Chapter Twenty-One

Branick peered over his shoulder for perhaps the third time since they had been ambushed in the clearing hours earlier. They were still moving at a brisk pace through the forest, without a word between them. It was best to keep focused, there would be time enough for questions and discussion later.

The path wound between a split in the rocky bluff. Stone cliffs rose like ancient monoliths on both sides, acting as a gateway of sorts. The path began to straighten again, hugging the hill that rose up on their left towards the north where the Obodoon Mountains stood over all other lands of Ael'Andar. A gully led into a deep gorge on their right, before falling off and becoming the looming rock wall that separated the Upper Fel'Thain from the lower. In the distance was a breathtaking view of the valley of Thain's Reach that stretched out hundreds of feet below. A river wound through the midst of it, snaking the full length towards the south. It split half way across the plains. One branch stretched out of the forest to meet the Everdeep, the other turned inland to the south east where it drained into the lands beyond the borders of the Reach. The sun, dipping lower in the sky as the afternoon waned, glittered off the river's surface like diamonds strewn across dark velvet.

Corlag stopped suddenly as he returned his gaze to the path, stretching out a hand behind him to catch Branick's attention, and signaled him to stop. Not more than a few dozen paces ahead of them was a robed figure sitting on a log overlooking both the path and the view of the valley below. His fingers weaved together repeatedly as he sat in silence, giving no sign of having noticed their approach. A gnarled walking stick rested against the log beside him.

After a moment of silent observation by Corlag, the figure tilted his head toward them, exposing one side of his face from within the drooping hood of his tattered woolen robe. The skin on his face was withered with age, and the one visible eye was dark in all parts. He was frail looking, his earth colored robe seemed to hang on little more than bare bone. Yet the stranger emanated power when he spoke, commanding attention from any who heard his words. His eye came to rest on Corlag's pack. He greeted them, his voice raspy at first, but clearing as he spoke.

"'Ello travelers, fair journeys to you. I am Borgolas if'n you're apt to inquire,' he stated matter-of-factly.

Corlag shifted his weight from foot to foot uneasily and nudged Branick when the old man glanced away down the path in the direction they were heading.

"What can we do for you old man," asked Branick?

Borgolas snapped his attention back to his guests, his eyes nothing but black orbs. They seemed to burrow right into them.

"I was merely greeting some fellow travelers happening by," replied Borgolas with a hint of displeasure.

He brushed back his hood with one bony hand, revealing the rest of his features. His eyes once again drifted to Corlag's bag.

"You both seem as though you could use a rest, care to share my log? It has quite a view."

"We're fine, thank you," replied Corlag.

"Aye, we have far to travel yet, and the day is not young," added Branick as he took a step forward and pointed down the path in front of them, "be well, and watch out for strange creatures."

Corlag began walking as Branick came alongside him. They passed by Borgolas side by side, Branick the closest.

"Creatures you say," rasped Borgolas after them.

"Aye, wild animals I mean," replied Branick with a backward glance, "there are many dangerous wild animals in these parts of late it seems."

Borgolas chuckled heartily.

"Indeed."

He flashed a toothy smile at Branick, his dark eyes giving him pause. They seemed to flare momentarily. Borgolas lifted his hood back in place over his bald head, the effort laboursome.

Branick turned his attention back to the path, and they hastened their pace to a brisk walk so as not to make it seem like they were hurrying away any faster than they had approached. No words needed speaking about the awkwardness of the encounter, nor the timing. They were disquieted by the situation, causing them to periodically check the path behind them throughout the remainder of the day.

Chapter Twenty-Two

Borgolas moved swiftly and quietly between the trees on the hillside following the path out of sight. His agility did not fit with the body he found himself trapped within. He knew the Crossroads would be the destination of the travelers. As he walked, he had to stop and rest periodically, propping himself against a tree or dropping to his knees on a patch of moss, small flashes of images from his past flooded his mind. A voice began to take root there, as if someone were narrating a story of ages long past from inside his skull.

'I don't know how long I have wandered this world, in the shell of a man, searching for an ancient power that is as lost to me as my former self. So long has it been that I couldn't recall what I sought, that now I am not even sure the ripples in my mind are real. The first sense of urgency came a day or so ago, waking from my slumber deep within the husk of a man I do not know, yet is wholly familiar to me.
I say this metaphorically of course, as I no longer sleep like a normal man. I am constantly roaming, searching, waiting. The ripples grew closer together, and I found myself

drawn here to the Reach. A wretched place of men in the cradle of the new world.

I can feel the source, it is close. Two travelers seem to be in possession of whatever it is my body seeks, one a bard if my observations are correct, and the other a seasoned warrior.'

Fearing he may fall over as the images became more intense, and the voice stronger, he sat on a rock propped between two trees. His head was pounding now. He cradled it in his bony hands, clenching back a cry of pain before sliding to the ground unconscious. The images overtook his mind and the voice drowned out the world around him.

'How do I know these things? These places across the world where I do not remember ever being? Why am I able to sense whatever it is they carry, and most of all, why do I have this ability? My mind has become splintered, my body a shriveled husk for a foreign host.

I find myself in dark company, hidden yet in plain sight. Have I become a puppet? Am I of this world? Am I even alive anymore?

Yes, that's it, this must be a dream, all a dream. No, a nightmare! Why can't I wake from it?

I need answers. I do not know how much longer I can hold out against whatever is awakening deep within me. Yes, yes, I must get answers. No... HE must have answers. We must follow these travelers and see what can be learned.'

Chapter Twenty-Three

Chieftain Dohmnall woke to a knock at the door of his quaint home that overlooked Garomvol. He slid out from under the blankets quietly so as not to wake his wife, and wrapped himself in some furs and groggily made his way to open the heavy wooden door. The cold hinges made a cracking sound in protest against the movement as they worked off the chill of winter, metal grinding on metal. Standing in the doorway was Syndara. Dohmnall cleared his throat gently.

"Good morning Syndara, welcome back. What brings you to my dwelling at such an early hour?"

"Sorry to wake you with the dawning of the day Chieftain, but I have some troubling news about our journey."

"I've told you a hundred times and more, don't call me that. Dohm will do for you," he gently chastised as he ushered her inside and closed the door.

He wrapped the furs tighter about himself and made his way to the hearth and stoked the fire, then set a kettle to boil for Javium.

"Blast, it's chilly out there this morning isn't it," he stated.

"I suppose so, I hadn't really noticed to be honest," replied Syndara with a smile.

"Of course you didn't. How silly of me. Now then, tell me this news while we wait for the Javium to brew."

Dohmnall set the lid on the iron kettle and took a seat at the simple wooden table next to the hearth, gesturing for Syndara to join him.

"I'm not sure where to start. It still seems so unreal to me," she said as she took a seat.

"At the beginning my dear, start at the beginning," replied Dohmnall.

Syndara fidgeted with the strap on her pack in her lap, and cleared her throat.

"Right then," she started, not taking her eyes off her bag, "We were about a half day's journey from the village when we discovered something shining in a chunk of jagged ice that was jutting out of the snow and rocks. We decided to see what it was."

She flipped the untied flap open on her pack and wriggled the cloth covered disk fragment free. It made a thumping sound despite her delicate touch in laying it on the table in front of her.

"This is what we found. I have no idea what it is. By the time we had gotten it mostly out of the ice, it was getting too dark to travel any further for the day, so we set camp under a nearby overhang."

Dohmnall flipped open the cloth, revealing its contents. He gasped in surprise as light from the window caught the gems in the surface of the artifact, sending a rainbow of colors splashing over the walls of the cozy home. He stood slowly, face contorted in thought. He stepped over to the hearth, lifted the lid on the kettle and gave the Javium a few stirs before returning to his seat.

"It's magnificent," he said finally, "But, my dear, is this what troubles you? Finding a treasure in the ice?"

"No Dohm, not at all. There's more, much more."

"More treasure?"

"What? Oh, no. I mean, maybe beneath the ice and earth. More to the story I meant, the troubling bit."

"Oh? Do go on then," he replied while picking up the object and inspecting it with the utmost scrutiny, turning it in his hands, weighing it gently.

Syndara rubbed her face with her hands before she continued. She could feel the warmth of the fire finally chiseling away the cold from her skin.

"We were woken by a creature, screeching, just before daybreak. I spotted a black skinned creature, short and lanky, with clawed feet. We were attacked by a second creature that dropped down in front of our camp. It just missed Aileesha with its claws. Luckily my reflexes were quicker than my senses, my bow shot killed the creature outright. A second creature attacked while we were distracted, almost getting the jump on me, but Aileesha's quick thinking no doubt saved my life. We dispatched the beasts, grabbed our things and left as fast as we could."

"This relic is fascinating. I've never seen anything like it. Its craftsmanship is masterful indeed. And these markings-," said Dohmnall, he trailed off, still entranced by the gem studded golden disk.

The fire hissed a few times behind him, causing him to jump up out of his seat. He set the jeweled piece of metal back down on the cloth and then swiftly removed the kettle from above the fire. He lifted the lid inquisitively, sniffing deeply.

"Ahh, it's ready."

Dohmnall scooped out two portions of javium into cylindrically carved wooden cups. He handed one to

Syndara and cupped the other in both hands, a smile growing on his face.

"I'm not sure if there were more of the creatures, I think we should double the watchers just in case. I will help if need be. I don't want to be responsible for bringing harm to anyone in the village," Syndara continued.

"Nonsense, I will let Braegar know. He can cover the extra watch with his men. You will have a much more important task," interjected Dohmnall.

He sipped noisily at the steaming liquid in his cup.

"I will do whatever is needed, winter is hard enough without extra troubles."

"Good, I'm glad to hear it, though I'm not sure you fully understand."

Syndara looked at him questioningly, her cup held to her lips.

"What do you mean," she asked?

Dohmnall set his cup down and wrapped the cloth over the relic as he spoke.

"This treasure has many questions attached to it, Syndara. Something in the back of my mind is making me think that the only people that will know what it is and whether it is dangerous or not, are the Aolfkin."

Syndara sputtered, almost choking on her swig of javium at the mention of the ancient race.

"Aolfkin? Me? Are you serious? You want me to travel across the Everdeep to seek answers from an ancient race that may or may not even reside there anymore but in tales? Have you gone mad old man? You know I love you but that's-"

Dohmnall raised his hands and grasped hers in his, pausing her onslaught. They locked eyes for a long while in silence. Much was said without speaking. She was like a daughter to him and he, like a father to her. Each in turn knew the others thoughts and hearts.

"They are no myth. Of that I assure you. I do not wish to see you leave, but it raises my hackles despite its beauty. Many tales of old stir in my mind when I gaze upon it, and it makes me uneasy. We must know what this relic is. If there is anything to such a treasure, the Aolfkin would know it."

"But why do we need to care about such things? What makes you think this treasure is something dangerous? Can we not just sell or trade it for supplies with the farmers in Thain's Reach to the south? Let it be someone else's problem."

"Just a feeling," replied Dohmnall, his face serious. The left side of his face twitched once, threatening to betray something unspoken. He took another sip from his cup and continued, "If this relic has history attached to it, we should not use it for our own gain. It would be even worse if there is some sort of foulness attached to it. I would not have our people be held responsible for bringing harm to our friends in the south. It's not an easy thought, leaving on such a journey, I understand this, but it is necessary and I do not trust anyone else to do what I ask with such a treasure. Despite the good nature of our friends and family here, most would disappear into the world with such riches in their grasp, and who could blame them for wanting a better life? Besides, I think you are the most capable of making this journey, and you should not be going alone. No that would be ill of me to suggest, you should take Aileesha with you, you're like sisters and I trust her as much as you."

Syndara stared at Dohmnall dumbfounded. Her cup, forgotten, tilted dangerously; the hot liquid within threatening to spill into her lap.

Dohmnall took the cup from her hands and set it on the table before the liquid could jump free and assault her.

"I-" she trailed off.

Dohmnall smiled and sipped his javium, giving her the time she needed to process.

Syndara knew there was truth in his words. A thousand thoughts warred inside her head for control. *Why did we have to find this blasted thing? Can't we just bury it?* She knew there was no other path forward than the one spoken of. With a sigh of resignation she found her voice again.

"I thank you for your confidence in me, Dohm, but if I am to take this journey, I won't bring any more of our people away from everything they know. If indeed you feel there could be danger attached to this trek, I would rather venture it alone. Tell no one of this until I am gone, especially Aileesha. I could never put her in harm's path. That is my only request, that and keep Aileesha from doing anything foolish in my absence."

"It shall be as you say," replied Dohmnall. He handed the wrapped disk to her, "Take a bit of time to gather your things and supplies. You will travel to Barroville in the south and seek passage on a boat from there. It's a friendlier port than Strandton."

He retrieved a leather purse, drawn closed with a fine woven string, from a sack of potatoes in the corner behind the table. It jingled slightly when he set it in her hands. He wrapped his hands around hers and pulled her to him for a hug.

"My dear child, how you've grown; a beautiful soul inside and out. Your parents would be so proud."

Tears welled in his eyes as he stepped back and looked her in the eyes.

"You will need to leave as soon as possible, the last of the boats to cross the Everdeep for sometime will be leaving when the spring festival ends, I should think."

"I should be ready by mid-day. I'll need a sled if I am to travel quickly. I will leave it at our southern watch post and continue on foot from there," replied Syndara.

"Of course, that's fine. The watchmen can return it when they change over next."

Syndara pulled the string open on the pouch gently and peered inside. It was filled with various coins and small gems. She drew the string closed and tucked it into a pocket inside her furs.

"Be safe, be smart, and may you return safely to us before the next season's change," said Dohmnall.

With that, Syndara returned the wrapped disk to her pack and made for the door. The hinges protested yet again as she opened it. Before stepping out into the cold, she turned to Dohmnall one last time.

"Keep a vigilant eye on the wilderness Dohm, I do not know what stirs in the woods, but I fear we have not seen the last of those creatures; whatever they are."

He nodded as Syndara turned and stepped outside. She closed the door behind her and tightened the last of the straps on her pack.

Hearing his wife begin to stir from her slumber in the next room, he scooped out two more portions of javium from the kettle and returned to his seat at the table awaiting her greeting.

"Good morning dear," his wife greeted while wrapping her arms around him from behind, her long hair falling about his face as she leaned in to give him a kiss.

"Dear lord, what has begun," he muttered under his breath, staring into his cup.

"What troubles you my love, who was here?"

Dohmnall looked up from his cup, a worried expression creasing his face.

"Syndara and Aileesha are back, but not for long. I have much to tell you," he said as he handed her the second cup of javium.

She sat next to him and listened to Dohmnall recount the events that had transpired.

Chapter Twenty-Four

Syndara knocked her feet against one of the logs next to the door of her home, kicking off the snow that clung to her boots before she stepped inside. With no fire crackling away in the stone hearth to warm it, the single room cabin was just slightly less cold than outside. She let herself get lost in the mundane task of setting a fire and collected her thoughts.

Before long, the fire had taken the chill out of the air and she set to gathering the things she would need for her journey. A tidy pile soon occupied the bed in front of her. A few sets of clothes, a collection of food in a woven sack, a tinderbox, a cooking pot, and a set of wooden dishes carved to fit one inside the other. She was packing her things into her travel pack when someone knocked on her door. Syndara sighed and rubbed her hands across her eyes, set the pack down beside the bed and answered the door.

Aileesha was standing in the doorway with a grin on her face from ear to ear, her long red hair flowed over her shoulders, and a spark danced in her marble eyes. Tendrils of steam rose from the loaf of fresh spiced bread in her hands. Knowing in that instantaneous moment that there was no escape from telling her best friend about her trip, she decided to invite her in. All she could do now was hope that she would understand.

"Come in then you goof, we have much to discuss," ushered Syndara with a wave of her arm.

A puzzled look replaced Aileesha's grin as she stepped passed.

"What is it Synd," she asked, closing the door behind her.

Syndara gestured to the two wooden chairs sitting in front of the hearth.

"Come, sit."

They each took a seat, and Aileesha set the loaf of spiced bread on the small table between the two chairs.

"I spoke to the Chieftain about the relic and our encounter with those beasts. He will have Braegar double the watch in case any more of them are skulking about," continued Syndara.

Aileesha broke the spiced bread loaf in half and handed one half to Syndara. "That is comforting. What did he say about the relic," she added, getting straight to the subject.

Syndara took a bite of the bread, her face warming slightly as the aroma from the loaf filled the room. After another bite she replied. "Mmm, that's one of the best batches of spiced bread yet I think," she started. "The Chieftain said he had never seen anything like it. He thinks it may be a relic of the old world, and so does not wish to use it for trade. He suspects it may have a foulness attached to it."

"A foulness? Like," Aileesha paused for a moment and picked pieces from the hunk of bread in her hands, "magic?"

Syndara burst out laughing and slapped Aileesha on the leg lightly.

"Surely not, don't be silly. You know those stories the minstrels tell are just that! Stories. Right?"

"Yeah, yeah, mock me all you want, but one day you'll see, there's something to all them tales. I mean where would they get such ideas if not from things that happened once upon a time?"

"Seriously though, Dohm wants me to seek out the Aolfkin across the Everdeep and show them the artifact, to determine if it's merely a harmless treasure or something else. That's how serious he was about it. He assured me they are no myth, that they truly exist."

"The Aolfkin," Aileesha exclaimed excitedly! She jumped out of her chair waving her arms and jumped up and down repeatedly. "No freaking way! You jest! What did he say of them? When do we leave? A real adventure! Finally! I got to get my thin-"

"Aileesha, wait, sit down. You don't understand," interjected Syndara. She locked eyes with her friend and prepared to shatter her best friend's heart. "*I* leave by midday. Alone."

Aileesha stopped her dancing about, hovering on one foot and stared at Syndara, her jaw agape. Her heart sank in her chest as Syndara's words crushed her dreams to dust. She collapsed back into her chair, a pained look creasing her brow.

"You wouldn't do that to me. You CAN'T," she choked! "No no no, you're not going alone. No WAY!"

Syndara sighed and gave Aileesha a caring look.

"I will not drag anyone else into this, especially you. It will be long, and not without danger. I spotted the relic and if there *IS* danger ahead, I will not be responsible for bringing you into its path."

"Nonsense, we were both there. Who's going to protect you if you get into trouble? Or lost, for that matter? We both know I'm the better tracker," replied Aileesha, animatedly poking Syndara as she cracked a smile. "I've wanted this my whole life, and now that there is a chance for such a journey, I will be damned if I let it pass me by, especially when my best friend is involved."

"I'll be fine, Aileesha. The village will need your hunting skills."

"Horse dung! There are plenty of others who can hunt. You're not swaying me from this Synd, I'm coming with you and that's a fact. The village has enough hunters and meat to last the rest of the winter here. Besides, there is nothing for me here. You know how badly I've longed for this, a real adventure, not just a trek into a part of the woods we've never been to before. This is my chance, our chance. It may never come again and I will not look back at my life with regret."

"But your parents-" pleaded Syndara.

"Will understand," Aileesha finished and added, "True friends stick together no matter the danger, and I won't be responsible for you getting into trouble because I didn't go with you."

Syndara quietly contemplated Aileesha's words for a moment before caving to her friend. How could she deny her this opportunity? It would be good to have company.

"Fine then, alright, you win. There will be no persuading you to change your mind, I know that much. Stubborn as an ox you are sometimes. You'd probably track me down even if I left without you anyways."

"Yes, yes, YES," Aileesha squealed triumphantly! She began hopping around excitedly again and pulled Syndara out of her chair into a bear hug. "This is going to be fun."

"You best get your things then," said Syndara as she playfully shoved her friend toward the door.

"I'll meet you back here shortly and I'll get us some more of that spiced bread too!"

Aileesha bolted through the doorway out into the snow, skidded to a stop in mid stride, spun around long enough to flash Syndara another grin and then continued quickly down the path.

"Don't forget your bow in your haste," Syndara called after her.

They had been friends since as far back as Syndara could remember, and she could not recall a time when her friend had been as excited as she now was.

Chapter Twenty-Five

Festus dismissed Maddi when he had finished the chapter. He forewent lunch to make the walk down the hill to the village of Maerin. He had two choices, he could take the road that wound around and between the hills, or he could take the footpath that had been worn along the hills by animals and people alike. It was more direct, but wove through the trees, and provided less sunlight.

The sky was clear, the sun warm, and the air crisp. He decided that the road would be the better choice as he had not been out in the sun in quite a while. The dirt path wound lazily down the hill, around a few bends, between a few more hills and out into flat farmland. Animals grazed in pastures where he passed by, penned in by log stacked fences.

It took him until mid-afternoon to reach the village, but he didn't mind. The journey warmed him, both in spirit and physically. Festus wiped sweat from his brow with a kerchief he had procured from one of his pockets, and he observed the village as he approached, noting small changes since last he had visited. New thatching adorned a few of the log homes, and new cobbles had been laid in the main street leading into the center of town where the villagers held their market. The new cobbles started from the fringe nearest the road to the Library and went all the way through the village center to the fringe of the main road on the western edge of the village.

Maerin was a quaint little place, tucked into the foothills east of Strandton, about a week's ride from the border to the eastern lands of Ael'andar. Composed of farmers, tanners, and tradesmen that plied their craft in peace. The only times they worried about the outside world was when travelers passed through, or they had to make the journey to Strandton or some other such place to sell their goods and buy what supplies they couldn't make or harvest themselves.

The Library had been established even before the village, further up in the foothills to the south east. The settlers were a few families of tradesmen that helped build the Library itself. In total, there were roughly fifty families that called Maerin home, at last census anyways. Festus wasn't sure that number was accurate anymore as he had spotted at least two new homes that had been constructed during the last summer season.

The village center was bustling with locals who all greeted him in turn when he passed by. They were carrying baskets of various trading goods and some children were laughing and running about chasing a chicken that really didn't look all too threatened.

He turned right at the village center and headed down the street leading north east. Zev favored being on the outskirts of the village, and when asked once long ago why he didn't live further away if he disliked people so much, he had replied that he preferred being further from the capital city than the rest of the folks here. His home was nestled up a small hill off the road a short ways outside the village, among a copse of alder trees. A bell hung from a fastened iron ring that had been nailed to one of the trunks next to the path. Festus pulled once, gently, on the bit of woven vines that hung from it. The bell clanged musically, jostling back and forth in the metal ring. Sunlight glinted off of it, dancing across the otherwise shaded copse.

"Zev, are you about," called Festus?

He stood there for a while with no response. He thought about leaving, but couldn't bring himself to give up so easily. Hesitating, he reached for the bell's vines again.

"Don't you even think about ringing that blasted thing a second time or I'll have to sick the Wicker Cat on you," shouted Zev from his open door.

"There you are old friend," replied Festus and lowered his hand to his side quickly. He smiled half heartedly, unsure if Zev was joking about the cat. One could never really tell with Zev, and so he continued to smile.

"What brings you all the way down here from your books?"

"I came to visit. It's been quite some time and I thought you would enjoy the company."

"Hog's arse. You know I like my peace as much as you like your books and your words. All the same, you might as well come in since you're here, I just made some Blood Vine tea and by the looks of it, you'll be needing it more than I after your walk."

"What? I may be getting old Zev, but I do get out more often than you. I appreciate the sentiment though."

They shared a laugh and Festus kicked his sandals against the stump outside the door and followed Zev inside.

A wicker cat stood where it always did, next to a handmade wooden chair covered in hides and cushions where Festus assumed Zev spent most of his time, reading he hoped, and not talking to the inanimate pet he was so fond of. It was one of the many quirks that had caused the villagers to dub him 'Crazy Zev.'

The cat had a new adornment from the last time he had visited, a tiny leather collar with a glimmering green gemstone hanging from it, along with a flat round disk made from what appeared to be gold. On closer inspection the disk had a name etched into it, *Wick*. Festus raised his eyebrows and gave Zev a sideways glance.

Zev didn't notice as he was busy scooping out the tea into two cups.

Half of the cabin was packed with shelves full of jars with various herbs, roots, fungus, plants (dried and living), and a wide assortment of bugs (dead and alive). A medium sized table stood amid all the shelves, neatly organized with all manner of utensils, mortar and pestles, vials, bottles, tongs and a neat stack of notebooks.

The other half of the cabin served as Zev's living space. A small fireplace, a simple bed with a straw mattress, a wood bin in the corner, a large chest for clothes and such, and his chair. A shelf with some dishes hung above the fireplace.

Zev turned from the fireplace with the cups, offered one to Festus, then sat in his chair.

Festus thanked him and looked for a place to sit.

"Mind if I sit on this," asked Festus, indicating the large chest across from Zev.

"Fine, but don't break it," replied Zev with a deadpan face. "So, Fes, what really brings you here? It sure isn't my cheerful demeanor."

"You got me," Festus chuckled. He reached into his pocket where he had put the letter, took it out and handed it to Zev. "I wrote it down to make things easier."

Zev unfolded the piece of paper and squinted while he read the thing at arm's length, holding it up to catch the light from the small window behind his chair. He *harrumphed* when he was finished and took a sip of his tea. "Sounds like this Maddi girl has been through a lot."

"Indeed. Do you have anything that could help her sleep?"

"Aye, I think I might have just the thing. It's good you have her busy with other things as well, that should help her mind suppress the bad things of the past. I doubt she will ever forget her past, but she will learn to cope with something good to focus on."

"That's excellent news. I'm glad I made the visit." Festus sipped his tea and involuntarily scrunched his face as the citrus flavor of the Blood Vine exploded his taste buds causing him to cringe and smack his lips.

"I like my tea potent," said Zev without skipping a beat and took another sip of his own tea.

"Wow, I'll say."

They sat in silence for a hand span before Festus decided to ask about the cat's new collar.

"I see you've named your cat finally."

"What? Oh, that? Nope, that was all Wick's doing. Just showed up with it one morning a few months back," replied Zev.

Festus just blinked and sipped his tea repeatedly.

Not much else was spoken of as they finished their beverages, and when Zev had finished his before Festus, he got up and started digging through his shelves for things which he placed on his work table. After he had gathered a handful of ingredients, he set to work grinding up a bit of this, squeezing drops of that and mixing it all together in a small bottle. He swirled the concoction around and held it up to a candle for inspection. Satisfied, he placed a cork stopper in the stem and spun around to face Festus who had been watching quietly from his seat on the chest.

"It's ready," said Zev. He held out the small bottle and waited for Festus to get up and take it. "A few drops in a drink of any kind before bed and she'll sleep like a Rock Hound."

Festus blinked at Zev before responding, not sure what to make of the Rock Hound comment. "Thanks Zev. What do I owe you?"

"Nothing."

"Come now, surely you use coin for supplies."

"No need."

"I-"

"If you insist on payment, then, my fee is that you leave me in peace for at least a month. That bottle should last at least that long."

Festus roared with laughter. "Fine, old friend, I can abide by that. I'll bring some new books for you when I next visit as well, how about that?"

Zev's face lit up slightly at that, but quickly returned to his usual serious demeanor. "I suppose that would be alright, just none of that lovey-dovey stuff the kids seem to be reading these days. Anarik Finabarin's stuff is OK though. Mostly because Wick likes the adventures and what not," he added with an unmistakable bit of enthusiasm.

"Deal." Festus thanked Zev once more and stepped outside. Zev closed the door behind him without another word. When Festus looked back from the top of the small path down to the road, Wick was sitting in the small window, a small ray of sunshine glimmering off the green gemstone. Festus shook his head and laughed, turned and made his way back through Maerin and on up to the Library.

Chapter Twenty-Six

Syndara and Aileesha pulled the last of the sled straps holding their supplies tight as Dohmnall made his way down the hill from his home to the front gate of Garomvol.

Jarmus and Devlin were busy prepping the Mammoth meat for the smoker and sorting what was to be used while the meat was still fresh.

Aileesha's parents milled about, fretting lovingly over their daughter as she prepared to leave them. They were full of joy and sadness which mixed together in their features, eyes watering, voices shaky, but smiles as big as the sky.

"Decided to take someone along after all did you Synd," stated Dohmnall, a faint hint of laughter in his gruff voice. He pulled Syndara into a bear hug. "A wise decision."

"She didn't get much of a choice Chieftain," Aileesha grinned and let out a laugh.

"No, I suspect not," he looked at Aileesha and chuckled, "Keep her safe Aileesha, and may you both have a safe journey." He turned back to Syndara. "I have not spoken of your journey to anyone else, so your mind can be at peace knowing no one else will leave the protection of the village to join you."

"Thank you Dohm. We will make all haste, in hopes of returning in time to help the village prepare for the next winter," replied Syndara. She embraced Dohmnall in one last hug.

"Your parents would be so proud of you," said Dohmnall. He took a step back and looked at both of them with pride in his eyes. "You're like daughters to me. Should anything happen to you, I fear I may break at the heart. Take no unnecessary risks on your journey my dears."

"We won't, I promise," replied Syndara, a lump forming in her throat. She moved aside to let Aileesha wrap him in a hug of her own.

Aileesha danced out of her skin with excitement to leave, grinning from ear to ear. She exchanged a half dozen hugs and kisses with her parents and soft promises to be safe and return home to them quickly.

"I don't think I've ever seen your face as bright as this moment Aileesha," said Dohmnall as they made their way to the open gate, waving farewell over their shoulders. "Oh, Synd, before I forget, take this," he added and handed over a small leather pack with a buckled leather strap running down the middle of a drawn flap. The mouth of the pack had a drawstring opening which was pulled tightly closed beneath the flap.

"What is it," asked Syndara. It was very light.

"I've filled it with various salves and treated bandages," he paused for a moment as she looked inside the pack. Worry crept across her face. He lifted her chin with the first two fingers of his right hand and locked eyes with her. "Just in case."

Syndara returned his nod and stowed the small pack away on the sled.

"Be safe girls, we shall see you soon."

"And you, Dohm," said Syndara.

"Be well Chieftain, take care of my parents for me," added Aileesha.

"Without question my dear," replied Dohmnall.

With that they were off. Syndara took the first shift pushing the sled. She planted her right foot on one of the wooden runners, and pushed with her left foot. Snow flew through the air behind her as she built momentum with each kick down the rest of the hill from their home. Aileesha was already jogging ahead of her down the hill.

Syndara took one last glance over her shoulder as she slid past Aileesha, her face half buried in the fur of her hooded coat. Dohmnall was watching and waving them off with Aileesha's parents next to him as they wound down the path towards the south and on into Obodoon Pass. She felt an emptiness creep into the pit of her stomach. She had no idea how long she would be gone from the only place, and life, she had ever known. At the same time, excitement welled up inside her unlike anything she had ever experienced before. Their adventure had begun.

Chapter Twenty-Seven

Syndara and Aileesha traveled south through the mountains for the remainder of the day, exchanging few words as they traveled. The sun cut through white puffy clouds in spots, speckling the valley of the Obodoon Pass with patches of bright orange light that danced off the white blanket of winter that yet clung to the ground. The snow sparkled all around them. It looked like crystallized lava, forever frozen in time. It seemed like a paradox to Syndara. How could something so warm looking, become trapped in something so cold? Spring would come soon, maybe a few weeks from now at most. This thought eased her mind as they put more distance between them and their home.

Aileesha broke her free of her thoughts, commenting on the view as they rounded a bend in the path. The valley opened before them, providing a breathtaking view of the pass further to the south.

"It's so majestic. Look at how the sunlight dances off the snow. Wow," gasped Aileesha. She stopped in her tracks and gazed off into the distance. "Look at that," she exclaimed excitedly, pointing south west! The Shimmering Tear could be seen through the treetops that reached up toward the sky from the gully below. "It looks like it's on fire the way the sun is shining off the water!"

Syndara stared in awe at the view. The warmth of it took her by surprise. It filled her with such a feeling of well being that she could have let herself get lost in that moment forever. It wasn't until the sun began to slip behind the western peaks, and dusk crept into the sky in its wake, that they continued on their way.

"We should make camp soon. Keep your eyes open for a good spot to make camp for the night. Something that is out of sight and defensible," said Syndara.

Aileesha went ahead and surveyed their surroundings for a suitable spot. She soon found a narrow path up to a ledge overlooking the trail leading south. There was a small copse of trees and bushes on the ledge that would provide shelter from wind and any storm that may creep up during the night. She returned to Syndara and pointed out the ledge not far to the south.

When they got to the bottom of the path leading up to the ledge, Aileesha grabbed the front of the sled and pulled, while Syndara pushed from the back. Before long, they had the sled placed under the trees. The ground was mostly bare and dry, sheltered by the tree boughs overhead. They set about making camp. Pleased with themselves at how sheltered and cozy the camp was, they set to making a meal.

"I get first watch this time," said Aileesha around a mouthful of roasted mammoth.

"Sure, that works for me. I'm exhausted. Wake me when you are feeling tired," replied Syndara. She finished the last of her meal and tossed a handful of winter berries in her mouth and grabbed her bedroll from the sled. She unrolled it next to the low burning fire and crawled inside, her back to the fire.

"What do you think it's like Synd," asked Aileesha?

"What," replied Syndara?

"Thain's Reach, the Everdeep, all of it I guess. I can't stop thinking about it."

Syndara rolled over to face her friend across the fire. She slid her right arm under her head like a pillow. "I imagine it's wonderful. Full of farmland and forest as far as the eye can see. The way the minstrels speak of the larger cities, I can only imagine what that will be like. It makes me nervous just thinking about it to be honest, that many people in one place. I don't know how they can live so tightly packed together."

"I'd go crazy living that way, but I imagine it will be something special to see. I can't wait to see the great stone cliffs that overlook the Reach. The minstrels make it sound like it can take your breath right out of your lungs," said Aileesha while she scooped snow into a pot to melt for a warm beverage.

Syndara laughed heartily.

"What's so funny," responded Aileesha, her own laughter mingling with Syndara's?

"I can't even imagine you being a farmer, let alone living in a city. The images in my head are hysterical. Your face all twisted up in frustration. It would never happen. I pity the man that would attempt to domesticate you," Syndara said through her continued laughter. She wiped her eyes with her hands as she tried to collect herself.

"Hey now, you'd fare no better you wild beast," replied Aileesha, throwing a bit of snow across the fire at her friend.

They both roared with renewed laughter.

When they had managed to stop laughing, Syndara bid Aileesha a good night and turned away from the fire again. She drifted off to sleep quickly, leaving Aileesha sipping at her warm cup of Javanth Tea while she leaned against a tree trunk and looked out over the moonlit valley below. The rest of the night passed uneventfully.

Chapter Twenty-Eight

The sun rose above the mountain peaks to the south east, spilling bright rays of light through the trees surrounding the ledge they had made camp on the night before. Syndara nudged Aileesha's foot to wake her, having taken over the watch duties halfway through the night.

"Rise and shine sleepy bear. Care for a mug of steeped frost sage," asked Syndara?

Aileesha stretched and rubbed sleep from her eyes then nodded. She cleared her throat without a word.

Syndara stoked the coals of the fire, bringing it to life. She added just enough wood to melt a pot of snow and brought it to a boil. Once it was bubbling, she reached into her pack and pulled out a pouch that contained dried frost sage leaves. She took a palm full and gently stirred them into the boiling water with a wooden spoon. She let the tea steep while they packed up their bedrolls and had a bit more of the dried meat and berries from the bushes Syndara had found the previous day.

"Almost time to move Synd, how's the tea looking," asked Aileesha?

"It's ready," replied Syndara as she filled both of their cups. She handed one to Aileesha, wrapped both her hands around the second cup and took a sip to test the brew.

Aileesha took a sip from her own cup, the bitter sweet flavor filling her with warmth immediately. "That's a good batch," she said, "thanks. Shall we have a bit of spiced bread to go with it before we start out for the day?"

"That's a fantastic idea."

Aileesha retrieved a fresh loaf from her bag and procured two hunks of the delectable bread before wrapping the remainder back in the cloth it was held in and placed it back in her pack. They stood near the edge of the landing to take in the view one last time before starting off on the day's journey.

"It really is breathtaking isn't it," asked Syndara?

"You can see all the way to the Shimmering Tear down the valley without obstruction," replied Aileesha.

"It seems like we're in for a warmer day, which is fine by me. The bridge across the Weeping Gorge will be free of ice for us hopefully."

"That will save us some time."

Syndara finished her drink as she gazed out over the valley. A large bird let out a long call as it flew past in the distance. Aileesha gulped down the last of her drink and packed up the pot and cups while Syndara doused the fire with snow. Little more than steam rose from its pit by the time she was done.

Syndara quickly stretched her arms and legs, working out the healthy ache from the previous day's exertions. "Ready," she asked?

"Yep, let's head out," replied Aileesha with a grin.

Syndara slung her bow over her shoulder, and started walking in front of the sled as Aileesha pushed it to the top of the path.

They Who Linger

They descended the narrow path back to the main trail with relative ease. Once on the main path, Aileesha took first run at pushing the sled while Syndara scouted ahead.

Most of the morning was spent traveling along the winding path toward the Weeping Gorge without stopping, and they sang a few ballads that they had learned when they were training as hunters.

A distant sound, like that of an injured rabbit caused Syndara to pause briefly. The hairs on the back of her neck tingled. She signaled for Aileesha to halt and stop singing. Hearing nothing more, she traded places with her friend, offering her fresh reserve of energy to hasten their pace.

"We should be at the Weeping Gorge watch post soon," whispered Syndara.

"Can we rest before we cross the bridge at the gorge," asked Aileesha?

"Let's cross first," replied Syndara. She scanned the forest over her shoulder one more time. "Something has the hairs raised on the back of my neck. I'd rather have the gorge between us and anything that might be following us."

"Fair enough, we'll cross first then."

They rounded one last bend in the trail, and saw the rope and wood plank bridge spanning across the Weeping Gorge not far ahead. Aileesha grabbed the front of the sled while Syndara lifted the rear, and they began to make their way across. Its damp rope creaked as it swayed and undulated slightly side to side. They stopped to rest their arms a few times. There was no snow or ice on the planks to allow them to slide the sled across.

Two thirds of the way across, they heard a chortling screech echo out across the valley behind them, much closer than earlier. It reverberated off the rocky cliffs of the gorge below, which magnified the pitch. Whatever it was, it was close. They scanned both sides of the gorge and lifted the sled again.

Once more, the sound broke the silence, even closer and louder this time. It rang out clear and shrill. Syndara's blood ran cold and her eyes grew wide with realization as full recognition shot through her mind; it was the same noise she had heard two nights prior, just before they were attacked.

"Do you recognize that, Ailee? It's the same sound that woke us two nights ago. I think we better move. Fast," exclaimed Syndara!

"I'm with you there," replied Aileesha.

"Keep your eyes on the other side of the bridge , if you see any movement be ready to drop the sled and grab your bow."

They continued as fast as they could with their burden. Not more than a few steps later, a loud snapping noise came from behind them and Syndara looked over her shoulder. She saw a large tree fall into the gorge, its trunk splintered near the base. Movement in the trees beyond the jagged stump caught her eye. Multiple dark skinned creatures were weaving between the trees, dancing in and out of the shadows provided by the forest cover, heading towards the bridge with unnatural speed. One of the creatures, much larger than the others, screeched and growled fiercely as it spotted Syndara and Aileesha. It burst out of the trees, raised itself up on its hind legs and scratched at the air with elongated clawed fingers. Darkness swirled and emanated from the creature like smoke from a fire. On its hind legs, the creature stood almost as tall as the mammoths they hunted in the northern tundra.

"We've got company Ailee," bellowed Syndara at the top of her lungs. She fought against the pangs of fear and terror that stabbed at her heart and mind, wrestling them into submission.

Coupled with the roaring of the stream that wound its way through the gorge below, the sound was all it took to set their muscles aflame with desire to be fully across the bridge. Without a word, both Aileesha and Syndara barrelled the remaining distance to the other side without pause. They dropped the sled in the snow as soon as they cleared the threshold onto solid ground. Adrenaline pumped through them like wildfire through tinder dry underbrush. They fought to catch their breath, hurriedly preparing to defend themselves.

"Where the heck are they coming from and what the hell do they want," shouted Aileesha, pounding a fist against one hip.

"No idea, but there's a big one this time," replied Syndara.

"How big," asked Aileesha, with a look of grave concern on her face?

Syndara breathed deep a few times, her hands on her knees. She stood straight, unslung her bow, and gritted her teeth. She sucked in air as she raced to set arrows in the snow before her. "Big!"

The last of the creatures cleared the trees on the north side of the gorge as the first of them closed the distance to the bridge. Aileesha raced to a snow covered rock near the lip of the gorge on their side of the bridge and readied her bow, following Syndara's lead.

With her bow in her left hand, she sprinted toward the bridge and unsheathed the axe on her right hip with her free hand. Everything felt like it was happening at once. The creatures howled at them, bounding across the bridge, the largest one in the lead. The old bridge protested heavily, swaying violently under the aggressive power of the creature's advance.

Aileesha loosed arrow after arrow, hitting a few of the beasts. One of them slumped forward and over the side of the bridge into the gorge; a feathered shaft protruding from one of its eyes.

Syndara reached the bridge posts and chopped wildly at the rope holding it up. The first one snapped with a twang. The combined weight of the beasts and their jumping, caused the bridge to twist to one side as the rope gave way. A few of the beasts clambered in vain to grip the tilting planks. They howled in defeat and rage, falling into the gorge onto the jagged rocks sticking out of the stream far below. The ones that didn't fall scampered along the swaying remains towards them, clinging to the remaining rope like ants on a stem of grass.

"We're not going to make it, they're going to get us," Aileesha shouted in panic. She fought against it as best she could, but was losing the battle quickly.

"No... They... AREN'T," Syndara protested between desperate swings of her axe at the remaining rope holding up the bridge. The intertwining strands of fiber unraveled with a *SNAP* as they were cut free under her onslaught. Her axe made a loud thud as it bit deep into the wood post beneath the rope. A cacophony of wailing beasts and debris smashed against rocks, the sound reverberating off the stone walls of the gorge up to them. Again time stood still as the largest of the beasts, seeing its demise coming leaped forward in desperation before the remaining strand was cut free from under it, all limbs stretched out to their full extent as it flew through the air towards Syndara.

"SYNDARA," yelled Aileesha. She threw her bow to the ground and launched herself off the ground to intercept the beast before it could catch her friend unaware.

Syndara instinctively threw herself to the ground at the sound of Aileesha's shout. She rolled to the side towards the rock that Aileesha had been using for cover.

Snow kicked up behind Aileesha as she ran straight at the giant creature with her axes drawn. She screamed like a crazy person, her face twisted in defiance.

Syndara saw Aileesha's predicament as her spin brought her around to face the bridge. Aileesha possessed every ounce of heroism described in tavern tales and story books in that moment.

Hair billowing like a banner, Aileesha tightened her grip on the axes, lunged off the ground in a full run and brought the weapons down on the beast with all the force she could muster as they collided. The blades bit deep, one into the creature's right shoulder, the other in its right side. The force of the impact sent them both reeling to the ground, a plume of snow obscuring Syndara's vision briefly. A pained howl and a loud cracking noise accompanied the impact.

The beast flailed in an attempt to gain its footing again. One of its hind legs buckled, giving out under its own weight with a wet crack. The creature began to lilt backward towards the gorge, clawing at the air as its body betrayed its desire to move away from the edge.

Aileesha was attempting to scramble backwards away from the creature on her back, all her limbs trying to find any purchase beneath the snow. She flipped herself over and started to get to her feet, but time was against her.

Syndara's heart sank into her chest as she saw what was about to happen. She lunged out of her crouch and ran toward her friend at full speed. "Aileesha, no, MOVE," she yelled. She leaped through the air and attempted to grab her friend by the arm.

Aileesha was pulled back to the ground by the flailing beast, putting her just out of Syndara's reach. It had thrown its weight forward away from the gorge in a last effort to avoid its fate, clawing at the stone beneath the snow for a perch. All it found was Aileesha's foot. She hit the ground hard, the air forced from her lungs. She screamed silently and kicked at the beast in desperation, catching it in the jaw more than once.

The creature managed to find a footing on the rocky wall of the gorge with its good hind leg, and in one smooth motion, launched itself up from the edge and back onto solid ground, flinging Aileesha toward the edge with its momentum.

Syndara landed in the snow where Aileesha had been and quickly scrambled towards her friend on her hands and knees. She clamped her hands around Aileesha's arm, stopping her from sliding any further towards the edge of the gorge. Aileesha's feet dangled in the open air. Syndara's muscles burned with fire as she pulled her friend back to safety.

"Synd, go, get out of here. I think it broke my ankle. We can't both die here, not like this. I'll distract it," Aileesha groaned through gritted teeth. She waved her free arm at Syndara, attempting to push her clear of the beast's gaze.

The beast roared, its whole body shaking. Ink black skin dripped equally dark liquid that evaporated into tendrils of smoke before striking the ground. Quills shivered along the length of the creature and its black orb eyes locked on its prey. Black lips curled back over a mouth full of even blacker fangs. The creature dipped its head, snorted like a mad bull and prepared to charge them.

"The burning bowels you will," Syndara shouted back in reply and lunged to retrieve her bow. She nocked an arrow, spun around on her heels to aim at the beast and fired her arrow in one quick motion. It struck the beast in one of its front legs. She turned to run as fast as she could, putting distance between herself and the beast for more shots.

"I won't leave you Aileesha," she yelled as she slid to a stop, grabbing another arrow from her quiver, nocked and loosed it.

The creature, stunned momentarily by the arrow in its leg, growled low in pain. It lunged.

"Syndara go! Get out of here. I won't be able to run from it," Aileesha yelled again, tears welling up in her eyes.

Aileesha mustered all her remaining strength, stepped forward and wailed as loud as she could at the beast to draw its attention. She almost fell with the first step as she put weight on her injured ankle, but managed to keep her footing long enough to launch herself against the creature, pushing them both toward the gorge again.

Syndara's second shot glanced off the creature's skull, adding to the momentum it carried towards the gorge. Her vision narrowed, and time stood still. She screamed in agony at the situation, tears filled her vision while it all unfolded against her will. Her bow dropped from her hands and she reached out instinctively with both hands toward her friend. She willed herself to move, to run to her aid, but it was too late and her body knew it. She watched helplessly, rooted in place as her best friend and the beast she still railed against both flew over the edge of the gorge and dropped out of sight. Spittle flew from her mouth and trailed down her chin as she erupted in sorrow. In an instant, her world shattered.

Syndara fell to her knees in the snow at the edge of the gorge. Tears streamed down her face as she wailed after Aileesha. She scanned the gorge for any sign of her friend, but only saw the largest of the beasts sprawled upon the rocks below; shattered and broken open from the midsection. She had no recollection of time passing while she knelt at the edge of the Weeping Gorge.

A fresh howl echoed off the stone walls of the gorge, snapping her back to reality. She looked over the jagged rocks below one more time. The creature that had claimed her friend was disintegrating before her eyes, wisps of black smoke roiling in the air currents from the raging water. She shook her head in disbelief, raised her head and pushed the hair out of her face. She looked across the gorge and spotted more of the creatures stranded on the other side, pacing back and forth, looking for a way to get to her. Some sniffed at the air, others pounced on each other in agitation. One looked down at the dissipating body of the shattered beast. Snarling and growling, the pack of creatures retreated into the trees.

Syndara got to her feet in a daze, took one last look down at the stream whisking through the bottom of the gorge, and still seeing no sign of her friend, turned to run. Bow in hand, she grabbed her pack, scooped up her remaining arrows and slid them into her quiver. She abandoned the sled with Aileesha's pack, wedged against a tree so it could not slide away and headed south. Her mind was racing, but she could not put two thoughts together. Alone and hunted, she would need to travel light, night and day, until she made it to Thain's Reach.

Chapter Twenty-Nine

It had been many days since Ingvar had fled from Melar's fate and he had mostly wandered without thought of its demise or a destination to guide him. The nightmares still plagued him and the previous night was no exception. He had slept amidst a copse of wild plum trees for protection from the elements as a storm rolled in. Once he had cleared the thick underbrush enough to be comfortable on the ground beneath the thick canopy of leaves that kept the majority of the rain to the outside of the copse, he laid down and closed his eyes. At first the rolling sounds of the storm were soothing and comforting, but not long after he had drifted off, the worst nightmare since the events in Melar struck him.

Ingvar dreamt of terrible shadow figures and demons of black smoke and skinless horrors rampaging across the southern low land farms and villages leading from the South Eastern coastal mountains, North West across the plains, consuming every living thing in their wake. The land scorched black, the skies filled with smoke and ash, blotting out the sun. Finally he dreamed of a shadowy beast finding him where he lay asleep beneath the plum grove, biting at his chest to rip it open and dig out his insides with its dripping black maw. It was then that he had startled awake.

The fresh scent of wet soil and grass was a thick contrast to his dreams, and his mind quickly cleared as the scent of wet earth wafted through the trees on a cool morning breeze. The first rays of sunlight glowed outside the low hanging branches, laden with the remains of the storm and plums that were just starting to ripen. They would make a nice change from his meager rations that he had managed to bring with him on his journey.

Ingvar was still wary of lighting a fire for fear of pursuers from the attack on Melar hunting the wilds. It was an entirely baseless fear he figured, but he couldn't shake the feeling of being hunted or watched. He climbed free of his shelter, stretched, relieved himself, cleaned his hands in the still wet grass and then gathered some plums before heading off into the western plains along a rolling ridge line that followed a small creek.

By midday Ingvar saw the white wisps of lazy smoke rising from the chimneys of a small village where a stone bridge crossed the creek and a dirt cart path ran out of the south through the village and off into the north. He didn't really want to go through the village, but he needed to get some supplies for the road. Wherever it was leading.

The dirt cart path gave way to cobbled stone work a short distance after Ingvar crossed the bridge. The stone work was not like anything he had ever seen. It was perfect. The stones kissed each other with no visible gaps, and all the stones were smooth and flat. The structures in the village were also of stone construction, and clearly older than the inhabitants that settled them. There were telltale signs of repurposed construction on all of the exteriors. Half a wooden wall here, newer, simpler rock work there, and large rough cut stone slabs making up newer ground stones for paths to gardens surrounded with simple wattle fencing.

A few of the larger buildings that were clearly not dwellings had carved wooden signs depicting their purpose. There was an Inn, a general provisions shop, an herbal shop, and a blacksmith amongst them. Ingvar made for the general provisions shop, opened the polished wooden door which was heavier than it looked, and stepped inside.

There were a few people milling about the shop, sorting through fruits and vegetables, picking out sacks of flour or requesting cuts of meat, butter, and cheese from one of the folk behind the counter to the left of the entrance. The goods lined the walls in neat sectioned baskets, wooden boxes and shelves. A cozy warm glow filled the shop from a candelabra hanging from a beam in the center of the large shop and a fire crackled in a bread oven behind a counter laden with baked goods along the back wall. A large figure filled his peripheral vision as he stared dumbstruck at the shop.

"Good morning to ya traveler, how can I assist today," asked a large round faced, balding man in simple woolen clothes dyed dark blue and brown? He wore a white apron over his shirt, fastened around a plump waist. A small marking on the inside of the man's right forearm caught Ingvar's eye as the man held out his hand in greeting. What looked like a flame seemed to dance on the man's skin for a moment before his sleeve slid down and covered it.

Ingvar blinked and found his voice as he shook the man's hand. "Nice shop you have here. Largest I've ever seen I think."

"Thank you, we make do. We get lots of visitors from the farmlands. Kind of a lucky little trading hub we've got here I guess. Looking for anything specific," the man inquired?

"Some food for the road, dried meat, cheese and the like. Probably some fresh bread too. It smells delicious," answered Ingvar, his mouth watering as he mentioned the fresh bread.

"I think we have everything you're looking for then. First time in these parts," asked the shopkeeper?

"It is."

"Where are you from?"

Ingvar hesitated a moment, images of the attack on Melar flashing in his mind.

"Melar," replied Ingvar hesitantly.

"Where are you headed?"

"I-" Ingvar cut short and looked at the man and shrugged.

"Ahh," the shop keeper, as if understanding without explanation. "None of my business really, just making conversation. I'm Gandrin, and that's my wife over there behind the bread counter, Lenda. Only been in these parts a few years ourselves. Used to run a place up in Beigaldi, but the business ran dry along with the crops up that way. Been a hard few years up there."

Ingvar had never heard of the place Gandrin was talking about, and didn't much care at this point in time.

"What's this village called," asked Ingvar, realizing he didn't know where he was?

"This be Kaldaross. Probably not its original name. Maybe it is. Who knows," answered Gandrin with a shrug as they walked around the shop.

Gandrin had a basket in his left hand and started pointing at supplies Ingvar had mentioned with his right.

Ingvar nodded when Gandrin pointed at something he wanted and they moved around the shop in a counter clockwise direction, trading small talk as they went. A few of the other shop visitors were doing the same, but with their own baskets in hand. Locals, Ingvar suspected. A few of them cast an inquisitive glance his way now and then, but for the most part didn't pay much attention to an outsider being present.

Before long Gandrin stepped behind the front counter with a full basket and Ingvar dug in his pack for his coin pouch. As he dug about in the depths of his pack, his hand brushed against something sharp and he yelped in surprise, dropping the bag on the wooden floorboards as he pulled his hand free to inspect it. A growing red blob rose on the pad of his right index finger.

"What on earth-" He cut himself short, wiped his finger on his pants to clear away the blood and pinched the small cut together with his other hand.

Gandrin looked on patiently as though this was an everyday sort of event.

Ingvar used his right thumb to keep the pressure on the small cut and retrieved his pack from the floor with his left. He peeled back the flap and looked inside to see what he had caught his finger on. At the bottom of the bag was a large amber colored seed, tucked into his spare clothes which he had hastily thrown into the pack when leaving Melar. He looked at it for a moment, completely baffled.

Gandrin greeted a new visitor from behind the counter, snapping Ingvar out of his ponderment. He was eager to inspect the seed, but it could wait until he finished up with his purchase.

"Ah, here it is," stated Ingvar triumphantly as he fished his coin pouch from the pack.

"That'll be five gold bits," said Gandrin plainly.

Ingvar picked out the small coins and held them out for Gandrin to accept.

"Need a cloth sack for any of this?" asked Gandrin.

Ingvar started to decline but then thought about it and accepted. He didn't know when he would next be near a village and he could tie the sack to his backpack and fill it with whatever food he found along the way. He finished packing the supplies, thanked Gandrin for his assistance and stepped out of the shop into the street.

The village was bustling with activity now, more than Ingvar would have expected for such a small place. Carts drawn by large horses and led by an assortment of farmers trundled along the cobbles and folk milled about in conversation. It was so peaceful. Too peaceful it felt. A sudden unease filled him, like unseen eyes lingering their gaze upon him and he felt the need to be away from this place. He walked with purpose north through the remainder of the village and out into the open countryside beyond, picking up the pace as he left its fringe. There were even more people on the roadway heading toward Kaldaross. He veered from the road up a hill to the west, and out of sight behind some trees.

Ingvar breathed a sigh of relief as he felt the unease lift from him, like the unseen eyes were no longer upon him. The countryside rolled off into the distance, a hilly valley weaving constantly north west. He sat down on a rock beneath the trees and opened his pack, carefully digging out the seed with a thick woolen sock to inspect it.

The seed glowed in the afternoon sunlight, its amber skin sparkling orange across the grass in front of Ingvar as he gingerly turned it over with the sock. It was tear shaped, fat at the bottom, narrow at the top and ridged with folding layers not unlike fish scales. Each of these scales came to a pointy tip where a dark red needle protruded from them.

As he handled the seed, the needles threatened to poke through the sock. He thought it was his imagination, but it felt like the seed was getting warmer to the touch. Suddenly, images of the Great Tree jumped into his mind.

The scent of the clearing, fresh fallen leaves beginning to turn to ash, the skies darkening; the ground shaking and stones rising in defiance of gravity.

A pristine image of the Great Tree from across the clearing that then gave way to a shriveled, decaying husk, a giant split tearing open in the middle of its massive trunk, the bark turning to hexagonal columns of stone. Hundreds upon hundreds of shadowy creatures were bursting from the dark rift at the base of the trunk.

Ingvar's skin chilled and his heart raced. He dropped the seed and the images suddenly ceased. His breath was heavy and a cold sweat spread across his brow. This was a seed from the Great Tree itself. He wasn't sure how he knew, but he knew it deep in his gut, without a doubt. The only reasonable explanation in his mind was that the seed must have fallen into his pack while he was sleeping beneath the bows all those days ago. He had no idea what to do with it, but he knew he couldn't just leave it in the middle of the countryside.

Using the sock to pick it up again, he wrapped it with a second sock. Another image jumped into his mind as he wrapped the seed, a sprawling forest of crimson and emerald trees with bark as black as night. A whispered thought followed the flashing image *'Find them.'*

Ingvar shook his head, quickly finished wrapping the seed and tucked it into his pack. He looked toward the north and felt a sudden urge to head in that direction, and so he set off, one foot in front of the other, a destination finally set although he did not know it.

Chapter Thirty

Five days passed while Ingvar strolled through the rolling hills north of Kaldaross. Each night he dreamed of unknown events in an unknown place. A vast kingdom of ancient giant folk; Cities of carved stone spread across an Oasis in the middle of an otherwise inhospitable landscape of cacti, cracked earth and dead plants.

The dreams grew longer and more intense with each passing night. Some were calming and inviting, others dark and violent. While he stopped one afternoon to have a bit of lunch, he had a lucid dream and woke in an entirely different place with no recollection of how he got there or where he was. On another occasion he was awoken by a strange group of travelers clad in chain mail and leather armor with long leather cloaks. A flaming torch emblem adorned the breast of their armor and cloaks. They thought he had been come upon by bandits as he was sprawled out, face first, in the grass next to a dirt path that wound through the hills. He assured them he was alright and that he must have just laid down for a rest but must have been more exhausted than he thought. He thanked them for their concern and they wished him well and then continued on their way.

Ingvar pondered the emblem for a while after the travelers had gone their own way. Something about it was familiar, but he couldn't place it. He felt like he had seen it before. It wasn't until sometime later that afternoon that he remembered where he had seen the symbol before. It had been tattooed on Gandrin's forearm.

The next day was no better. He woke at the bottom of a hill and sore muscles, having no recollection of how he got there or knowledge of where he was. His belongings were close by, but scattered, as if he had tumbled down the hill.

At that point he began to worry. What was happening to him? Who were these mysterious giants, and where were these memories coming from?

An entire history of these unknown people in his dreams began to take root in Ingvar's mind and he grew increasingly uneasy when it came time to sleep. Eventually exhaustion would win out, but his sleep was not all that restful.

The lush green farmland valleys and coniferous strewn hills had given way to a vast sea of golden-yellow grass plains dotted with clumps of gray-green bushes and the odd cluster of large stones. He hadn't seen a farmstead or any other signs of life aside from the odd animal in three days.

On the sixth day of journeying north, or at least he thought it was the sixth day but it was getting harder to keep track with the blackouts, he came across some ancient stone columns that jutted from the landscape. Feeling the exhaustion catching up with him, he decided to stop for a while and have a gander at the ruins.

Ingvar walked around the stone pillars in awe, admiring their craftsmanship. He dragged his palm lightly across the surface of one that tilted toward the ground in an easterly lull and felt slight ridges where his fingers passed. He stepped closer to see what they had found. It was a weather worn carving on the underside of the pillar, where it had been protected from the worst of the weather's effects over time. He laid his right palm against the stone and gently followed the carved lines of the symbol with his thumb.

The carving was of a large beetle with what appeared to be a saddle on it. Ingvar inspected the pillar beneath the carving for more. There was another carving roughly two hand spans beneath the first. This one of a tall figure wearing decorative armor adorned with scarab symbols on large shoulder guards with indentations that looked like they had been scooped out with a circular tool. A sphere sat in each of the indentations, appearing to float free of the shoulder guards themselves. The head was adorned with a full helm that had a beetle head for a face guard. In the figure's left hand was a large three pronged spear. Each prong was longer than the next, making up a three tiered spear head.

Ingvar was elated with his discovery and his curiosity was piqued. He searched all of the other pillars, eight in all, forming a giant circle which he imagined once held up a magnificent stone structure. There were a dozen or more such carvings still discernible, and many others that were mostly worn away with the passing of time.

Hours passed, afternoon gave way to early evening, and Ingvar decided this was as good a place as any to camp for the evening. He still worried that he would awaken somewhere else as had been happening with increasing frequency, but he was too tired to care overly much, and so found a comfortable patch of grass to lay upon in the shelter of the ruins.

Chapter Thirty-One

Ingvar's dreams were filled with visions of a vast, ancient empire being built up among shimmering dunes of golden sand that quickly changed into cultivated and irrigated landscapes where trees and plants of all kinds were being tended by throngs of unfamiliar people of varying sizes and races, the lush foliage coaxed into embracing the harsh landscape over the course of centuries.

Moon cycles flowed past in a blur, clouds formed and emptied their burdens upon the land forming rivers and ponds where the sand and stone had been shaped to catch it, then dispersed.

The visions flooded forward to a time when the landscape was dotted with colorful foliage, occupied by all kinds of wild creatures, and bustling trade routes that were traveled regularly to and from settlements all throughout a vast empire.

Ingvar recognized some of the races he was seeing but could not connect the dots in his dream state.

Monolithic structures were built, stone pillars carved with symbols of a language he did not know, border walls constructed and armies formed to guard them.

Next came the wars. The destruction of those walls, the crumbling of those massive structures that stood for a thousand years or more, and one final event that ended all that remained in an explosive flash of light and a sundering of earth that surged upward into the sky.

When the flash subsided and his dream vision was restored, the land was once again desolate, but forever changed, and at its heart there was a great tear in the earth that had swallowed the civilization that once called this land home. Nothing but dust and ruin remained.

Recognition hit his dream-self like a brick.

O'Marah, the Fallen Kingdom.

What he had witnessed caused his breathing to hitch, his heart to pound in his ears, and his vision to go dark.

~*~

Ingvar gasped awake, his breaths coming in rapid succession. He attempted to clamber to his feet from where he had fallen asleep among the ruins, but his legs failed him. Every muscle in his body was shaking. He was stricken with panic. His eyes searched the darkness in random directions for signs of danger. It took him what felt like hours to calm himself enough to gather his wits about him. He sat with his back against one of the stone pillars, taking in slow, even breaths, and even still the dream vision replayed in his mind like he had really been there.

He was aware that this was more than a dream but didn't yet know how, or why.

How was this possible? It couldn't be what really happened, could it? Why did none of the historical texts that exist mention any of these events?

Ingvar's mind was a complete mess of questions and rapid thoughts. The sun had not yet risen, but he felt like he needed to leave this place. Something was causing the hairs on his neck to stand on end and his sense of unease was constant. He gathered up his belongings and made off into the early morning mist to the north, every so often looking over his shoulder to assure himself that nothing was there.

Early morning darkness gave way to dawn, and before he knew it, the sun was beating down behind him as he traversed the rocky landscape toward the foothills of the Balithain Mountains that loomed barely on the horizon far to the north.

Something was drawing him toward the north, whether it was the fear at his back pushing him, or something else, Ingvar did not yet know, but one thing was certain, this is where he needed to go. Unsure how he knew, he trusted that answers to his future and what to do with the seed lay in the mountains or beyond.

Chapter Thirty-Two

When Ingvar woke to hushed voices, he did not immediately open his eyes. The ground was hard beneath him and the air smelled of damp stone. He had no recollection of having slept and was not yet sure if he was having another lucid dream or if the voices he was hearing were real.

Ingvar slowly opened his eyes, his head tilted towards the sound of the voices. Three shadowy figures stood a few feet away with weapons held out in front of them, dim light from behind them glinting off the surface of the weapons as they spoke in a hushed tone. They were going back and forth quickly, making small gestures in his direction.

Suddenly they stopped conversing aloud, their heads lilting toward him. The figure on the left, taller than the others and heavier set, nodded as if in acknowledgment to an unspoken question. The middle figure echoed the nod and the third figure, on the right, the slenderest of the three, stepped backward out an entranceway that had been hidden by their silhouettes. The middle figure stepped backward into the entryway, blocking it, all the while maintaining focus on Ingvar.

The remaining figure motioned slowly with its weapon for Ingvar to get up, to which he obliged, slowly. He raised his hands and sat up. Sweat beaded his brow and threatened to run into his eyes. He felt nauseous for a moment after he sat up, but kept the contents of his stomach inside his body with great effort.

The figure reached into a pouch on his belt with his free hand and retrieved from within it a glowing orb. White light flooded the room revealing the figure and Ingvar's surroundings.

Ingvar's eyes went wider than he ever thought possible, and before he could stop himself, laughed. Surely he was hallucinating.

"Damn the above, I've gone mad." blurted Ingvar.

The figure tilted its head to the side inquisitively and placed the orb on a stone ledge nearby, then sheathed its blade. The weapon was like nothing Ingvar had ever seen before. Curved slightly down from hilt to mid-blade, then ridged with in-cuts as the blade rose back up and forward to a point. It was semi-transparent and was held in a wide sheath made from an unrecognizable material. The sheath was fastened up the middle of the figure's back with a number of straps that held it secured to the armor without hindering movement.

The figure's armor shimmered iridescently in the white glow, like it was made from shells of some kind, yet appeared sturdier than plate armor. The shoulder guards were magnificent, with spherical indentations amid a similar material, where orbs of emerald green floated freely, one in either shoulder guard. The helmet was the defining feature that had made Ingvar burst out so. The visage of a beetle stared back at him, complete with fuzzy antenna like plumes, and it fit seamlessly with the gorget at the figure's neck. Every bit of the armor fit together so that it appeared to be one single piece.

Here stood a Legend made real in front of him. He had been told stories about Beetle Knights as a child, but they were thought to be nothing more than that. Stories. Myths. Legends.

They could not be real.

Could they?

"I do not speak your tongue well hu-man, but have other ways to communicate," said a voice in Ingvar's mind suddenly.

"They... you... are real!" exclaimed Ingvar.

"Indeed, we are."

"Telepaths, Mind speakers. I've heard many stories of your kind as a child. Can you hear my thoughts?"

"Not as such. It's more like seeing images full of intent. Thoughts always have intent, and we are good at reading these intentions," The voice paused for emphasis on this before continuing, *"How did you get here, hu-man?"*

Ingvar could feel the edge in the voice. Goosebumps spread up his arms.

"I truly do not know. I don't even know where *HERE* is." Replied Ingvar as he looked around the room. He was in a smooth stone chamber. There was a staircase carved into the stone near the entranceway where the middle figure stood guard that wound up into the darkness beyond the glow orb's reach. Barely visible beyond the darkness above, he could make out a faint hint of light that indicated there was another opening much higher up.

"You are within our realm." Stated the voice plainly as if that would answer all his questions.

"Until now, I didn't even know your kind were real, let alone where your realm existed. Please..." Ingvar answered the unrepeated question that hung in the air before them. "I am lost."

"*Lost?*"

"Aye. I've lost track of time. I've traveled without being awake, and I know not where I am. I know it sounds strange, but it's the truth."

The figure shifted forward slightly, his beetle helmed visage glaring intently at Ingvar for a number of heart beats.

"*Fear not, hu-man, I see your mind truth. It is as you say. You traversed the foothills through night, day, and night again. Your mind visions show me what your mind does not tell you. It has been three days since last you recall.*"

"Three days! How is that possible?"

"*Most likely more. There are dark spots in your mind visions. Between the ones I can see. I do not know how this is possible, hu-man. Normally we can see all things in one's mind.*"

"Ingvar."

"*As you say, Ingvar, hu-man.*"

"And what do I call you-" Ingvar stopped, unsure how to address the figure in any way.

"*Ah. Yes. Forgive me. I am Brov. A male as you would identify,*" said Brov, placing his right hand over his chest, his fingers spread wide as he introduced himself. "*This is Vodroc, another male of our kind.*" Brov continued, indicating the figure in the entranceway with a sweep of his right hand from his chest. "*And our third is Des.*"

"A female, yes," Ingvar guessed, based on his recollection of the slender figure that had exited the room earlier?

"*As you say, Ingvar hu-man.*"

"Just Ingvar, please."

"*As you say, Ingvar-*" Brov cut himself off from adding the racial moniker.

Ingvar rose slowly to his feet and stretched away the aches in his muscles from sleeping on the stone floor, took a deep breath and swallowed hard. It was then he realized how parched his throat was. Before he could reach for his pack to get his water skin, Brov procured a round, wooden vessel with an ornately carved wooden stopper.

"*Water.*" Brov answered before he could ask what it was.

Ingvar marveled at the Knight's ability to read his mind. He took the water vessel and after a moment of figuring out how to open it with a slight twist to unseal it, he drank deeply. The water was cold, and crisp, as if it had just been pulled from a fresh mountain stream. It had a slight sweetness to it.

"*Nectar, for energy and health.*" Brov answered again before the question could be asked.

Ingvar could feel the liquid working its way through his body. His muscles quickly relaxed and the aches receded. He replaced the stopper and handed the vessel back to Brov.

Ingvar bowed slightly and said "Thank you for your kindness."

"*I fear I gave the wrong impression. It was practical, not kind. You will need your strength for our journey.*"

"What journey?" asked Ingvar with a look of confusion.

"*We must take you with us to our council. They will know what to do with you.*"

"What to do with me? What do you mean? Point me in the right direction and I can just be on my way."

"*You do not know where you are to journey. Your mind visions reveal as much, and we cannot take the risk that you will remember the way to our kingdom. We have remained hidden this long, away from the world and the troubles your kind brings with them. While it is possible for us to move the kingdom, it takes great effort to do so and we would rather not have to do so unnecessarily."*

Ingvar slouched down against the wall next to his belongings.

"I see. So I am to be a prisoner of circumstances then?"

"Not a prisoner. A guest. For now."

Ingvar's mind raced with thoughts of running, of pleading his case, of fighting his way out of his situation to avoid being held captive.

Brov straightened slightly, tensing, but did not react.

"Can you see my thoughts now? I do not mean disrespect, but I also cannot control my thoughts. My words, well, that's another thing. I am not used to articulating thoughts before thinking them as your kind are said to do."

"They are not pleasant. I understand. We wish there was another way, but this is how we have survived and maintained our ways without corrupting influences from the outside world."

"Have there been others that have found their way here then?"

Brov hesitated before answering.

"Once, long ago."

"What happened to them?"

"That is not for me to say."

"Who then? Him?" asked Ingvar, pointing at Vodroc.

Brov shook his head side to side once.

"Nothing I say will change your minds or convince you otherwise will it?"

"No. Your mind is-" Brov paused and tilted his head to the left slightly before adding, *"broken, incomplete, missing pieces. We cannot discern whether you pose a threat or not.*

162

The Council may be able to see more. They are much stronger in our ways."

"Ah. I see."

Ingvar scratched an itch beneath his beard. A beard! The realization that he had been traveling long enough to grow a full beard struck him like a hammer against an anvil. How could he have traveled for so long without being cognoscente of it? He worked to keep his breathing calm, fighting the panic that threatened to rise in him and force him into a stupid reaction.

"Ingvar hu-man, it will be alright. We do not wish you harm. You simply have to be counseled," stated Brov. His voice in Ingvar's mind made him jump out of his thoughts once more.

"What does that mean?"

"I cannot say. That is for the council to determine."

Vodroc shifted in the entranceway, sheathed his own blade, which Ingvar had not realized had still been drawn, and nodded once in Brov's direction before he turned and walked outside.

"Do you speak to each other telepathically?" asked Ingvar curiously.

"Not as such. We are trained to guard our minds from birth, but we have other subtle ways of simple communication."

"Fascinating."

It was growing lighter out, and with Vodroc no longer in the way, Ingvar could see that there was a large stone ledge outside that went on for some distance before suddenly ending in what he assumed was a sheer drop. Fog or low cloud cover prevented him from observing anything more about his surroundings.

A series of clicks and humming whistles from outside bounced off the stone walls around him. Before he could ask what the sound was, Brov stood, gestured with his left hand toward the entranceway and extinguished the glowing orb.

"When you are ready, Ingvar hu-man."

Ingvar cleared his throat, gathered his things and walked outside with Brov right behind him. Though he knew the tales from the story books, Ingvar was not prepared to see the giant beetles that the Knights used, loitering off to his left. Vodroc and Des were removing what Ingvar guessed to be feed bags of some sort from the nose tusks and pincers that jutted from the back of the beetles' jaws on either side of their skulls. They flicked their fuzzy antennas excitedly in anticipation, carapaces shimmering in the growing light of dawn. Their wings, unlike other beetles Ingvar had seen unfolded from pouches on the side of the creature's belly, between the front and middle leg. Small recesses in the carapace formed natural saddles for up to two riders on the creatures backs. Two of the beetles were dark green with hints of yellow on their undersides, and the third was a dark red with a vibrant blue underside.

Brov placed a hand on his shoulder, breaking him from his revere and gestured toward the red beetle.

Ingvar closed his mouth which had fallen open. He walked towards the beetle and when they reached its side, Des stepped around from the other side to meet them with a curt nod.

Brov bowed slightly and stepped back.

It was then that Ingvar noticed the special markings on Des's armor, clearly marking her as in charge. He could not see her face beneath her helm, but he was certain that she was amused with his stares.

"Watch where I step, hu-man, and climb up behind me," said a new, feminine voice in his head. It was baffling to

164

Ingvar that he could distinguish their voices without them ever speaking aloud.

Without waiting for his acknowledgment, Des climbed her beetle's middle leg, using the black bony spikes as foot and hand holds.

What took her seconds to do, took Ingvar much longer with his shorter reach. When he had settled into the groove that formed the seat of the saddle behind Des, she instructed him to wrap his arms around her waist and to hold tight.

"The beetle will not drop us, but just in case you feel yourself getting light of head I will keep you from falling." Des explained as he did as he was instructed. *"It is much like riding a horse, only larger. You'll be fine I'm sure."*

Des performed a series of toothy whistles and tongue clicks, and the beetles began their ascent, their wings buzzing harmoniously.

Ingvar looked in all directions, taking in the view. It was breathtaking. Tall stone pillars covered in trees, vines, ferns, moss and all other manner of foliage dotted the landscape. A misty fog crept through dense forest at the base of the pillars and over the edges of jagged mountains in the distance. Flocks of colorful birds like nothing he had ever seen before flew over the treetops far below.

The building he had been sleeping in was no normal building. It looked like it was naturally shaped, not constructed. The ledge outside of it jutted out from the side of an immense jagged faced mountain.

Ingvar was at a complete loss as to how he could have ended up in such a place.

The sun continued to rise at their backs as the beetles glided almost lazily down into the valleys between the pillars. The air grew humid and warm. Water cascaded from the sides of many bluffs as they traversed canyons and valleys in weaving patterns until his mind was a twist of directions.

No doubt it was intended to further confuse him in case he suddenly recalled how he had gotten here.

After what seemed like hours, they broke free of the jagged stone pillar jungle into a wide open landscape of flower filled fields, roaming animals of all kinds and sizes, most of which he did not recognize, and a magnificent stone city jutting up from the heart of the flat land. He knew without asking that this was their destination. The beetles swooped lower to the ground, the downdraft of their wings buffeting the long grasses of the fields as they passed, making the fields look like an ocean of green, its tide pushing on toward their destination.

Chapter Thirty-Three

It was dusk by the time Ingvar and his new friends landed in the stone city and Ingvar's mind was overwhelmed with all the revelations and sights the day had brought. He slid off the beetle's back and landed on the smooth stones next to Des and took a moment to stretch away the stiffness of the day in the saddle.

The city was stunning, everything was made of stone, but none of it had brick or cut stone patterns that Ingvar was used to seeing in architecture. It all looked smooth, without blemish of any kind, like it was naturally formed into buildings.

After the riders had dismounted, the beetles took to the air again, and entered individual nests in the side of a rectangular granite structure that must have been a stables of sorts. A handler stood at the ready to feed and wipe down each of the beetles once they had settled into their nests. Baskets of melons and eggs lined the walls behind the handlers.

With a wave of her hand, Des directed Ingvar towards a large set of wooden doors that were ornately carved with images of beetles and other creatures along their edges. The doors were not square like the ones Ingvar was used to, instead, they were round. Flat along the bottom, wide enough that one of the beetles could pass through them. Ingvar started toward the entrance with Des right behind him. Brov and Vodroc followed.

Beyond the entrance was a large room with numerous nooks along the walls with stone benches and small glowing orbs in settings on the walls above each nook table. To either end of the room a rounding staircase of stone led up to another floor. Marble and granite columns filled the open space, rising from the floor into the ceiling with no hint of a seam or cut. They were one solid piece each, and seem to be part of the rest of the building.

"The work of our Stone Shapers," Brov's voice echoed in his mind. *"Welcome to the Shifting Kingdom."*

Another set of doors loomed across the room straight ahead of them, smaller, but a mirror of the building's main entrance. Two guards in similar armor to his escort's own stood to either side of the doors. As they approached along a red stone path, the guards stepped forward two steps, turned toward each other and reached out a hand to open both doors simultaneously. They bowed low and stepped back to clear the way for them to enter the chamber beyond.

Ingvar was led into a giant hall of shaped stone columns with large marble carvings of men and women in various poses, some heroic, some kneeling, others in vivid battles, set inside large oval alcoves on each wall.

Instead of tapestries or painted murals, every flat stone surface was covered with a mixture of different stone veins. Red granite, obsidian, rose quartz, sandstone, limestone and many others. It was a stunning display.

Lush plants wound around the stone columns and overhead between arched stone beams, and above those, glowing orbs floated freely near the ceiling, their light reflecting off of some smooth, glassy gemstone inset in the stone ceiling. The light danced as the orbs spun.

A dark wooden table stretched the length of the hall, with woven wooden chairs spaced every other foot, and ornate symbols embedded into their backs. Each chair had its own symbol, and behind each chair stood a tall figure clad in regal looking clothes. Ingvar suspected the symbols represented the individuals that stood behind the chairs.

There were nineteen figures standing behind the seats, leaving one empty in the middle of the right side of the long table. The emblem on that chair was that of a serpent. Ten women in regal robes of emerald green and golden lace, nine men in equally regal robes of sapphire blue with silver lace, skin the color of red clay and eyes a silver white that glimmered like diamonds. Each pair of eyes became a piercing glare when they looked upon Ingvar, unsettling him deeply. He felt his skin chill and his legs shake.

The doors closed behind them. Des remained directly behind Ingvar. Brov and Vodroc stood guard to either side with their gauntleted hands crossed.

"*Be calm, young hu-man, you are in no danger in this place. We will discern your intent, and the truth of your journey. Then we will decide your fate,*" echoed a new voice in his mind. He looked around at each of the figures in the room until he discerned the one whom was speaking, face calm, his eyes more focused than the rest. The figure dipped his head and closed his eyes in acknowledgment when Ingvar had sussed him out.

Before Ingvar could say anything in reply, the new voice continued in his mind, "*Nothing ill is to be your fate, but if it is decided that your leaving this place puts us at risk of exposure, after remaining hidden from the world for centuries, then you will be bound to us, never to leave again. Do you understand?*"

Ingvar nodded his head in agreement slowly. There was nothing else to say or do. He was completely at their mercy.

"Then let the mind meld begin." With that, the council members stepped forward and took their seats. They all looked upon Ingvar with renewed intensity, and a cacophony of prodding questions and discussions reverberated in his mind, causing Ingvar to grow slightly dizzy and lightheaded. Brov and Vodroc guided him to a seat at the end of the table and lowered him into it.

Images flitted before his eyes and dissipated quickly. A tapestry of his life and that of those he did not recognize. He felt unsettled, yet at peace. It was unlike any feeling he had ever experienced.

Ingvar had no idea how much time had passed, but he was exhausted. It became a struggle to keep his eyes open and his head from drooping, chin to chest.

All at once the multitude of voices probing his mind ceased, and a single baritone reverberated in his skull.

"We have completed our beginning inquest and have determined that you pose no immediate threat, but there is yet much to explore and discuss about your past. We will let you rest and recover before continuing, as your mind is not yet strong enough for this undertaking," announced the voice that had initially greeted him from the council.

With that, the council members stood and exited the chamber without another word or glance in Ingvar's direction.

"Come Ingvar hu-man, let us get you some food and find you a room to rest in until the council is ready to continue." Des's voice chimed.

Ingvar stood, shakily and followed Des from the Council Chamber, Brov and Vodroc to either side to aid him.

They Who Linger

~*~

Ingvar awoke to a thumping on the stone door to the bed chamber he had been assigned for the duration of his stay, however long that would be. Des had shown him how the door worked before all three of his escorts had left him alone in his room hours earlier, ensuring him that he was not a prisoner as such, but more an indefinite guest.

Des greeted him with a nod when he opened the door and beckoned for him to join her and the others for some food before heading back to the Council Chamber.

It turned out it had been almost a full day since then. He had been so exhausted by the council's mind probing that he had slept away an entire day.

It was a simple meal of oven toasted bread with a sweet molasses and cinnamon flavor, grilled eggs and tomatoes with diced potatoes and mixed vegetables.

When the group arrived at the Council Chamber, the council members were already present and seated. The same baritone voice from the first encounter greeted Ingvar as they entered and wished him a fair day, then the man gestured for Ingvar to take the seat he had used the previous time he had been questioned.

Once Ingvar was seated, the voice continued.

"This council was once twenty strong, now nineteen of us remain. Our fallen member fell to corruption ages ago and was imprisoned. Until now. We sense his taint creeping back into the world of men and now you appear on our doorstep with a mind full of missing memories of your journey to get here. There can be only one answer, the seal is broken and you carry the seed that could once more seal the door to that dark realm. You will need to know our history to understand, though we fear your mind will break further."

They Who Linger

Ingvar looked the council members in the eyes, those piercing, silver eyes, and sighed. "Show me."

Chapter Thirty-Four

Corlag and Branick came upon the crossroads near dusk. With a sigh of relief, they set their bags on the ground next to one of the many stone megaliths that used to be the cornerstones of a keep and watch tower. These giant stones and a few bits of crumbling stone walls were all that remained of the keep now. A wall of stone and mortar four feet high blocked the edge of the jagged rock face that fell hundreds of feet into the valley below. The great trees of Thain's Reach covered the valley like an ocean of green, swaying in a light breeze. The view was nothing short of spectacular. Corlag approached the lichen covered stone wall and gripped the top of it with his left hand. He stood there for a few moments, soaking in the view and the warm breeze rushing from the valley below. He tested the durability of the aging wall that protected him from a potentially fatal slip to the valley floor far below. The capstone he gripped with his left hand came loose with minimal effort. He raised his eyebrows in surprise and stepped back as the stone slid forward into the void. He listened to it hit a jagged outcrop of stone on its sudden voyage toward an unsuspecting end; the bits that broke free careened and echoed their earthen cries off the cliff face.

"Whoa, careful there, these stones are well weathered," called Branick. He had already started making camp in the center of the ruins.

"I see that," replied Corlag with his eyebrows still raised. He whistled and retreated back into the safety of the ruins.

"It will be dark soon," said Branick, pointing at the descending sun.

"Aye, I'll see if I can't get us some fresh meat for dinner."

Branick nodded and continued with his menial task.

~*~

It wasn't long before Corlag spotted a pheasant strutting along a narrow game trail in the tall grass on the north side of the junction where the three paths met in front of the ruins. It was slowly making its way up a hill toward the trees, scratching at the ground here and there. He took one slow step after another, making no sound as he attempted to sneak up on the majestic creature. Its head bobbed as it walked, and it paused near a small fern, pecking at the leaves. He was a few feet away. He silently unsheathed a throwing dagger from his belt, ever so carefully raised his arm, ready to throw. The bird stretched to its full height and turned suddenly towards him, its grey chest puffed up. It tilted its head this way and that, trying to make sense of the danger it felt nearby. It showed its orange and red plume and vibrated its feathers rapidly in warning. Before it had a chance to dart away in fear, Corlag flicked his wrist toward it. The dagger whistled through the air in the blink of an eye, catching the bird in the chest, piercing its heart and killing it instantly. It was a clean kill, no suffering and no pain. He gave silent thanks for the coming nourishment and mourned the loss of such a beautiful being at the same time.

He retrieved his dagger and bled the bird before he cleaned it on a clump of grass and re-sheathed it. He picked his catch up by the feet and turned to make his way back down the hill. Something to the north caught his eye as he was turning, giving him pause. A lone figure approached along the northern road, coming down out of the Obodoon Pass. As the woman approached, he noticed that she carried a bow in one hand and was constantly looking over her right shoulder as she staggered along the path.

Corlag signaled Branick with a loud whistle. When he poked his head out of the ruins, Corlag pointed up the north road at the approaching woman and then cut across the hill towards her himself.

Branick dashed up the road to meet Corlag, who had now set his catch down on a patch of grass next to the path. Corlag held his hands out to his sides as he approached the woman.

"Hey there, are you alright," Corlag called out?

The woman jumped in surprise, noticing them for the first time. A look of relief crossed the woman's face. Slowly, they moved towards her, cautious yet friendly.

Branick watched the hills behind her, looking for any threat, but could see nothing.

"Yes... I think so," she replied between labored breaths. "I... will be... fine," she stammered as she attempted to shoulder her bow. Her limbs began to shake as exhaustion caught up with her. She lowered her guard a little, letting the tension and strain that had gripped her, subside.

"You look as if you've been traveling for a long while without rest. Come, join us at our fire and warm yourself.

We were just fixing some dinner. You are welcome to join us," said Corlag.

"Thank- Thank you- kindly," the woman replied, struggling to stay conscious. Darkness flooded in from the edges of her vision, taking her completely as she muttered the final word.

"Whoa, easy friend," said Corlag, catching the woman before she could tip forward. "You're safe now."

He hoisted her left arm over his shoulders and placed his right arm gently around her waist, supporting her weight, and waved Branick to help. Together, they walked the woman back to their camp. They set her down gently, propping her up against one of the old foundation stones closest to the fire.

Branick went about preparing the food and a warm drink for everyone while Corlag inspected their guest for injuries, being as unintrusive as possible. Satisfied that there were no major injuries of any kind that he could discern, he set her pack, bow and quiver to the side, against a stone next to her. He then removed his blanket from his bedroll and draped it around her. All the while, Branick sat with his back to the fire, his eyes on the hills to the north, watching for any sign of trouble from where the woman had come.

Corlag couldn't figure out what it was, but something was bothering him. Whatever it was, it had the hairs on his nape on end and his skin crawling. Dusk had settled in, and would not last much longer. Already the shadows crawled along the ground, stretching their dark tendrils toward the east. He scooped two cups of fresh brewed Javium from the pot over the fire while he pondered the woman. He gently nudged Branick on the shoulder with the bottom of one of the cups to shake his gaze from the hills to the north.

Without averting his eyes, he offered up his right hand near this shoulder to accept the cup.

"Something is terribly wrong, I'm not sure what yet, but I can feel it in my bones," said Branick.

"Aye friend, I feel it as well," replied Corlag. "If there is one thing I've learned over the many years of our travels, it's to trust your instincts. We'll let her rest a bit. We can find out what is going on after she wakes."

"There will be little rest tonight. I do not trust the darkness to stay where it belongs, beyond the light of the fire."

"Agreed. I assume since you have averted your eyes from the fire for some time that you are saving your night vision and taking the first watch?"

"Aye."

"Very well then, I will tend supper and bring it to you when it's ready."

"I'll be near the broken arch of the ruins, where I can keep a better eye on our surroundings, and be far enough from the fire so as not to disturb my vision," replied Branick. He stood and moved toward the front of the ruins.

Corlag turned his attention to roasting the pheasant.

Chapter Thirty-Five

Syndara jolted awake, scrambling to get free of the blanket draped over her and instinctively reached for her bow, which wasn't there. She frantically looked around, only calming when she laid eyes on a red haired man huddled by the fire, watching her. He had his hands outstretched to indicate he meant no harm. Recollection came to her that they had met on the road, but it was all a blur; only bits and pieces came back to her.

"Easy friend, you're safe," said the man.

"Where's my bow? How did I get here? Who are you," she blurted all at once.

"Beside you," the man pointed to her right, "we carried you when you passed out, and I," he placed his hand on his chest, "am Corlag."

"We," asked Syndara as she looked around again?

"Aye, we. My associate, Branick, is keeping watch at the moment."

Syndara reached for her bow and quiver, then, with great effort, stood and walked closer to the fire. She kept her bow close at hand as she sat and warmed herself by the fire.

Corlag offered her some food from a cook-pot, scooping it into a wooden bowl. He set a wooden spoon in the contents then passed the bowl to her. "Fresh roasted pheasant stew. Please, sit and let us make introductions."

Syndara accepted the bowl slowly. The smell of the food wafted over her and melted her defenses. She sat cross-legged, hunger taking over. She ravenously dug into the food, taking a number of bites before replying. "I am Syndara," she began, gently dabbing her mouth with the back of her hand, "a huntress from the village of Garomvol to the north."

"In the Obodoon Mountains," replied Corlag with a hint of surprise. "What are you doing so far south alone?"

"I was traveling south to Barroville with my friend, Aileesha, to seek passage on a boat across the Everdeep." She hesitated for a while before continuing with the rest of the information, visually judging the character of Corlag. "I suppose it doesn't matter now if I tell you this or not. We were set upon by a pack of wild beasts, black of skin, unlike anything I've ever seen before. We were just passing over the Weeping Gorge when they came upon us from the trees. I managed to cut the ropes on the bridge, dropping most of them into the gorge, but one made it across. It was massive. My friend, Aileesha-"

She choked up. Tears welled up in her eyes and crept out at the edges. The firelight reflected off of the tears as her emotions threatened to take control of her.

Corlag looked on without a word, his face betraying his own emotions.

"Aileesha saved my life. When we came under attack at the gorge, she did not hesitate to throw herself in the path of the beast. I couldn't save her..." she clenched her free hand into a fist. The tears streamed down her face as the dam broke. She cried out mournfully and uncontrollably, her body shaking as she wept.

Corlag remained silent, staring intently across the fire. He was surprised by her description of the creatures and the similarities to the ones that had attacked him and Branick in the forest clearing. Surely that couldn't be mere coincidence? He waited for her moment of grief to pass, giving her time to collect herself before speaking.

"Those beasts you described, we've encountered them as well. It would seem our paths are intertwined, truly. We were attacked in a clearing at the heart of the Fel'Thain Forest on our journey through it. If not for Branick, I would surely be missing an arm, if not my head. It would seem that we could benefit from each other's company. Would you be opposed to traveling with us to Barroville? That is, in fact, also our destination. We are heading there for the spring festival. What say you," offered Corlag? He bent and scooped three fresh cups of Javium from the pot and offered one to Syndara.

"Your company would be very welcome. I will travel with you to Barroville," she replied. She accepted the cup and thanked him. "I must find passage on a boat once I arrive there, I cannot tarry from my people longer than is needed."

"What takes you so far from them if I may be so forward," inquired Corlag?

Syndara thought about the question for a while before answering. She did not wish to let on about the artifact to strangers. Deciding it best to avoid the full truth, she gave a simplified answer.

"I seek wisdom. I travel to the Blackwood at the request of our Chieftain."

"Don't we all," replied Corlag. He poked the fire with a stick, sending a cloud of sparks up into the night. He gave her a curious look but pried no more.

"Have you ever been across the Everdeep," asked Syndara with curiosity in her eyes?

"Aye, once, long ago."

"You sound pensive about your journey there," she replied, picking up on his woeful tone.

"That is a tale for another time," said Corlag as he poked the fire some more and added another log to it.

She sensed that she would get no more out of him about the subject. She uncurled her legs and stretched out beside the fire, placed her right foot over her left knee, and proceeded to crack her back.

"I feel as if I have been through a great war," she said with a sigh of relief when her back popped in several places.

"How long were you traveling alone after your-" Corlag hesitated, "you lost Aileesha?"

Syndara pondered the question for a moment, thinking back on her travels since the attack.

"A few days at least, but I can't rightly recollect the exact number."

A night bird's call echoed through the silence, and Corlag turned his head to the north again. He folded his hands to his mouth in an interlocked manner. He breathed out sharply, sending a mimicked reply through the darkness.

"Branick wishes to speak with me, I had best go see what he wants," he said, then stood and brushed dried grass and leaves from his leggings. "Help yourself to some more food and drink if you like." With that, he stepped out into the night, an extra cup of Javium in hand.

Chapter Thirty-Six

Borgolas gripped his walking stick with both hands, resting his left temple against it, his chin on his knees. He looked down on the crossroads from his perch on a boulder hidden in the tree line to the north west of the ruins of the keep that once stood as a bastion of trade and travel, lost to the ages long since passed, in conflicts most had forgotten about. He had found the spot just before dusk while the two travelers had been gathering firewood and hunting a colorful bird. A pheasant by his recollection, or the mind of the body that hosted him at least seemed to think that was the name of the bird. A voice he both recognized and did not boomed inside his head.

I must know if the memories I wake with are things that have truly happened, or if I am just dreaming. Night after night, I have what I would assume are nightmares. I have visions of creatures running through the night, hunting, killing, and feeding. Dark skinned beasts, claws like steel, and mouths full of fangs. I taste what they taste; blood.

He spit on the ground attempting to rid himself of the taste from the passing thought. He took a deep breath and reached for his water skin. The voice returned while he was drinking, causing his head to throb with every internal word.

They show no remorse, nor do they contemplate, they just act. Even as they feed, their hunger grows. I feel their hunger. Come to think of it, I have begun to feel it even as I wander in the daylight, no longer just at night. They begin to grow bold, no longer afraid to roam from the shadows. I feel tense, angry, yet calculating. I fear it is not long before I lose even the simple abilities I have left to distinguish myself from what dwells within. It wants... No, it NEEDS to surface.

Images of a past not his own flickered in his mind once again, this time pertaining to some mysterious powers, and a woman at his side he did not know; yet knew better than anyone. Her beauty radiated through his body. Just when he felt like he might fully remember this past, she melted away like dust in the wind, and he was alone in the woods once more. The walking stick cracked between his hands, as rage gripped him.

Why now? What changed to cause this re-emergence of chaos within my mind? A second source... NO! It can't be. What is it? A woman from the north! Again the creatures, I can taste the blood, hear the screams, one has escaped! I must find her. I must find the source before it tears apart the remaining parts of my mind.

He bolted upright, flinging back his hood and watched the woman approach down the road from the Obodoon Pass. A new strength welled in his limbs, the shattered walking stick lay at his feet, all but dismissed. A cold wind rippled through the trees, rustling his robes about him as he watched intently.

Chapter Thirty-Seven

Branick sat near the fire, warming himself. It was cold amongst the old stone ruins. Corlag had taken the second watch and the woman, Syndara, was fast asleep. He sat with one arm over a knee, and poked the fire with a stick with his other hand as he quietly contemplated all the events that had transpired over the past few days. The similarities of the creatures and their attacks that the woman had described to Corlag were troubling. He couldn't put his mind at ease about it. There had to be a link, some reasonable explanation. Ancient memories haunted him about the wars he and Corlag had fought in many long years ago. The beasts they had encountered reminded him of other creatures they had encountered amongst the throng of the southern armies that had marched against the kingdom of men, in an attempt to eradicate the young race.

Unable to focus his thoughts on anything for more than a few seconds, he crawled into his bedroll. He lay there for a long while, staring up at the clear night sky, scanning the heavens for stars he recognized. Before long, he began to doze off. He signaled to Corlag with a soft bird call that he would be asleep soon, a faint reply echoed back in his ears as night took him in its embrace.

Chapter Thirty-Eight

Corlag sat with his back to a stump not far from the camp, his pack next to him. He was thinking about the Blackwood, dwelling place of the Aolfkin. He could not put it out of his mind once Syndara had mentioned it. Not many knew whether or not they still existed among the trees at the heart of Thayrium, and even fewer sought to explore the woods there. They were not safe, nor were they easily accessible. It was a journey for the desperate and the hardy. What could possibly drive her Chieftain to send her there? He had a suspicion itching at the back of his mind. One that formed together when she had described the creatures that had attacked her and her friend. There was no way it was a simple coincidence that the two attacks had occurred. The timing of the attack he and Branick had suffered was not without its own suspicion. Their journey had become increasingly bizarre from the moment they had unearthed the artifact. His thoughts wandered and he found himself reflecting inward.

I have never traveled the Blackwood myself, but many a tale I have been privy to and have shared in taverns far and wide. If the tales are true, and the Aolfkin still linger among us, with as much knowledge and wisdom as the tales depict, I would be curious to meet them as well.

He undid the straps on his pack, reached inside and procured the artifact absentmindedly. Enough light from the fire reached out into the darkness to illuminate its surface as he ran one hand over it before becoming lost in thought again.

I have also heard the tales of O'Marah and its haunted ruins. They say that among the ruins, buried deep underground, lies the remains of an ancient civilization that was all but erased from the face of Ierolden during a great cataclysmic event, thousands of years ago.

He flipped the artifact over and examined it further. He noticed strange notches on its backside and some unknown script around the edge.

Some claim to have heard voices in their minds as they skirted the expansive landscape at the ruined kingdom's border, lamenting their tale of being buried alive. Monolithic pillars pockmark the land even now, outlining paths that no longer guide so much as misguide weary travelers and would be treasure hunters. There are more tales of lost adventurers than there are of the ruins themselves. In one of the few recordings that have surfaced, an adventurer claims to have discovered a crack in the world, a ravine that does not appear to have a bottom. To his recollection, it seems to split the southern part of Thayrium that is covered with the ruins of O'Marah, almost in two.

A faint glow from the artifact snapped Corlag out of his memory trance. He shook his head and looked again at the relic, but the glow was gone. He rubbed his eyes and wondered if he was seeing things. He traced the lettering with his index finger, pausing for a moment before returning it to his pack.

Perhaps that landmark has something to do with the disappearance of the race of ancients buried beneath O'Marah, that is, if it truly exists at all. Then there is the Everdeep...

That vast expanse of water, an Ocean they call it, seems to have no bottom in places. Of the charted routes crossing the open waters, there are dozens of islands, each with its own tales. One such island, supposedly, is home to the soil of Ierolden in living form. Sailors claim that the earth walks like a man. There have been sightings of giant men with one eye in the middle of their brow, and fish the size of ships with glowing orbs resting on singular antennas that hang in front of them; lighting their way through the dark waters. There are even tales of a creature with tentacles that can wrap around a ship's hull and drag it below the surface, whole. The Everdeep is young compared to the rest of the world. It never used to exist according to ancient documents I read when I visited the great library long ago.

I can't help but wonder if this Borgolas fellow we met knows more about our situation than we do. His visage haunts me still. I found everything about him unsettling.

His hand that had held the artifact began to itch and he scratched it with the other. He put the artifact back in his bag and returned his vision to the dark hills beyond the ruins. Corlag found himself thinking of the mysterious figure they had encountered on the path as he watched the dark hills.

Each time I think about the relic, his face appears, clouding my thoughts. Why did he continuously look at my pack? Does he sense the relic somehow? Is he responsible for these strange creatures and the attacks on us? His eyes were certainly as dark as their skin. I will be keeping a wary eye on our path; I do not wish to encounter him unawares again.

He stood and slung his pack over his shoulders, then found a shrub to relieve himself on. Night had begun to give way to dawn. It would soon be time to wake the others. He did one more patrol, scanning the hills around the camp. Satisfied there was no immediate danger, he returned to the camp to stoke the embers to life in preparation for breakfast.

Chapter Thirty-Nine

The trio broke camp shortly after dawn, their bellies warmed with porridge and Javanth tea. Branick stomped out the fire and took up the rear of their column. Corlag led the way. They followed the meandering trail through the rocky hills that decorated the valley leading along the Upper Reach, eventually beginning a criss-crossed descent along the valley's cliff face, down into the Lower Reach and on to Barroville.

Only a few thin, white clouds spotted the otherwise clear skies; the sun danced through the trees as they traveled. The surface of Thain's Reach River glistened like a field of gemstones on green silk as it weaved throughout the farmlands. The roar of Thain's Maw echoed faintly along the cliffs from far to the west where the giant waterfall fell hundreds of feet from the Fel'Thain down into the valley. They could see the small smoke plumes from chimneys rising up through the trees far to the south, at the edge of their viewing distance now.

"There it be," exclaimed Corlag, pointing down the valley towards the rising shafts of smoke. "Barroville. We should reach it by late afternoon if all goes well, and it looks like the weather favors us today," he finished as he raised his face to the sky, taking in the warmth of the sun and sighed.

"Beautiful. It's-" Syndara paused for a moment, taking in the scene from half way down the valley's cliff side. "It's absolutely beautiful."

"Aye lass," replied Branick. He placed his hands on the straps of his pack and stretched. "It is that."

"Let's push on, we will take a break once we reach the main road at the bottom," said Corlag, leading them down the cliff side again.

They reached the main road at the bottom about an hour before midday. They found a grassy area next to the road with a log and some boulders to sit on. It was a light meal of bread, cheese, and water, followed by some wild apples from a natural orchard not far off the road. There were plenty of travelers on the road, farmers and their animals, families with their children, and merchants with plenty of wares. They were all headed to the festival at Barroville from their homes and villages that spread all throughout the Reach.

When they were sated and rejuvenated, they fell in between a merchant and a farmer herding his animals to the spring market. The sounds of bells rang occasionally as cattle and sheep were herded back in line by his dogs, and horseshoes clip-clopped on rocks buried in the old dirt road as they pulled the creaking wooden cart carrying the merchant in front of them. The crowd of people was a welcome change, even when it became thicker the closer they got to Barroville. The rise in noise indicated that there were many more within the city's walls.

Corlag caught himself instinctively resting his hand on the hilt of his sword at his hip. "We've become rather on edge wouldn't you say Branick," he asked as he looked over his shoulder at his burly friend, who also had his hand on his weapon hilt.

"Aye, that I would. 'Tis not without merit," he replied, cracking his knuckles.

"True indeed. We need to be cautious of everyone and everything while we are within those walls. Do not speak of the events that have transpired. Folk get squirmy over such things and it tends to get out of hand quickly. We do not want to be responsible for panic amongst the farmers and woodsmen now do we?"

Branick and Syndara nodded in unison.

"I'll get us a room at the Hog's Head once we get through the gates, and make arrangements with the Inn Keep to spin my tales in exchange for meals and lodging. Maybe we'll get lucky and earn a little extra."

"That'd be nice for a change," jabbed Branick with a smirk.

"Smart arse," replied Corlag. "Once we have put our belongings in our room, you should take Syndara to the docks and find out when the next boat is leaving across the Everdeep to Thayrium and if they have room for three."

"Why's that," asked Branick?

"I'm thinking we're long overdue for a visit to the other side of the world," answered Corlag, giving Branick a knowing look that had become common between them over the years.

Branick nodded his silent acknowledgment.

"Interesting times ahead, wouldn't you say old friend," asked Branick?

"Interesting times indeed."

They walked through the gates to the city and down the bustling streets.

Chapter Forty

Borgolas watched the three travelers descending into the Lower Reach. While he observed them, more images from his past flooded his mind, accompanied by a terrible ringing in his ears. He stifled a cry of pain and fell to his knees, hands shaking as he placed them over each ear, trying to soften the noise within. He fell forward onto his elbows, the pain searing into his skull. He took deep, slow breaths, and waited for it to pass. When it had, he sat up, hands on his knees. His mind was clear, and the ringing in his ears dissipated.

A recollection of the ancients had emerged in his mind. Could this be? Had the pieces of the keystone truly appeared from the ashes of ruin? His eyes blazed with an unnatural hunger. He wiped his hands over his robes, dusting off dried foliage.

Yes, this is a prison, I remember now.

He spat on the ground and balled his bony hands into fists, the knuckles no longer cracking with arthritis.

I was banished to live within my own puppet's body for an eternity, forever wandering mindlessly. The grip of the ancients must have weakened for me to be able to escape my fleshy cage. Do they remember me, or have they forgotten and now they seek the power for themselves? Or do they even know what lies within the tombs? How long have I truly wandered like this, lost to my own illusions? I will find the keystone again, and I will make them pay for what they have done to me. I will burn this world to ash if necessary! How dare they banish me!

An image of a man covered in dust, sitting on a throne surrounded by darkness flooded his vision. Eyes alight with blue-white light, ever watchful. They fell upon him in the vision, burning him to the depths of his soul. He screamed in agony, a third voice filling his mind this time.

'You will remember surely, that you brought this on yourself, for your actions condemned us all. We linger beneath the ruins. We wait. We remember. If you seek to return, you will find the Everlight remains as strong as ever, and it hungers to devour dark souls like your own.'

He was filled with rage. Words could not describe the depths of the anger he felt. He remembered his pets and his powers that made them do his bidding. Their actions, the things of nightmares, his powers are enough to make even those who dwell in the shadows tremble.

Faces danced across his vision. The travelers, even the woman whom he had not met. He knew then that they were not memories from his own eyes, but rather those of his pets as they had strove to put down those that would rob their master of the keystone.

Mmm, the furnace of hatred licks at my mind like the sweet nectar of a lover. It's threatening to consume me and I can't say as I would stop it if I could, now that I have learned the truth of my fate and awoke from my prison sentence.

He slammed his fist into a nearby tree, splintering it up the length of the trunk. It tilted away from him. Chunks of wood and bits of bark showered the ground around the cracked trunk.

They Who Linger

Was it so wrong to seek higher power? Do they blame me for their sorrow? Is it wrong that I wanted to save the one I had loved with all my being? I never meant to lose control, but when I was hunted down like a rabid animal, I lost my hold on the power. The Cataclysm... That—That was my doing... I was provoked, prodded; HUNTED!

He wailed in agony again and brought his hands together like a hammer against an anvil. He swung them down on the ground in front of him, the ground ruptured and the grass turned to ash around him.

"It wasn't my fault," he bellowed at the sky.

He breathed heavily, hunched over on his clasped hands which were buried in the loosened soil and rock. Tears streamed down his wrinkled cheeks. He remained there for a long while, no longer caring to follow the trio; he knew their destination and he had eyes that could travel unseen or heard. After he had regained his composure, he straightened up again, got to his feet and wiped snot and drool from his face with the back of his hands. His resolve steeled, he cleared his throat and started through the trees at a leisurely pace, taking in the sights and smells as if for the first time.

"Oh such power," he whispered to himself, a smirk creeping across his face as a long stemmed wild flower withered beneath his caress. "My love, they killed you to get to me! Are you lost in the darkness as I was? My own kind... HOW COULD YOU FORSAKE ME!? You will all pay!"

He lifted his head toward the sky and screamed viscerally; His hands clenched so hard that his unkempt fingernails dug into his palms. Blood welled up and ran down over his knuckles. He clenched his jaw, severing the scream and his eyes flared as all semblance of age emptied out of him; replaced by youthful strength and nimbleness.

They Who Linger

He sniffed the air and smelled smoke. He saw flames licking their way hungrily across the dry forest bed in his wake, sparked by his previous outburst.

If a mere recollection can bring this kind of power to the surface, I wonder what else I am capable of in this body. Perhaps I will play with these abilities before I go after the keystone. My kind has had centuries to advance while I roamed the world like a mindless insect, and I am sure they have been keeping their powers in check. The fools, their world shall become their prison, forced to watch it unravel. I will kill all that they know and I will burn it down around them.

My love... I will deliver vengeance like no other, they will know how wrong they were, and they will be helpless to prevent it. The cataclysm was a reaction, but if channeled, the power I discovered is capable of so much more. They have no idea what they threw away. I will need more puppets, and I will have them. The dead are perfect subjects. They don't struggle against the moral bonds. Rest now, that is what I need to do, I need to gain my full strength once again. Tonight we hunt!

Breathing rhythmically now, he laid himself down on a bed of moss. His mind danced with visions from multiple sets of eyes all at once as his pets crawled and darted through underbrush and down shaded crevasses in pursuit of his prey. He dreamed of fire and it circled around him as he slept, but did not touch him or his bed of moss.

Chapter Forty-One

Owain walked toward the lake from his secluded cabin in the forested hills on the western edge of the Shimmering Tear. The morning was crisp, the sun glistened off the surface of the water and the snow on the ground; birds chirped in the trees all around him as he walked along the snowy path he had packed down with his daily trips for water. He breathed deeply and basked in the beauty of the new day.

He crested a small hill just before the final descent to the shoreline and stopped in his tracks. A woman lay half floating in the water, half ashore. He looked across the glassy surface of the lake for a boat or raft that she may have fallen from, or for signs of anyone else on the shoreline or lake. Small waves from the light morning breeze lapped around her, slowly pushing her up on the gravel. She had a number of cuts, scrapes and bruises visible on her face, arms and through patches of torn leather armor and fur lined clothing. He rushed to her side and checked to see if she was alive. Finding no pulse, he quickly pulled her the rest of the way up onto the shore and immediately started trying to resuscitate her.

He cupped his hands over her mouth and nose, gulped in some fresh air and immediately exhaled through his hands. He then wrapped his fingers together, one hand over the other, pushed the heel of his palm down gently on her chest above her heart and pumped rhythmically. He repeated the process a number of times and then flipped the woman on her side when she began to cough up water. While she coughed and sucked in great gasps of air, taking a tenuous hold on life once again, Owain calmly went and scooped some fresh water into his wooden bucket from the lake. He helped the woman to her feet and the woman grimaced in pain as she put weight on her right foot. He offered his free arm to the woman to help support her weight and she attempted to speak through her chattering teeth. She frantically looked about in all directions, a puzzled expression on her face, and nearly fainted from exhaustion. Owain caught her before she could fall.

"Hush now my dear, conserve your energy, there will be time enough for introductions and questions after you've rested and warmed up. Come, let's get you by the fire and into some dry clothes. My cabin is not far," Owain answered her unuttered question and pointed up a small hill to his log abode amidst a small copse of trees. Smoke listlessly rolled up from a stone chimney.

It was a short walk up the hill to the cozy looking cabin, but took a lot longer than usual as they stopped a number of times to avoid the woman straining herself beyond the little energy she had left in her. They stepped inside the cabin, as quaint on the inside as it was on the outside, and Owain helped the woman down on a bearskin rug in front of a crackling fire. He poured some of the water from his pail into a kettle and hung it over the fire on a hook to boil. He then turned his attention to rummaging around for some dry clothes and offered them, along with a blanket, to the woman.

"You can change into these in my room back there, then let's get a warm cup of Frost Sage tea in you. The sooner you are out of those wet garments the better," he said as he pointed out the room at the back of the cabin.

The woman accepted the clothes and blanket, nodded and slowly made her way to the room, propping herself up against the log wall when she staggered. She returned a short while later, wrapped in the blanket. She fumbled her way back to the fire and sat down on the rug again. She looked around the sparsely decorated interior of the cabin as they waited for the tea to steep, her eyes sagging continuously. A small hand carved table and two chairs were off to one side along the back wall, a few shelves, also hand carved, with a variety of wild herbs and dried meats in woven reed baskets stood along the wall that divided the bedroom from the main room. A handful of hooks were fastened to the log wall next to the door for cloaks and hats.

"It's not much," said Owain as he watched her take in her surroundings, "but it's home."

She smiled with effort and looked at the kettle over the fire.

He checked on the tea. Satisfied that it was done, he scooped two cups out and handed one to his guest.

She thanked him with a nod as she took the cup of tea in both hands, outstretched from beneath the blanket wrapped around her. The warmth of the fire and the tea washed over her as she drank the liquid, barely waiting for it to cool at all.

He offered her more tea, but she politely declined, her voice raspy and soft.

"No... thank... you," she managed, and waved off the cup as she curled up on the rug, barely able to keep her eyes open as she did.

Owain watched as she succumbed to her exhaustion.

"Rest well frail one," he said and draped a second blanket over her.

~*~

The woman came too in the middle of the first night, panicked and feverish. She barely remembered parts of how she had gotten to the cabin, and was fearful of the dark corners of the room where the firelight failed to reach. The man that had helped her was sitting close by. He reassured her that everything was alright and that she was in a safe place now. She was weak, the fever sapping any strength that she had left. The man offered her some stew, aiding her as she could barely prop herself up, and then he gave her a cup of warm liquid she did not recognize the taste of. Soon after that her eyes became heavy again and she gave into sleep once more.

Owain stoked the fire and then went to bed as well, confident that the woman would not wake again until morning.

Chapter Forty-Two

Aileesha bolted upright, gasping in deep quick breaths, arms raised up in front of her, clawing at the air. Sunlight was pouring in through the single window off to the right side of the door, across from the stone hearth where she had fallen asleep. The man who she vaguely remembered helping her emerged groggily from his room, greeted her with a smile and stepped past her to stoke the embers in the fireplace. His silver-gray beard was disheveled and stuck out in all directions. He was older, wrinkles lined his freckled skin; hazel eyes glimmered in the sunlight spilling through the window. Although he did not look like it, she suspected he was strong and capable.

"Where am I," asked Aileesha?

"You are in my home, along the western shore of the Shimmering Tear," replied the man. He cleared his throat, "And my name is Owain."

"Well met Owain, my name is Aileesha," she said with effort. She stretched her arms and tried to work out some of the pain in her muscles. "What happened? The last thing I remember is falling from a cliff into the Weeping Gorge."

"Ah, that explains why I saw no boat or raft on the lake then. You must have tumbled along down the River of

Tears and out onto the shallow shoreline. You were lucky to wash ashore and not be sucked deeper into the lake by the currents. Remarkable, truly. Clearly you were present enough throughout the ordeal to swim towards safety before you lost consciousness. You had almost expired when I lucked across you on the shoreline. You were very lucky."

"Syndara," exclaimed Aileesha, remembering her friend! "Have you seen my friend? Her name is Syndara. Is she alright?"

"Whoa, one question at a time, lass. I saw no one else."

She threw off the blankets, saw her clothes were not her own and frantically looked around the cabin, searching for them.

"I must go, I need to find her and make sure she is alright," she said hurriedly as she spotted her clothes hanging on the backs of two hand carved chairs where they had been set to dry next to the fireplace. She scooped them up and headed for the back room before Owain could respond.

"You are in no shape to travel yet. You almost drowned and you look like you've been through a war. You'll be lucky to make it to the shore let alone go hiking across the mountains in pursuit of your friend. Rest. I'll fix the tears in your clothes and armor as best I can while you heal. At least another couple of days to regain your strength," protested Owain.

Even as he spoke, she was already beginning to wobble about on her feet as she made her way to the back room to change. He caught her by the shoulders before she could fall into the side of the table.

"Easy does it lass," said Owain as he helped her to one of the chairs to sit. "It will be a few days before you have your strength back. You're in no shape to travel now."

Aileesha dropped her torn clothes at her feet in frustration. She started to remember everything then. The artifact, the attacks, and their journey south through the snowy pass; the battle with the giant beast and her fall into the gorge. She placed the heel of one palm against her forehead and the other hand on the table as she gritted her teeth against a new wave of pain and nausea.

"I must get some water from the lake, you need to rest. Sit here or lay down on my bed, whichever suits you. Just do as little as possible, as I believe you've suffered a solid blow to the head. It will take days for the dizziness to subside," said Owain as he put more wood on the now crackling fire and excused himself as he stepped through the door to get the water. A cold breeze swept across the room and engulfed Aileesha, forcing her to action. She made her way to the bedroom, bracing herself against the wall as her legs threatened to buckle beneath her the whole way. Within moments of collapsing onto the bed, she was dreaming of shadows and gnashing teeth.

~*~

A short while later Owain had a fresh pot of tea steeping away and another bubbling with porridge. He woke Aileesha with a tap on the shoulder and a soft voice.

Aileesha jolted awake and immediately took a defensive pose, scrunching her knees to her chest beneath the covers.

"It's only me, lass. You are safe," he said.

She was sweating and her eyes gave away the fact that she was fighting with a fearful frenzy to dash from the bed.

"Here, I've made some tea to help with the pain," he said as he held the cup up to her. He aided her with the food and warm liquid.

When she had finished the porridge, she gripped the sides of her head and groaned in pain.

"Here, finish the tea, it will help with the pain," he said as he held the cup to her lips. "That's it, drink it all down. Good, now let's get you tucked back under the covers."

He drew the blankets up over her shoulders as she rolled against the wall, still clutching her head in her hands, but no longer groaning. Within minutes she was fast asleep again.

He stayed with her a while longer to make sure that the tea did its work, then retreated to the front room. He sat in one of the chairs in front of the fireplace and contemplated things.

What seemed like mere moments had turned to hours and the setting sun cast an orange glow over the trees, their shade darkening his window and alerting him to the fact that the day had trailed on without him.

Aileesha was mumbling and audibly tossing in her sleep. He retrieved a dried herb from one of his clay containers and ground it in his mortar and pestle, then knocked the contents into a wooden bowl. He sniffed at the bowl tentatively. With a satisfied nod to himself, he took the bowl with him into the bedroom and wafted it in front of Aileesha's nose until she calmed.

"There, troublesome dreams no longer, my dear," he whispered and smiled as he walked back into the front room and set to roasting some meat on a spit for supper.

Chapter Forty-Three

"Syndara, watch out," Aileesha cried out as she bolted upright from her deep slumber once again, her arm reaching out in front of her for her friend that wasn't there. Realization of her surroundings sunk in once more and she let her arm drop to the blankets. She pushed them aside and climbed out of the bed, testing the stability of her legs as she got up. Confident that she would not tumble to the floor after a few steps, she made her way to the front room. There was no sign of Owain, but there was a loaf of fresh bread and cooked meat on a plate at the table, and she could see steam rising from a pot hanging over the fire. The scent of frost sage wafted through the air from the steeping tea.

The smell of the meat made her stomach rumble audibly. It was then she noticed a tiny piece of paper with one word scrawled on it next to the plate.

'*EAT*,' it read.

She sat and devoured the food ravenously. Once every last crumb on the plate had disappeared, she noticed the cup next to the plate. She took it and ladled out some tea. She could feel the strength returning to her body even now, the meat nourishing her muscles.

She put on her boots and opened the door. Daylight assailed her, forcing her to shield her eyes with one hand until they could adjust as she stepped outside. She took in her surroundings clearly for the first time. Owain's cabin stood on a small hill overlooking the Shimmering Tear, surrounded by trees on all sides but the front, and was nestled up against the foot of the mountains on the north western edge of the lake. It was mid-morning, and the sky had only a few clouds.

She spotted Owain sitting cross legged on a rock near the shoreline, looking out across the water.

Not wanting to push her luck too much, she took her time as she walked down the winding path to the gravely beach. The sun warmed her face and filled her with energy. The fresh air bathed her in life and all her worries melted away. For a moment there wasn't a single thought of anything other than the present. The rocks rubbed together beneath her feet as she took her first step onto the beach.

"Owain, how long was I asleep," she asked as she approached?

Owain opened his eyes as he turned his head towards her, delight awash on his face.

"Three days," he replied.

He patted the rock next to him. "Come, have a seat with me."

She climbed up on the rock and sat next to him, and looked out over the water. The surface rippled lightly in an unseen breeze, the crisp, fresh air cleared away any remaining grogginess that remained from her lengthy slumber. She breathed in deeply, closed her eyes, and sighed.

"How do you feel," asked Owain?

"I feel-" she began, then paused as she opened her eyes, "Better. The walk and the fresh air helped."

"Your cuts seem to have mostly healed, and there is no infection, thank the light."

"I cannot thank you enough for your kindness Owain, I owe you a debt I fear I can never repay for saving my life. I have no doubt that if you had not found me that I would not be here now."

Owain waved one hand at Aileesha and '*tsked.*'

"Twas no more than any self respecting person would have done," he replied.

"I'd like to think so, but nonetheless, you saved my life, no doubt. For that, I am forever in your debt."

"No debts here," he said. "I heard some strange howling last night, to the south. Probably near the pass down into the Upper Fel'Thain at the south end of the lake. Wolves I'm sure."

Aileesha's eyes grew wide at this news.

"I need to be getting on my way; I have to catch up with my friend. I fear that whatever attacked us may still be tracking and hunting her through the pass. I remember more of our ordeal now as well."

"Come, let us return to the cabin. You can tell me about it on the way," replied Owain. He slid down off the rock and offered his hand to her.

Aileesha accepted the offered hand and slid off the rock next to him. She told him everything she could remember about the attack as they walked back to the cabin. What the creatures looked like, how they moved, as if they were compelled against their will to continue forward even at the risk of their own peril; how they fought, and how she fell. She was careful not to mention the artifact.

"Hmm, most unnatural. There is definitely more going on here than we can comprehend," Owain stated as he opened the door to the cabin and ushered Aileesha inside.

"I have prepared a concoction that should help with any remaining dizziness, and help to keep your energy up as you travel. You can take it with tea, water, or food, but do not take it alone or it may upset your stomach, something fierce," he said as he gathered a small pack and filled it with supplies. He held a couple of vials up to indicate the concoction and then wrapped them in some cloth before placing them in the pack as well. He then retrieved her mended clothes and armor from a small chest in one corner of the front room.

"I fixed these up as best I could. I will not convince you to stay and rest further, as I know your fear for your friend's safety compels you onward. A noble thing that. She is blessed to have a friend that cares so much. But, please, heed my words and take your medicine as instructed, twice a day until it's gone."

Aileesha thanked him as she gave him a big hug, and went to change in the bedroom. When she returned to the front room Owain was standing at the door with the small pack held in his hands.

"You are too kind. I can't thank you enough Owain," she said as she slung one strap of the pack over her shoulder. "We were making for Barroville, but with the bridge out and no boat, I must find another way around to the pass-"

"There is a game trail that winds along the mountains around the western edge of the lake. It will bring you to a winding path near the Weeping Falls at the southern tip of the lake that winds down into the Upper Fel'Thain. From there you can cut back towards the Crossroads south of the pass," Owain said with a smile, cutting off her contemplation.

"I will be sure to repay your kindness upon our return home. Although that could be some time-" she trailed off. She thanked him again as she gave him another bear hug and stepped out into the afternoon.

"A safe journey Aileesha, there is much more that will take place before your journey ends. Beware the ancients," said Owain as he stepped out after her. "OH, your axes. They are next to the pile of firewood there. I found them yesterday when I went to get water," he pointed to the wood stacked against the west side of the cabin.

"Wow, another stroke of luck," replied Aileesha with a big grin. She retrieved her axes and slid them into the hoops on her belt. She thanked Owain one last time and made for the game trail.

"Mercy upon your travels. Vengeance binds itself in strange ways to this world," he whispered to himself as he watched her climb the trail out of sight. He rubbed his beard, deep in thought, and went back inside, letting the cabin door swing shut on its own behind him.

~*~

Aileesha wound her way up the game trail, using a stick she had discovered to help brace her weight as best she could and keep her from becoming exhausted too quickly. She still wasn't at full strength, but she couldn't wait around any longer. By mid-afternoon Aileesha had climbed to the flat of the trail that snaked along the mountains along the western shore of the Shimmering Tear. The sun shone down between the trees that lined either side of the path.

Aileesha was deep in thought regarding Owain's comment about the ancients. She pondered what he could have meant by that as she continued along the trail. The breathtaking view of the lake from a cliff top stole away her thoughts a short while later, causing her to pause for a short rest. She edged her way to the tip of the outcropping and sat on a log. The great expanse of the valley stretched out in all directions. The view filled her with renewed energy and excitement. After a quick sip of water and a bit of bread, Aileesha continued on her way, desperate to cover as much ground before nightfall as she could. A warm feeling filled her body as she walked on and relished in the realization that she was once again on a real adventure, but this time all on her own. The thought was terrifying and exhilarating at the same time.

Chapter Forty-Four

Merchant stands had been erected on both sides of the bustling streets, wherever there had been space. The awnings hung out over the booths enough to form a rainbow canopy over the navigable portions of the streets that remained for customers to walk and browse in comfort out of the sun. Merchants hawked their wares at any passersby that made eye contact. They were eager, yet civil. The festival had been held in Barroville every spring since its founding, and the rules were well known. The guards were tough, but not unkind, and everyone respected them. Travelers flooded the streets in every direction looking for a place to stay or to set up shop. The city had clearly outgrown its size. As many as could safely fit were permitted inside the walls, but once the limit had been reached, all others had to make camp outside the walls, along the main roads leading to the city gates. The lineups into the city would be hours long come morning, each traveler waiting their turn to peruse the merchant stalls or make trades of their own.

Children ran through the streets and alleyways, screaming and laughing as they played. Corlag, Branick and Syndara crossed the center of the village, having entered from the north gate, making their way towards the Inn along the south east wall. As they rounded a corner to the side street where the Hog's Head stood, a dog scampered across the cobble stones to bark at chickens in a pen. They clucked and fluttered about as their owner shooed the dog away. The streets were all paved with cobblestones, and every fifty feet or so there were wooden posts with simple lanterns hung from cross beams supported by ornately carved supports that connected to the post. All of the buildings were simple clay and wood with a mix of slate or wood shingles, except for the mayor's house, the jail house and the guard barracks, which were all made of square cut stone.

Corlag pushed open the aged wooden door to the Inn and entered. Branick closed the door behind them, taking a quick scan of the crowds of people in the square. No one paid them any mind.

Syndara and Branick took seats at a free table, and removed their burdens.

Corlag made his way to the counter against the back wall, directly ahead of the door, and flagged down the serving maid.

"Excuse me madam, might I speak with your Inn Keep a moment," he asked kindly?

"Oh my, arn't you a kind spoken sort," she replied with a hefty giggle as she set her tray of dishes down on the counter, "How can I say no to that face? There's no rooms left if'n you're inclined to inquire."

"I'm looking to make arrangements with him for the festivities."

"Ah, a bard then," she stated as she gave Corlag another once over, "Let me see if'n I can find him. Have a seat there with your friends."

"Thank you kindly," he replied with a warm smile and a slight bow.

"Ohh," she laughed, "You're a right proper gentleman aren't you! You're too much. Go on then, off with you." She dismissed him with a forward wave of her hands, as if ushering a child from the kitchen, and then disappeared behind the counter shaking her head and giggling to herself as she went through a doorway behind the counter to what Corlag assumed was the kitchen.

Corlag sat next to Branick and looked about the tavern that made up the lower level of the Inn. It was warm, quaint, and well cared for. Large oaken beams, iron lantern sconces, a stone hearth with a raised stone platform for performers, and a combination of hand carved benches, tables and stools cluttered the room in an orderly manner. All of the seats were arranged to have a view of the hearth.

A short while later, the Inn Keep entered the room from the doorway behind the counter, wiping his hands on a rag hanging from a stained white apron around his waist. He greeted them in a gruff, but warm and friendly voice.

"Ello there. I be Bhaltair. What can I do fer yeh," he inquired, extending his hand to Corlag.

"My name is Corlag, and these are my companions, Branick and Syndara. I am here to spin tales for the festival. Have you a room to put us up in for the duration in exchange for drawing a steady crowd," he asked and shook the man's hand?

"OH, the crowds won't be an issue either way, but all the same, I'd rather have ye here to keep 'em occupied as opposed to 'avin them at each other's throats over bad trades an' the like. Aye, I saved one room for a minstrel. You're in luck, you are the first one to arrive. It be the last room upstairs, at the end of the hall. There be only two beds, however. Will that be a problem?"

"No, that will be fine, I can take the floor."

Syndara eyed Corlag while he talked with Bhaltair, a small smile crossing her face.

"Very well then, what be yer price minstrel? I'll give yeh the room for free, provided yer tales don't rouse the rabble, an' the coin keeps comin' in for drinks an' the like," asked Bhaltair?

"Fair enough, five gold coins is my price."

"HA! A fair minstrel you are. Never thought I'd see the day," replied the Inn Keep as he nodded and smiled, "Aye that works for me. I'll feed you and your companions for the duration of your stay as well. If'n you want drinks, I can only offer you a few with your evening meals as I need my supplies to last for the festival. Any extras you'll have to purchase like the rest. Fair?"

"That is more than fair. You are kind, thank you Bhaltair," replied Corlag offering his hand to seal the deal.

Branick nodded at the Inn Keep as he handed Corlag the key and reminded them which room was theirs. They gathered their belongings and made their way to the room to drop them off. The room was on the south east corner, with a window that overlooked the roof of the building next to the Inn, across the many homes and shops that sprawled to the south and out towards the harbor. A number of ship masts could be seen and if they craned their heads to the edge of the window frame they could see a glimpse of the ocean waters beyond the docks, and the lighthouse out across the bay. The beds lay against the east wall, and a small table with some candles and a wash tub sat against the south wall. Satisfied with the room, they returned to the tavern to have some dinner.

"It's good to have a hot meal not cooked over a campfire for a change hey Bran," commented Corlag through bites of stew, "You and Syndara should seek out the dock master and find out when the next boat crosses the Everdeep. See if we can book passage. I'm going to get my tales ready, and tune my lute. We'll get to it all after breakfast."

"Oh," exclaimed Syndara as she patted her belly, "Let's not speak of breakfast for a while yet, that meal filled me to the bursting point. I've not had a meal like that in ages." She took a sip of her water before continuing. "We ought to sleep well with a hot meal in our bellies and a roof over our heads."

"To the morrow then," exclaimed Corlag as he held up his mug and smiled.

They thanked Bhaltair for the meal when they were done and headed up the stairs to their room.

Chapter Forty-Five

They woke early the next morning, before the roosters could climb atop their coops and greet the dawn, and had a quick breakfast before going about their tasks ahead of the majority of the hustle and bustle. Branick and Syndara made their way to the docks to find the dockmaster, while Corlag stayed behind at the Inn tuning his lute and picking what tales to spin for the coming evening. Having finished by mid morning, before the others were back, he decided to use the extra time to check out the market.

He grabbed his cloak and fastened it around his neck, pushed it back over his shoulders, and clasped it in place on the shoulder pads of his interwoven leather cuirass. The cuirass was covered in ornate patterns of dancing golden music notes. He tightened the straps of the cuirass along both sides of his ribs, and then belted on his sword. Lastly, he grabbed his lute and slung it over his back and made his way outside, locking the room behind him.

As he stepped out into the bustling city, the sun assailed his vision as his eyes fought to adjust, and the cacophony of sounds washed over him. He perused the market stalls, casually looking at various hand crafted knickknacks and baubles with no real interest. A group of children laughed and giggled, chasing each other between stalls near the town square. One of them spotted Corlag while dodging a little girl who had attempted to tag him in a game of tag. The boy pointed at Corlag and yelled to his friends to come see the minstrel. Before he could duck into the crowd, Corlag was surrounded with a dozen children all cheering and asking for songs and tales. A warm smile spread across Corlag's face and he nodded to the children in agreement.

"Only a few though, little ones, as I have other matters to attend to," said Corlag as he unshouldered his lute and began to sing a children's melody. The children clapped along and laughed at the funny bits. Corlag followed it up with a popular fairytale and when he was done, bowed to the children and politely excused himself, slowly working through the crowd that had formed and dismissing the requests for just one more tale.

Not long after, he entered the market proper. There he spotted a man approaching a woman at a trading stall. He appeared to be inquiring about her wares like any normal person, but it wasn't the man that had caught his attention, it was the woman. She seemed overly agitated by the man's presence. He continued to watch out of curiosity.

The man, seeing that the woman was upset, apologized to her as he backed away from the stall, dodging a couple other shoppers as best he could. The man's features said it all. He was genuinely confused by her reaction to his inquiry of her wares. When the man turned his back to her to leave, the woman burst out from behind her stall like a firestorm racing through dry underbrush.

Utterly frozen with surprise, Corlag looked on, fixated at the sudden turn of events. The woman's right hand looked as though the flesh had all but rotted away. The hand was gone, replaced by elongated, pointy bones, leading up to bony plates where her wrist would normally have been. She screamed with ethereal energy as she lunged on the man from behind, and before anyone could react, or even realize what was happening, buried her bony appendage through his back and out the front of his chest.

The man didn't have a chance to cry out in pain as his life drained out of him, his face awash more so with shock than pain. He fell to one knee, one hand propping him up, the other limp at his side as he fought his own end; the woman still shrieking, clung to his back, trying to pry her arm free of his torso.

A nearby guard, having realized what was happening far too late to save the man's life, recovered his wits and before the dying man hit the cobblestones completely, nocked and fired an arrow at the woman. It looked as though it might take her head clean off her shoulders as it *thumped* into her skull. It connected just as she got her arm free, and the force of the impact combined with her reeling, launched her backwards off of the man. Her body landed awkwardly in the street, ending her bizarre attack as quickly as it had occurred.

The man she attacked, still on his knees, stared in silent horror at the gaping hole in his chest. He attempted to straighten up one last time, and as his final breath left his lips, he slumped back against the corpse of his attacker, propped up against it, his face towards the sky.

The guard rushed toward the fallen man and woman, others joined him soon after, yelling at anyone nearby to get back. They quickly formed a circle around the scene and waited for another guard to bring the cloth from the deceased woman's nearby market stall awning to cover the bodies.

Corlag moved toward the scene as the guard captain arrived, seeking to explain what he had witnessed.

The guards hastily covered the bodies. Blood slowly crept out from under the fabric, giving away any illusion of what it now hid from sight.

The captain of the guard saw Corlag approaching and held out his left hand, his right on the hilt of his sword.

"Halt your progression. Keep clear, in case there is more danger from that," he pointed at the covered heap hesitantly, indicating the deceased merchant woman, unsure what to call her.

"I witnessed the event, and I wish to give a statement to the happenings," clarified Corlag. He held out his hands and stopped in his tracks. "To whom do I do so?"

"That would be me. I must tend to the scene first however. Are you traveling through or are you from the area?"

"Traveling through. I am a minstrel and am staying at the Hog's Head for the evening, spinning tales."

"Very well then, I'll seek you out after I have this mess taken care of and can start making sense of it."

"I will await your arrival there then."

"See to it that you do. The people of Barroville are going to be inquisitive of this to say the least, and rightfully so. We've not had a murder, or any violent act inside these walls for decades. At least nothing more than fist fights between a couple of drunks or sea captains with a dispute to settle. They will need to be reassured, and we will need to know whether or not we should be keeping our eyes open for more trouble."

"I will be there when you are ready," assured Corlag as he nodded his agreement.

Corlag left the guards to tend to the dead and hurriedly made his way back to the Hog's Head. He recounted the event in his mind, the images of the woman's hand and her attack playing over and over in his mind.

Chapter Forty-Six

Borogolas walked among the market crowd, watching a woman at her stall. She was weeping periodically and was clearly agitated.

"Ah yes, a perfect subject," he thought aloud.

He looked about to ensure no one had paid him any mind, then ducked into an alley where he could be in shadows. He propped himself between the two buildings, angled so as to both be at rest and to have line of sight on the woman's market stall. He raised one hand towards her, and closed off his mind to everything else going on around him. The sounds of the market faded away, the clanging of smithy hammers, the clip-clop of feet against stone; the ship bells in the harbor tolling their various warnings. Soon the only sound was his slow, steady breathing as he focused intently. Recent images of her life flashed in his mind. Her agony and rage were almost overwhelming. Her mind was completely unprotected, void of any faith whatsoever. If ever she had any, it had been buried beneath her hunger for vengeance over the loss of her husband in the mines east of Barroville, near the border. It amused him greatly how the favored of the Volskaian had forgotten their heritage, and how to guard themselves daily. Neglect of their beliefs and prayers had made them susceptible; weak. The perfect puppets.

'So, you seek to escape from the pain of losing a loved one. I do believe I can aid you in that quest,' the voice in his head continued as he smirked, *'It just so happens I need more puppets to assist me. A little twist of will ought to suffice.'*

He uttered something under his breath and threw back his hood, intensifying his focus on the woman.

"Let's see how you fare with your new gift," he whispered to the wind.

Almost instantly, the woman appeared calmer. She stopped fussing over her stall and greeting onlookers. A short while after Borgolas uttered his inaudible words, the woman began to take on a new look of agitation. The woman picked at the flesh of her right hand, keeping it from sight and she became short and curt with would be customers. As Borgolas watched, a man approached her stall and began to inquire about her wares, and she became even more disturbed by his presence and inquiries. The man, weary of her reaction, backed away while apologizing for inconveniencing the woman.

To Borgolas' surprise, the woman exploded out of her stall and attacked the man from behind, her scream sending shivers up the spine of his fleshy host. He had forgotten how quickly the vulnerable could be possessed. It was all over in a matter of moments. A guard had put the woman down with a quick shot from his bow, the arrow protruded from her forehead. More guards rushed to the scene and the bodies were covered with the cloth from the awning of her market stall.

'Magnificent,' he thought excitedly. *'I forgot how efficient the turning could be. Her mind was lost to rage within minutes. A shame really, that she attacked that man so quickly.'*

222

He scowled as he saw the guard that had killed his puppet shouldering his bow while staring at the covered bodies.

"I shall deal with you later," he uttered at the guard from his shadowy perch.

I will have to be more careful with my subjects in the future, and be more prepared to take control, even if it means decimating everyone in the area. There are bigger things at play; I can't be bothered with avoiding petty village guards and pitchfork wielding farmers now can I?

He pondered the speed of the turning again and rubbed his hands together, then scratched at his chin.

Could the keystone fragments have magnified it somehow? Could they be here? I must find them. Come nightfall, I will have my answer, even if I have to burn this entire place to the ground.

Chapter Forty-Seven

Corlag did not notice Syndara and Branick sitting at a table not far from the front door of the Hog's Head when he returned. He passed by them, heading straight up to their room.

Branick knew something was off right away and suggested to Syndara that they should go and find out what happened. They abandoned what remained of their lunches and followed after Corlag.

"What's got you so preoccupied Cor," asked Branick as he nudged the door shut behind them with his foot. "Is something wrong?"

"You seemed in a mighty big hurry, you didn't even see us sitting by the door when you came in. Is everything alright," added Syndara.

Corlag paced silently back and forth for a moment before sighing heavily and sitting on the edge of one of the beds, facing them and the door.

"There's been an-" he paused, looking for the right word to describe the situation, "Incident. In the market." He scratched his head and curled his lips, trying to find the words to continue. "A woman murdered a man after he inquired about her wares."

"What," blurted Syndara, gasping in shock? "Why, what did the man do?"

"What makes this so troubling," inquired Branick? He cleared his throat and quickly added, "I mean, other than the murder bit of course?"

"Something is terribly wrong. Her arm was disfigured, like the skin had melted away, and the bones in her hand had fused together to form a single claw; complete with ridged bone plates along the forearm all the way to the elbow. She ripped right through the man's torso from behind... and the scream..." he shook his head once, looked at the floor and then tilted his face toward them again, "I haven't seen or heard its like since the southern war Bran. It chilled me to the bone. I was frozen in place, unable to react before it was all over."

"That doesn't sound good at all. What do you suppose is going on? Do you think it's related to our troubles back on the road," replied Branick? He caught Corlag's unspoken suspicion in his mentioning of the war.

"I don't know, but I have a sickening feeling that we need to be away from this place, and soon."

"What are ye thinking then," asked Branick, looping his thumbs through his belt?

"If I had any doubts about our need to join Syndara on her journey, they are gone now. I have to give an account of what I saw to the captain of the guard when he is done processing the scene of the crime. He will come here for that. In the meantime, we'll eat and then I'll spin my tales tonight, and we will depart at first light. I'll smooth things over with Bhaltair. Any luck finding a ship?"

"No luck with the ship. They are all docked until the end of the festival at least," Branick nudged Syndara with his elbow, "let's prepare our things and get some supplies ready."

Syndara was staring at Corlag in disbelief. She blinked a few times and shifted her weight, snapping out of her daze.

"What about Old Strandton," she offered hesitantly? "We could surely get a boat there if need be. Maybe we should leave tonight just to be safe?"

"We have no way of knowing for sure that there would be any boats left to catch there. The current trade season is nearing its end, and we're lucky to have found the boat here at that. No, if push comes to shove, we'll find a way," Corlag assured her.

"Very well then," she replied, as she crossed the room and grabbed her pack. "I'm ready when you two are."

Branick stepped toward Corlag and placed a big meaty hand on his friend's shoulder and looked him in the eyes.

"We'll figure out what is amiss, but there's not much else we can do until the morrow. Perhaps we can locate and persuade one of the ship captains to leave early."

"Aye, you are right. That may be the best course of action," replied Corlag as he clapped Branick on the shoulder and got to his feet.

They packed up anything not needed immediately, assuring they were ready to leave at a moment's notice.

Chapter Forty-Eight

They had just finished their dinner of roast beef with herb speckled potatoes and gravy, broccoli, carrots and peas when the captain of the guard arrived. He spotted Corlag, made his way through the crowd of people, tables and chairs and stood at the end of their table. He greeted them courteously.

"Good eve to you three," greeted the captain.

"And to you captain," replied Corlag as he set his fork down on his now empty wooden plate and stood to offer his hand to the man.

"I'm sorry to catch you at supper, but it was a right mess cleaning everything up without disturbing more folk than necessary."

"No apology needed sir. Please, have a seat if you prefer," offered Corlag, indicating the seat across from him next to Syndara.

"Thank you," replied the captain. He waved down the serving maid as he sat. She took his order and was off to the kitchen. "Shall we get this over with so you folk can get about your business then?"

"Aye," replied Corlag as he pushed aside his plate and folded his hands on the table in front of him. He recounted the events in full while the captain received and ate his dinner. The captain held his questions until Corlag finished recounting what he had seen.

Branick and Syndara listened to the full account intently, and said nothing.

"Anything else," asked the captain? He swallowed the last bite of his roast beef and sopped up the remaining gravy on the plate with the last of his bread, popped it in his mouth and proceeded to wipe a handkerchief across his face that he had procured from a pouch on his belt.

"Yes, one question, what do you make of her hand? The one that looked mutated," asked Corlag?

The captain hesitated before answering. Clearing phlegm from his throat and stuffing his handkerchief back in the pouch. He looked weary and had clearly not seen home in many days, for the candlelight revealed the shadowy bags under his eyes. He placed his right forearm on the table, leaning towards Corlag.

"Quite frankly, I have no idea. Never seen anything like it," he shrugged and brushed something off the emblem on his breastplate with his left hand. "It would be best not to bring it up until we know more. The last thing we need is a panic among the people during the festival. Keep this to yourselves, and say nothing more of it. Do you understand?"

Corlag stood and offered his hand across the table once more.

"Understood sir," he replied as the captain shook his hand, "not a word."

The captain stood, shook Corlag's hand, and thanked him again for giving his account, then excused himself and returned to his duties. The tavern had filled up even more since the captain had arrived, and Corlag excused himself from his friends, grabbed his lute and took a spot by the hearth against the north wall. It was facing the center of the tavern, not far from where the stairs led to the upper level. He settled on a stool, and introduced himself to the crowd.

"Good evening one and all, and welcome to the Hog's Head. I am Corlag the Bard, and I have the honor of spinning tales for you this evening. Please, sit back, grab some food and drink from our good host Bhaltair and his staff, and enjoy," be bowed slightly.

His address was met with whooping, whistling and cheers from the crowd. The serving maids wound through the tables greeting all of the new visitors and taking their orders.

"I shall start with a grim tale which you all may have heard before, but I trust do not bore of; The Shaping of the Terror Woods."

The crowd whooped and hollered their pleasure at his announcement, and once the din had died back down, he began his tale. He plucked at his lute strings all the while, matching the melody to the tone of the story.

"Many tales are told in taverns across the world of Ierolden of a forest of the dead. It is said that the trees themselves rose from the ashes of a war torn land amidst an ancient battle between the beasts that dwell in shadow and the humans of the southern portions of Ael'andar, enveloping the beasts within themselves. It brought finality to the struggle, forever entombing the beasts within the trunks of the giant trees so that the creatures would be unable to repeat their attacks and tread no further north toward the kingdom of men. There have been no sightings of the beasts since, other than the horrid visages that are now as one with the trees of the Terror Woods. The beasts are now contorted limbs of the trees that reach up to the sky, as if seeking moonlight that shall never again touch their skin. Their faces, frozen into the bark of the trees in whatever pose they had when they were entombed, forever."

"But not all evil creatures were stopped that day. Many more across our world avoided the fate of the beasts in the south." Corlag went on telling the full account of the war and the sacrifice made by the Ancients to form the forest prison known as The Terror Woods.

After Corlag finished telling his tale of the southern war, he spun a great number of other tales that evening, bits of history, cherished folk tales from across Ierolden, and a variety of poems and songs.

All but the bard had been gripped with silence as he spun his tales and sung his songs, broken only by cheers of satisfaction between each tale or song. This lasted for hours, and the crowd had grown to fill every empty space available; the windows were open for those waiting outside to hear and the walls were lined with eager listeners and onlookers. Even Bhaltair was enthralled, listening as he cleaned cups and steins with a rag behind the bar. The outside world melted away for the moment.

Syndara and Branick had given up their seats to newcomers at some point, and now stood near the hearth, leaning against the wall, smiling.

He announced his final piece of entertainment and thanked the crowd for joining him for the evening. He finished and was met with a raucous standing ovation, the crowd eager to hear more. He took a bow, and thanked them again, excusing himself as he stepped away from the hearth to greet his friends.

Branick patted him on the shoulder with a grin on his face and handed him a drink.

"Excellent crowd tonight."

"Aye, and well behaved," replied Corlag. He accepted the cup from Branick and took a sip. "Thanks for the drink. I'll meet you two upstairs, I need to go speak with Bhaltair and smooth things over in regards to our early departure."

"We can help explain the situation if you like," said Syndara, stepping forward.

"It will be alright. It's probably best if I do it alone."

With that, they parted ways. Corlag wound his way through the crowd of people, whom had turned to drink and merriment of their own making. Some stopped him briefly to thank him and greet him as he passed by. He excused himself politely as he squeezed through one last group near the counter and waved down Bhaltair, who greeted him merrily.

"Ah Corlag, what can I do fer ye lad," asked the tavern keep as he set the mug he was cleaning down on a stack near the kegs on the back wall, and began wiping the counter top in between them.

"I need a moment of your time to speak about our stay if you can spare it," replied Corlag as he pulled on his right earlobe gently.

"Is everything alright with the room lad? I hope we didn't-"

"No it's nothing like that," Corlag cut him off before he could worry about the standards of his Inn and pointed at the end of the counter away from the crowd nearby. "Shall we?"

Bhaltair nodded. They moved down to the end of the counter near the stairwell to talk privately.

"Bhaltair, I want to apologize, something has come up and we cannot stay for the duration of the festival."

"Are ye sure? It's shaping up to be the best festival I've ever had the pleasure of being in business for. Tonight was the best night o' me life as a tavern keeper. Honestly! I'm

231

not just blowing smoke. You are a gifted bard. We could make a fair bit of extra coins together."

"I wish I could, you are a generous, and kind host, but it seems fate has other plans. We must leave first thing in the morning. I truly apologize; I know we had an agreement."

"Think nothing of it, friend, no hard feelings. Ye're the best damn bard I've had the pleasure of hosting here. Ye brought in the largest crowd I've ever seen, an' probably covered my expenses for the duration of the festival an' then some in a single night. Ye're welcome back anytime. There be a number of other entertainers about, looking fer work. They won't bring a crowd like this mind ye, but I can't complain." He chuckled and grinned at Corlag. "It be all profit from here on out."

"Glad to hear it, and thanks for your understanding."

"Don't mention it," said Bhaltair as he offered his hand, forearm extended over the counter.

They clasped in the old fashion, hands locked around each other's forearms, and shook once, sealing both their new friendship and concluding their business.

"See ye in the morrow, or if'n I miss ye, next time ye be passing through."

"Until then," replied Corlag, nodding one last time and then turned and headed up the stairs to bed.

Chapter Forty-Nine

A figure crept through the shadows, hunched on all four limbs, weaving in and out of the alleyways of Barroville's outskirts. It scuttled along in the shadows, pausing to raise itself up on bent legs, licking and sniffing at the air. A guard came around a corner while it was crossing one of the main streets and it skittered the rest of the way across into darker shadows before it was seen. It watched the guard pass by before turning and climbing up the side of the building next to it. Once more it licked the air, clinging to the peak of the roof it had climbed onto, and chortled to itself as it locked its gaze on a larger building a few rooftops ahead, just beyond the town's stone wall. Sensing its prey nearby, the figure lunged from roof to roof. Finally it came to a tall building next to the wall. The creature sank low, then leapt with all its strength, clearing the distance between the building and the roof of a guard post on the wall. It landed with a slight thud as it scrambled to keep its footing on the clay shingles. Next, it lunged from the guard post onto the slanted roof of a large building next to the wall not far from the guard post. It scuttled to the south side of the roof, dug its claws into the hard wood beam that capped the end of the roof and peered over its edge at the window not far below; its muscles tensed as it prepared to jump again.

~*~

Corlag opened his eyes at the sound of a thud on the roof above their room. He reached for his sword in the dark, crawled out of his bed roll and looked towards the window.

"Bran, did you hear that," asked Corlag in a hushed yell?

Branick was already on his feet, weapon in hand scanning the room behind Corlag. He nodded as they made eye contact in the moonlit room.

"Stupid question," muttered Corlag under his breath as he blinked sleep from his eyes.

Branick pointed a finger toward the ceiling and signaled for him to back up near Syndara, who muttered something in her sleep and rolled over on her bed, the straw mattress rustling slightly. Nothing but the sound of their breathing could be heard as they waited.

"Bah, maybe it was just the wind. Can't we get a solid night's rest for-" Branick was cut off as something crashed through the window suddenly, followed immediately by a loud shriek. A familiar shadowy creature came rolling to all fours and slid across the floor into the dark recess by the door to the hall, melding into the shadows.

Branick and Corlag recoiled back defensively, and covered their ears as best they could without dropping their guard. Syndara, startled, reeled out of her slumber and scrambled up against the wall, frantically looking around for the source of the noise.

"What the heck is going on," she yelled and fumbled for her bow and quiver.

They Who Linger

~*~

Borgolas stepped out of the shadows of an alleyway across from the Hog's head. Moonlight cast a shadow from his hood across half of his face as he watched the creature on the rooftop, preparing to lunge at a window on the side of the upper level of the Inn.

"Find what we seek and kill any who get in your way," he whispered when the creature met his gaze.

The creature tilted its head to one side and let out a chortling sound in acknowledgment, then lunged at the window. The sound of shattering glass tore through the silence of night. Borgolas pushed back his hood, his weathered face aglow with delight. He walked out of the alley into the town square and slowly made his way to the front of the Inn.

~*~

"I see it," shouted Syndara! She pointed toward the creature, now slinking up the wall behind the door in the shadows. "What are these things?"

"No idea, but this one is about to have a bad day," replied Corlag. He put his back against the wall and slowly approached the corner leading from the main part of the room to the small recessed entrance by the door, sword raised in front of him.

Branick grabbed his shield that was leaning against the bed next to him and jumped into action with Corlag, doing his best to avoid the broken glass strewn across the floor so as not to cut his bare feet. He moved to stand between the broken window and the door preparing to pincer the creature, shield raised.

"C'mere you filthy cretin," he beckoned the creature, tightening his grip on the shield straps.

"Oh no you don't, not again," added Syndara. She crouched down between the beds, nocked an arrow and prepared to fire at the dark corner. She scanned what she could see of the wall and ceiling, but could no longer see the creature.

"Can you see it, Syndara," asked Corlag? He spared a glance at her, averting his attention from the corner of the wall ahead of him.

She shook her head and crouched a little lower, waiting.

Corlag began to hum, smoothing his free hand over the blade of his sword. Its cold steel surface began to glow with a faint yellow light and musical notes danced along the edge of the blade.

"Alright demon," he uttered, his eyes flared up with the same yellow glow, and what appeared to be wisps of cloud or smoke trailed from the corners of his eyes, "Time for you to go back to whatever hell you came from."

With that he lunged toward the dark recess ahead of him, the light from his blade danced off the walls, illuminating the creature where it huddled in a corner against the ceiling; claws dug into the wooden walls, blocking the door. It squealed and shrieked as the light from the blade washed over it. Instinctively, the beast lunged from its perch.

Syndara's arrow caught the creature in the neck as it sailed over Corlag towards Branick, claws bared. It shrieked, the force of the impact throwing its weight off center, and it slammed into the wall before hitting the floor. It recovered quickly, somehow kept its momentum as it ran at Branick and slashed at his legs.

Branick dropped his shield arm down to block the creature and jabbed over top of its metal rim with his right hand. He stabbed down at the beast with his blade, catching it in one of its shoulders.

This time it did not flinch, but instead, pushed into his shield, biting at the edge with its jagged black maw and shook furiously, attempting to raise itself up on hind legs, front claws flailing for purchase in Branick's chest and it tried to rip his shield from his grip.

Branick planted his feet, left leg forward and his right foot sideways. He leaned into his shield, attempting to hold the creature at bay.

Corlag shouted and leapt clear across the room, bringing his blade down in an arc on the creature's side. It bit deep, causing the beast to flail frantically as it fell back against the wall. He kicked out hard from his landing, with both feet, sending himself plowing towards the creature; his blade held out in front of him like a spear. It buried into the beast's side and slammed against the wall boards, pinning it in place.

It let out one last cry of pain, started shaking rapidly all over as the same light that had surrounded Corlag's sword spread through the veins beneath its skin, making them glow. The creature burst into white flames and crumbled to dust. A flash of light lit the entire room, and the flames scorched the wall slightly before they dissipated as quickly as they had appeared. The arrow Syndara had fired clattered to the floor at Corlag's feet, scorched but intact. His sword remained wedged into the wall boards, no longer alight.

"What did you just do," gasped Syndara, blinking in disbelief at the pile of ash on the floor where the creature had been. "What just happened?"

"It was a banishment hymn, and I think we have unwanted attention on our trail. There's much more going on here than we understand. We have to leave tonight, we cannot wait until morning. Grab your things. I don't want to be responsible for bringing harm crashing down on these people. We make for the docks immediately," replied Corlag, breathing slightly heavier.

Branick rolled his shoulders, stepped forward and spat into the pile of ash, then looked at Syndara.

"What did you mean by 'not again'," he inquired, and pointed his weapon at the ashes. "Is this what attacked you and your friend in the northern pass?"

"Yes, but there were many, about half a dozen or more; and a larger one," she answered. She stood and gathered her things hurriedly.

Branick looked at Corlag for a long moment, concern cemented on his face. He gathered his belongings as well and strapped on his armor.

"They seem to like you," said Corlag. He fastened the final strap on his leather cuirass. "You'd best start sleeping with your armor on."

~*~

Borgolas heard the screeching of his minion as it died, and saw the flash of light through the broken window illuminate the rooftops across from it. He winced, feeling the creature's pain. He put a hand to his throat and rubbed it. He cleared his throat and shrugged off the pain.

"Hmm, bard indeed," he said aloud, with a smile. He rubbed his throat once more, then turned to enter the shadows of another alley across from the Inn.

"Show me what you're up to," he added and lifted his hood back into place. He slid back into the shadows and watched for signs of activity.

~*~

They Who Linger

The trio made their way down the hall from their room, waving off the odd onlooker that had been awoken by the commotion. They made it downstairs and paused to grab some bread rolls and dried meat, hastily put the supplies in their packs before dropping some copper coins on the counter to cover the cost and slipped into the kitchen.

"We'll leave through the back. I don't want any prying eyes on us as we leave. We need as much of a head start as we can get, and I don't think that's the last we've seen of our fiendish visitors," said Corlag, looking back over his shoulder at his companions. He prepared to open the door to the alley at the rear of the Kitchen. "Ready?"

They nodded. Branick placed a hand on Syndara's shoulder.

"Have an arrow ready just in case," he said, raised his shield and stepped into the alley in the lead.

Syndara nocked an arrow, letting it rest between her fingers and stepped out into the darkness right behind him; Corlag followed her, gently closing the door so as not to make a sound.

Chapter Fifty

Branick stepped beyond the threshold, checked left and right before leaving the shadow of the recessed doorway. The back of the Inn butted up against the eastern wall of the town, leaving a narrow alley roughly five feet wide. Seeing no immediate threat, he signaled to the others to follow. He led them through the dark passage, following the towering stone wall towards the docks.

As they approached the end of the alley, where it intersected with a cross street leading to the east gate out of town, he signaled for them to stop. He looked around before deciding to duck down a side alley, hoping to skirt around the gate without anyone seeing them. He had no desire to be answering any questions, or potentially putting innocents in harm's way if there were more beasts hunting them.

They reached the main street leading through the middle of Barroville a short while later. The main street would take them the rest of the way to the docks, and was covered in enough merchant canopies to provide adequate cover. There was no sign of guard patrols anywhere. That did little to settle Branick's nerves.

"What's the plan once we reach the docks," Branick whispered to Corlag? "The boat we found doesn't leave for another few days."

"We'll just have to convince the Captain that it's in his best interest to depart sooner, rather than later. If we can't convince him of such, then we'll have to procure transport through other means," replied Corlag, giving Branick a serious look.

"Aye," Branick nodded, then added, "supposing the Captain will listen to reason, we should make it without any trouble."

~*~

Borgolas grew impatient watching the front of the Inn from the shadows. He crossed from his hiding place to the side of the Inn, following the wall around to the back alley behind it. Seeing no one, he found the back door and entered the kitchen. He slunk through the dark interior and made his way up the stairs. He stood outside the door of the room he determined he had watched his minion crash into, and listened for any sign of the travelers within. After a number of moments of nothing but silence, he flung open the door, ready to deal with anyone still hiding within.

He scanned the room quickly and spotted the pile of ash at the base of the scorched wall. His jaw tightened in anger. A cold wind swept through the room from the gaping hole that was once the window, flapping the curtains and pulling at his robes. A growl emanated from his throat as he thrust his hands out in front of him. The windowed wall exploded outward with a resounding *BOOM,* the wooden boards and support beams shattered into pieces. The debris rained down on the ground and roof tops all around the south side of the Inn. The wind died down as fast as it had come, and he strode to the jagged edge of the room, peered out across the city towards the docks, looking and listening for any sign of the travelers.

"Come my friends, now we hunt in earnest," he shouted into the night.

A screech echoed over Barroville in answer, followed by another and then another. This went on for some time as he stood watching the night, hands balled into fists at his side.

"Wha- what is going on he- here," a nervous voice brusquely shouted from behind him.

Borgolas spun on his heels toward the plump figure standing in the doorway, who he assumed was the Innkeeper. A maniacal grin danced across his face and he began to laugh.

In a move that defied his fragile appearance, Borgolas turned and launched himself from the broken wall, landing on the cobblestones below in a crouch. He stood and casually began walking down the back alley along the east wall of the city in search of his prey.

Shouts of confusion and alarm echoed out through the night, dissolving the facade of peaceful slumber.

~*~

A shadowy creature scurried through the darkness just outside the walls surrounding Barroville, licking the air and squawking as it moved. Catching the scent of its prey, it turned toward the wall and clambered up a nearby tree. It lunged from the trunk of the tree, and landed on the inner edge of the parapet, its clawed front appendages gripped the edge and it leaned forward to let out an ethereal screech. Black ooze dripped from its mouth. It licked its lips and leaped onto a nearby roof inside the town's wall.

A patrolling guard spotted the beast when it lunged from the parapet ahead of him, and shouted in surprise at the top of his lungs. He spun around and bolted for a nearby watch tower to raise the alarm, warning of impending danger.

Another guard, coming from the opposite direction, saw his friend in panic mode and immediately reached for his crossbow. He eyed the creature as it spun to focus on the shouting guard. It was gangly and dark skinned. Realizing what was about to happen, he fired a bolt at the creature in haste, and yelled out his own warning to his friend, waving an arm frantically at him.

"Look out Jeb!"

The creature shrieked when the bolt thudded into the roof next to it and snapped its head in the direction of the second guard. It shifted its weight and spun to charge at the new threat, its claws *clacking* off the clay roof tiles as it charged forward.

The second guard saw the beast refocus on him and fumbled to reload his crossbow as fast as he could, to no avail. His hands were shaking so badly he could barely draw the string. He abandoned the crossbow, let it clatter to the ground and unsheathed his sword.

The creature launched from the roof and slammed into him just as his sword cleared the sheath. It struck him full in the chest, the momentum knocking him back and pinning him beneath its bulk. Claws dug into his arms and legs; he screamed in agony.

The beast gnashed its jaws at his face, but he managed to hold it at arm's length, the clacking fangs narrowly missing the tip of his nose. It reared on its hind legs, snapping the bones in the guard's legs under the weight of it, and slammed down on his chest with its front claws. A third guard came running from another watchtower not far away, bellowed at the top of her lungs and rushed the creature.

Still clawing at the guard under it, the creature raised its head and bit at the second, catching her by surprise. She jumped back just in time to avoid losing one of her legs.

The guard beneath the beast managed to free his sword arm while the creature was distracted, and with numbness threatening to fully overwhelm his senses, he gave a desperate swing with every bit of strength he had left. Before the blow could land, the creature bit down on his throat with lighting speed as it returned its focus to finish off its first victim. His hand released the blade. He sputtered and gurgled, grasping at the beast's maw, desperately fighting to prevent his imminent demise.

The guardswoman looked on in horror, hiding behind her shield, sword at the ready. She watched her fellow guardsman fade away, his legs kicking as his lifeblood drained out of his body and over the side of the wall. His free arm fell limp against the cold stones a short moment later.

Moonlight glinted off the beast's eyes when it raised its head and slowly stepped off of the guard's now lifeless corpse toward her, black orbs piercing her soul. Blood dripped from bits of flesh that had become wedged between its fangs. She blinked in disbelief, unable to move as she took in the full horror of the creature in front of her, seemingly made of pure shadows and malice. Every bit of it was blacker than the night, and the surface of its skin shifted like a smoke cloud. It continued its slow gait towards her, tilting its head to the side, claws clicking against the stones of the parapet. If not for the very real sounds and the stench of its sulfurous breath wafting

244

toward her on the wind, she would not have believed the beast to be real.

The bits of flesh that dangled from its fanged maw flung gore in all directions as the beast roared and rushed forward.

She shook her head, finally breaking out of her stupor, and banged her sword against her shield once, twice; a third time. Rhythmically clanging the blade against the shield to steel her nerves and hopefully intimidate her oncoming opponent. That was what they taught them in guard training, victory through intimidation whenever possible. Finding her resolve, she bellowed at the top of her lungs and lunged to meet the creature. Her sword cut a gash in its hide along one side, her sudden onslaught catching it by surprise. It growled and leaned back out of the way of her follow through attack, then pounced on her.

She raised her shield and pushed into it hard, rolling with the impact, positioning herself beneath its belly as she did so, and kicked against its ribs with both feet, sending the beast sprawling back over her head. She continued rolling with the momentum, righted herself, and windmilled her arms to keep her balance as she teetered on the edge of the parapet. She desperately tried to catch her footing, but before she could succeed, the creature got back to its feet and swiped at her, catching her in the midriff with its claws. The chain links of her armor tore open like they were made of cloth; she fell back off the wall, flailing in silent disbelief the whole way down. She landed awkwardly on her head, breaking her neck on the cobblestones of the dark alley below.

Wasting no time, the beast jumped from the parapet to another rooftop, then another, bounding deeper into the city.

In the distance, a guard tower bell began tolling.

Chapter Fifty-One

They heard a guard call out from somewhere off in the distance to the east, followed by the sounds of combat. Branick halted their progress with a raised hand clenched into a fist.

"That doesn't sound good Cor, and after whatever the big noise was before it, I don't think we've got much time. We have to move fast, it's not far now" said Branick.

They hurried through the streets and alleys, weaving toward the waterfront as directly as they could. They burst from a side street into a giant, stone paved street littered with crates and barrels a short while later.

Branick pointed out the dock master's hut, raised up on wood pilings at the front of the central pier. The docks consisted of three piers, all full with ships of various sizes.

"Right, I'll rouse the dock master. Syndara you get to the end of the dock by the boat; be ready for anything. Branick, watch our backs," said Corlag, taking charge now.

Syndara and Branick took their places, and Corlag ran up the stairs to the hut. He rapped his knuckles on the door and waited for a moment.

"Excuse me sir, sorry to bother you at such a late hour, but it's an emergency," offered Corlag as he rapped his knuckles on the door again. *Silence!* He knocked a few more times, and finally the door creaked open. A haggard looking elderly man poked his head out into the night, smacking his lips and blinking out of sync.

"Who- who is it? What do you want at this awful hour? BEGONE!"

The man flailed a hand dismissively while he tried to focus his vision, and before he could get a word in edgewise, the door was shut in Corlag's face. He banged on the door again with the heel of his left hand.

The man quickly swung the door open again.

"Don't people know how to let an old sailor rest in peace anymore? I should have the guards-" the dock master began to mutter before he was cut off.

"Enough! Forgive my curtness, but it's an emergency. I need the captain of that vessel at the end of your pier. Where can I find him?"

"Alright, alright! No need to lose your head son. His name be Barthus. He be at the Pigeon Hole just up the street. Why you be needin' him at this hour," the dock master replied with a surprised look on his face?

"I really don't have time to explain sir, but it is no doubt a matter of life and death. Stay in your hut, it's not safe in the city this evening."

The seadog looked at him for a moment, curling his lower lip in thought. He waved a hand at Corlag dismissively from behind his door. "Bah, it makes no difference to me. Be on your way then and let me get back to my sleep," he said then quickly closed the door in Corlag's face again.

Corlag shrugged and jogged back to share his information with Branick.

"The Captain is at the Pigeon Hole just up the street apparently. Stay here with Syndara, I'll go talk to him," said Corlag.

"Aye, be careful friend. Whatever we heard earlier is more than likely looking for us. Hurry back," replied Branick.

"I'll be quick, I regret this already, but I don't think the Captain will be getting a choice in the matter. Don't worry, I can get him to accompany us without harm."

"I have no doubts. Many things about your trade have puzzled me, and I learned long ago not to question it. Now make haste," Branick ushered him on with a wave of his left hand.

Corlag ran quietly up the street the dock master had indicated, in search of the Pigeon Hole, and their Captain.

Chapter Fifty-Two

Borgolas let out an amused sound when he heard the din of battle off in the distance. He stopped in the middle of the main street and listened for a moment.

"That's it, find the bard and his friends." He extended a hand toward the sky, index and middle fingers held together, the rest lazily bent towards his palm, "no need to delay this any further. Let's see if we can burn them out."

He balled his other hand into a fist and gestured with the upraised one, swirling it around once and then jabbed it out in front of him; fingers pointed at one of the buildings down the street. A brilliant bolt of lightning sheared through the cloudless night and struck the building. Fire erupted up its side. The flames quickly engulfed the dry wood as it spread to the roof in a matter of seconds. Thick acrid smoke billowed up and began to form a plume above the city.

"Ahhhh, that's better," he exhaled joyfully. "There's nowhere to run bard, you'll learn that soon enough."

Borgolas lifted his head to the night and cackled with delight.

Chapter Fifty-Three

Corlag couldn't help but chuckle when he spotted the sign for the Pigeon Hole. It had a wooden pigeon carving smashed head first through the wooden sign, its head making up the 'O'.

"Cute," he said to himself, approached the door and began banging on it. After a few moments, a burly man angrily flung open the door, his brow furled, prepared to tear a strip off of whoever was disturbing him and his guests so late in the evening.

"What d'ya want at this hour? I have no beds, no food cooked, and no drinks to serve. The sky best be falling down around us for you to be waking myself and my patrons this late in the night. I ought to have-"

Corlag cleared his throat, cutting the Innkeeper off before he could finish his rant.

"You know, that's the second person to say something like that this evening, ENOUGH ALREADY," he bellowed, then promptly apologized and recollected his patience.

Startled, the man glared at him for a moment, his mouth opening as if to protest, and then decided he had best not push his luck with the stranger at his door.

"Alright then, no need to go getting all in a huff about it. What can I do for you?"

"I'm looking for Captain Barthus. I was told he is staying at your establishment. It is urgent that I speak with him."

"Very well," replied the man. He quickly disappeared into the dark interior, the door closing behind him. He returned a short while later with a candle holder in hand, and a bearded and haggard looking man in tow.

"Here he is. Good night," added the Inn Keep dismissively as he pushed the man groggily out into the street and closed the door again.

The bearded man stretched and rubbed sleep from his eyes. He stepped toward Corlag, commanding answers without uttering a word.

"Evening Captain. I was told that is your boat at the end of the central pier at the docks, is that the case," asked Corlag?

The man cleared his throat and spit into the street, just missing Corlag's feet.

"Aye, what d'ya want boy? What be yer interest with Tabitha," he replied?

Seeing that he was on the verge of a standoff with the man, Corlag muttered something under his breath quickly and waved his hand in front of the captain's face as he finished; a warm glow emanated from his hand when he next spoke.

"My friends and I were seeking passage aboard your ship when it sets sail in a few days, but it seems a situation beyond our control has arisen, and we need to make our departure before sunrise. Is there anything important that you are waiting on for departure?"

"Nay, I suppose we could be on our way this morning. Let me rouse the crew with my boot, and meet me at the dock shortly," replied the man with a distant look in his eyes.

Corlag smiled, pleased with the answer.

"I shall see you there," returned Corlag. He repeated his previous gesture and the glow faded from his hand.

Barthus shook his head slightly.

"Well what are ya waiting for boy, get a move on, we don't have all day," the captain bellowed and then stepped inside the Inn yelling for his crew. "Up ye lazy scalawags, we got a boat to prep!"

The door slammed shut behind him, and Corlag turned to head back to the dock, smiling. It was then that lightning and fire lit the night sky, and the smell of acrid smoke hit his nostrils. A fire had broken out not too far from the Pigeon Hole. It was time to leave.

Chapter Fifty-Four

Corlag returned to the docks and found Branick and Syndara talking with one of the dock guards.

Branick waved him over when he saw him running along the seawall. He had an irritated expression on his face, and was clearly gritting his teeth to hold back his anger.

Seeing Branick wave, the dock guard turned and greeted Corlag with a terse nod.

"Ho there, your friends here were just telling me that you are looking to set sail before sunrise," said the guard, holding up a hand indicating for Corlag to stop, "you know there be no ships leaving for a few days right? What business do you have with the Tabitha at this hour without her captain present?"

Branick glared at the back of the guard's head while he spoke with Corlag, then added his own retort.

"Our new friend here doesn't seem to remember my mentioning that you were getting the captain of this fair ship here," he sarcastically stated and pointed over his shoulder at the ship with a thumb.

"Mind yer tongue," returned the guard, glancing back at Branick.

"Aye, he's on his way. Barthus is getting the crew and meeting us here. We are setting sail as soon as the ship's anchor can be lifted. Is there a problem," answered Corlag?

"What," blurted the guard in surprise, "I was told there were no ships set to depart for a few days by the dockmaster just this afternoon. None of them have even been loaded with their designated cargo. Was this cleared in the logs with him?"

"Are ye satisfied that we're not here to plunder the ship now," Branick asked with a grin?

"Don't go anywhere. I'll be talkin' to Captain Barthus when he arrives. I'll not tell you to mind yer tongue again neither, lest you be spending the rest of the night in a cell," replied the guard, jutting a finger in Branick's direction.

"Suit yerself," replied Branick as he stepped back and leaned against a crate.

"Let it be. No sense getting into it with him," said Syndara patting him on the chest, "we have enough to deal with as is."

Branick looked at her for a moment, then turned and stepped back toward the ship muttering under his breath while he rolled his shoulders.

"Will there be anything else," Corlag asked the guard?

As he opened his mouth to reply, the guard's eyes grew wide in horror, and he started down the pier towards the town quickly.

"FIRE," he yelled and gave the group one last look before he picked up his pace into a full run. He continued shouting for help as he disappeared up the street towards the flames that now danced high into the night sky, his inquiry forgotten.

"Oh no! That looks like the direction of the Hog's Head. What's going on," exclaimed Syndara? She had not seen the plume of dark smoke, or the flames dancing along a rooftop in the distance, having been distracted by the guard. The coastal breeze was quickening the fire's spread and the smoke cloud was growing ever larger above the town, billowing on the wind to the north east.

"Our troubles are not over. It seems we are due for some more company. Be ready," he replied loud enough so Branick heard him where he fumed at the end of the docks.

Branick unsheathed his sword and swung his shield off his pack in tandem.

"Syndara, you should get on the ship. You'll have a better vantage from up there if we have unwanted guests," said Branick pointing at the bow of the Tabitha.

"Let's just hope the captain and crew get here soon," she replied, then jogged up the gangplank onto the ship.

"That shouldn't be a problem," replied Corlag with a grin.

"Why, what did you do," she asked?

"Oh nothing, Captain Barthus was very understanding is all," he answered, smiling innocently.

Syndara looked at him curiously from the top of the gangplank, Branick chuckled and rolled his neck to loosen up his already tense muscles, and Corlag unsheathed his own sword with his right hand. He started humming a tune and took up position at the front of the pier. His left hand started to emanate a light blue glow while he waved it over his blade, as he had done before, transferring the glow to the blade. He finished the tune and began a new one.

Syndara watched in amazement from her new vantage point on the Tabitha's bow.

~*~

The wounded creature bounded across a number of rooftops before landing on an overhang overlooking the docks. It sniffed and licked the air, looking up the seawall towards the dock house. It spotted the bard at the foot of the pier, his blade alight with blue flames. It clacked its jaws together and chuffed, crouched low and shook its body. It ruffled its quills, then lunged into the street. It screeched as it pounded towards its prey across the cobblestoned seawall.

~*~

Corlag focused on the advancing beast, his hymn growing in pitch. He planted his feet and angled his sword out in front of him in a parrying stance. Branick now stood beside him with his shield raised.

"Time to die, beast," yelled Branick.

Corlag brought his hand up and clasped his sword in both hands, bowed his head slightly and closed his eyes. His song reached its peak, he snapped his head up and shouted with all his might, thrusting the sword point towards the creature. Sparks danced from the glowing blade, spreading all over the ground around where he and Branick stood. A wall of light shot up into the sky from the edge of the circle of glowing ground that now surrounded them forming a dome over where they stood.

The creature collided with the wall of light in front of Branick and clambered to shield its eyes. It hissed and gnashed its teeth. Branick stepped forward to meet it with a backhanded swing of his shield. The attack connected with the creature's jaw with a resounding *thwump*!

The beast's cat-like agility saved it from Branick's sword swing that quickly followed the shield slam. It leaped out of reach and scampered away from the wall of light. An arrow sunk into one of its shoulders as it skittered away, and a second one bounced harmlessly off of the cobblestones near its front feet and hit a barrel.

Corlag hummed another tune and stepped through the barrier, flanking the creature, placing it between them and the sea. It snarled and bit at the arrow shaft jutting from its shoulder, succeeding only to shatter the arrow shaft between its teeth. The beast launched a flailing assault with its claws at Branick as he too stepped out of the barrier of light. He caught the first few blows on his shield, but the creature relentlessly pressed its attack and Branick was swatted aside by an errant blow that struck his sword arm.

Branick laughed through the pain and quickly recovered, brought his wounded arm to bear, growled through his teeth, and aimed a punch at the creature's snout with his sword hand. The hilt of his sword connected, snapping back the creature's head, which gave him an opportunity to bring his shield arm back around to connect with the other side of its head, sending it flailing to the ground.

A second volley of arrows from Syndara met their mark, leaving two new arrow shafts protruding from the beast's back.

Corlag saw his opening, and moved in quickly from the side to finish the creature off with a thrust of his glowing sword. He charged the last few feet to close the gap before it could recover again, flipped his blade over in the air, caught it by the hilt and slammed the tip downward through the beast's head. The blade sunk into the ground beneath, cracking the stones around it. He held onto the blade for a moment to make sure the creature wasn't going anywhere, then released his grip on the hilt, and stood back as the creature was enveloped by the flames from the blade, quickly turning to ash, leaving the sword standing freely on its own. The glowing barrier dissipated into a cloud of glowing particles behind them.

Branick was staring at the ash pile, his mouth agape.

"Are you alright," asked Corlag while he pulled his blade free and clasped a hand on his friend's shoulder?

"I'm fine," he answered and shook his head. "Just a scratch. What the hell are these things?"

"Hell indeed! I'm not sure, but they definitely have something in common with that place."

"Corlag, your hand," exclaimed Branick, his eyes wide with surprise!

"What," asked Corlag, with a confused glance at his free hand? It was engulfed in swirling yellowish flames.

"What's happening to you friend?"

Corlag balled his hand into a fist slowly and opened it again, flexing it. As he examined his hand, the flames dissipated and he looked at Branick, leaving them in near darkness again, save for the moonlight dancing off the water and a torch hanging in its clasp on a dock post flickering off in the distance. His sword had ceased glowing when the creature crumbled to dust around it.

"I'm fine. Just some bardic residue is all," he said, eying Branick.

"There's more than that going on. I've seen a lot of your tricks and that's not one of them," grunted Branick and pointed at Corlag's hand.

Corlag looked at his hand again, and slowly wiggled his fingers before averting his gaze.

"Let me see your arm," Corlag said, changing the subject.

"You know I don't like the feeling your mending leaves behind. Besides, it's not that bad," Branick shied away slightly and shook his arm for emphasis, and gritted his teeth, "OK, maybe a little bad."

"A little indeed, you're dripping blood all over the cobbles," replied Corlag. He placed his left hand over the gouge marks in Branick's sword arm and sang a brief hymn, his hand flashed with a yellow glow briefly, then returned to normal. He slapped Branick's arm where the wound had been, "there, how's that?"

"Better, but damn the itch," said Branick as he scratched at his arm some more.

"Could be worse," Corlag laughed and slapped his friend's arm again.

"Everything OK over there? What was that light," yelled Syndara across the docks?

Corlag and Branick looked back at the ship.

"We're fine. It's dead. Do you see the Captain at all," Corlag sent back?

"Not yet. That fire has grown," she said and pointed up the street.

They jogged back toward the pier, and as they approached the ship, the door to the dock master's shack swung open.

The old man poked his head out and began to shout at them. "Can't you people leave me in peace? What's all the noise about anyway? Don't make me call the watchman back here or-"

Branick spun on his heels and glared at the dock master, cutting off the remainder of his onslaught of questions.

"The city burns, creatures formed from the very shadows themselves roam the night, and there be trouble afoot. You'll do best to mind yer tongue, gather your things, and be on your way to safety outside these walls if'n you value yer life," shouted Branick all in one breath.

Corlag placed his hand on his shoulder.

"Gentle," said Corlag.

"Aye," replied Branick, shaking Corlag's hand off.

"I don't know what you folks are up to but-" the dock master began to retort then trailed off, burrowing his gaze into Branick's back as he watched him stroll away toward the end of the pier.

"NOW old man! I'll be damned if I'll have your blood on my hands because you were too stubborn to know when trouble was breathing down your neck," shouted Branick without turning around.

The hinges on the door squeaked as the dock master shirked away into the darkness of his hut, followed by the sounds of frantic rustling and clanging.

Chapter Fifty-Five

Borgolas ducked into an alley after igniting the blaze and rounded a corner, exiting near the eastern town wall. He spotted a guard's body, a woman, awkwardly sprawled on the ground, neck bent unnaturally far to the side. He looked up at the parapet above and saw blood dripping over the edge a little further south from where the woman's body lay.

"Effective little beasts," he said, pleased. He watched the droplets of blood splatter down the side of the angled stone wall for a moment. A pool of it had formed at the base of the wall and was slowly, oozing along through the spaces in the cobble stones.

He looked back at the woman's corpse and flicked his left hand upward towards the fallen guard, as if beckoning her.

"No sense you lazing about now, come on, on your feet; we've got work to do."

Her corpse quivered momentarily, and then rose slowly to its feet. Borgolas picked up the rogue sword and shield that had clattered in opposite directions of the body when it hit the cobbles and handed them back to their departed owner. The husk of the guard stared at him with glazed eyes and it wrapped its stiffened fingers around the hilt of the blade and through the straps of the shield.

"That's it, here we go," he added and started down the alley again, his new pet unsteadily waddling along behind him.

A scraping noise echoed down from the parapet above, bouncing off the walls of the buildings around him, followed by a gurgling moan. Borgolas looked in the direction of the noise, a grin on his face.

"Ah, so there are two of you, excellent."

The dead guard from above swung his newly animated limbs over the edge of the wall, fingers clawing him forward. He fell off, and landed hard on the ground with a sickening crack; his helmet clanged off the stones and blood flew out of his gaping wounds splattering across the alley. It was like watching a heavy stone land in mud. Without pausing, he clawed to his feet, his body bent to the left a bit now.

Borgolas shrugged like it was nothing out of the ordinary, turned and continued on his way as the two corpses shuffled along behind him.

Chapter Fifty-Six

Borgolas doubled over when his minion was dispatched. His new puppets shambled up on either side of him protectively, and stared blankly ahead towards the end of the alley.

"Curse this bard," spat Borgolas angrily and straightened himself up, "It's time to bring this charade to an end."

He wove his hands in front of him in an intricate pattern as he spoke to his new friends.

"Hungry my puppets?"

The two corpses let out a ghastly moan and looked at him.

"Go, and don't stop until they, or you, are dead," he chuckled to himself and clapped his hands together, "well re-dead in your case."

The dead guards stumbled forward out of the alley into the harbor towards the docks, shrouded in darkness and shambled along the southern wall that soon met up with the seawall.

Borgolas weaved through side alleys until he found an opening facing the docks. He watched his reanimated guards lumber up the street through the shadows at a brisk, shambling pace.

He spotted his quarry speaking to someone in a shack on the central pier, and without hesitating, he made another gesture and pointed his finger at the hut. Lightning arced out of the cloudless sky and struck the roof as the bard and his friend were moving away from it. The roof exploded out in all directions, the remnants igniting into flames, and a massive thunder clap shook the area as it boomed over the town.

"That ought to distract them long enough."

The bard and his bulky friend took cover behind a pile of crates and barrels and looked all around. Borgolas had not spotted the third traveler yet, and chose to remain in hiding until he had found her. He gestured toward the water with his right hand and watched as the dead male guard lowered itself quietly into the water.

An old, wrinkly man burst from the shack at the front of the pier and frantically looked around. He shouted and pointed very animatedly at the destroyed roof of his home. He had a number of belongings strapped to a giant travel bag on his back, some of them *clanged* as he shook about in anger. He jabbed a hand toward the stack of crates and continued to yell, blaming the giant of a man next to the bard. The old man quickly shied away from the burly traveler he had been accusing as the giant rose to his feet and bellowed back menacingly. The old man turned towards the town and started running up the street away from the docks, yelling for help, alerting anyone that could hear him of a fire at the harbor. Not soon after, a guard ran up to the pier to assess the situation. He finally spotted the third traveler, perched on the bow of a giant ship at the end of the pier. She was very distracted by the recent happenings and the guard. Borgolas grinned and stepped out of the alley. He watched his other shambling puppet approach around the side of the burning hut, coming up behind the unaware guard.

"That's it, they are cornered like frightened rats, get them," he said under his breath and laughed menacingly.

~*~

A thunderclap directly overhead made Corlag, Branick and Syndara all duck behind cover as it shook their bones and the earth beneath them. It was immediately followed by a flash of light, and a storm of debris, shingles and timbers exploded out over the harbor, sending scorched and burning wreckage from the shack roof raining down all around them. Luckily the ship was far enough away from the flaming debris storm to avoid catching fire.

Branick and Corlag poked their heads up from behind a stack of crates and barrels to have a look around, checking for danger. Just then, the dock master burst from the hut screaming at the top of his lungs, travel bag and belongings strapped to his back. He spotted Branick peering over the stacked goods, and immediately waved his hand in his direction accusingly.

"You! What did you do? I know it was you, ye bast-" he was cut off as Branick bared his teeth and yelled in return.

"Did you not just hear the thunder clap? Lightning struck your roof you old fool. There's trouble brewing I tell you, do you see any clouds in the sky? Get out of the city; NOW," Branick bellowed at the man and pointed commandingly away from the harbor!

The man cowered back, clamped his mouth shut, stopping any further rebuke. He then turned and ran fleeing from the pier. He didn't look back again while he scurried up the street out of the harbor. They could hear his shouts for help getting further and further away. Not soon after he had disappeared another watchman ran up to the pier from down the harbor to the west.

"Oi there, what's happened here," he asked tersely, making eye contact with Corlag and Branick?

Corlag threw an arm in front of Branick and stepped forward before he could approach the guard.

"Lightning has struck the roof of the Dock Master's hut there. He's gone up the street for help, you should do the same. We must make sure the fire does not spread to the pier, or worse, the ship here," answered Corlag, gesturing to both the building and the ship in turn.

"I'll be fine doing my job without your telling me how to do it, thank you kindly," replied the guard.

Corlag quickly uttered a hymn and looked the guard straight in the eyes.

"You should really get help and stop letting your pride get in the way."

The watchman blinked at Corlag, then looked at Branick, and back to Corlag, as if trying to recall where he was and what was happening.

"That's a good idea, I should go. Make sure the fire doesn't spread," the guard droned on, pointing at some buckets on the pier then the lapping surface of the water below.

Syndara had returned to watching the harbor for danger, and spotted motion behind the guard on the seawall, coming from the shadows cast by the shack. She called out a warning as a menacing figure approached the guard, but was too late.

The figure buried its sword in the watchman's back, right through his heart. He gawked at the point protruding from his chest, palms raised towards the blade in disbelief. The blade receded back through his torso slowly, leaving him to waver about unsteadily for a moment before his dead weight carried him to his knees; his gaze fixed in place. He slumped to his side against the cold stones. The last thing he saw was a sideways view of a hunched woman's figure shambling past where he had stood, his own blood dripping from the blade gripped in her hand; then darkness. His metal helmet rolled across the stones, over the seawall, and splashed into the water.

Syndara watched helplessly as the scene unfolded and she scrambled to nock an arrow.

Corlag and Branick had closed the gap and were approaching the front of the pier when the watchman's body slumped to the ground, revealing a hunched guard woman. She had a hollow look in her eyes, and her neck bent unnaturally to one side. She clacked her jaws together and elicited a groan as she shambled past the watchman's body towards them.

A scraping noise from behind them alerted Corlag and he spun to find another guard, the remnants of one at least, half out of the water on its belly, at the far end of the pier. It dug its fingernails into the boards and clawed itself the rest of the way up onto the wooden planks.

"We've got another one here," he shouted, put his back to Branick's and faced off against the approaching second guard. Its chest was torn open, and its entire upper body leaned to the side, eyes vacantly gazing at its prey.

"Is there no end to this," Syndara cried out rhetorically and fired her arrow at the corpse that had pulled itself out of the water.

The guard didn't so much as grunt when the arrow slammed into its left thigh, and without flinching or pausing, lumbered on.

"They're Undead," yelled Corlag.

Branick sighed heavily and rolled his eyes.

"Damn," Branick uttered, barely loud enough for Corlag to hear.

Branick swung at the undead guard in front of him. It made no effort to dodge or block the blow. His sword cut through the guard's shield arm just above the elbow. The arm hit the wooden planks with a wet Thud. The guard groaned then swung its sword at Branick, mimicking his own motion. He caught the blow on the rim of his shield, the impact denting it. The force of the blow pushed him back a step. He counter attacked, hitting the guard in the leg, but did no real damage. She pressed on.

Corlag shouted and charged the second undead guard, unleashing a flurry of attacks, inflicting many wounds as he dodged the wild swinging of its arms. A normal man would have keeled over in agony from such an onslaught, but the undead creature didn't even flinch. It tried to get hold of Corlag, all the while gnashing its teeth at him.

Syndara fired arrow after arrow into each of the undead, peppering them with quills, the shafts protruding from all angles. She fired the last of her arrows, dropped her bow on the ship's deck, unsheathed both of her axes, and ran for the gangplank. She kicked at the undead guard Corlag was battling as she reached the pier, buckling one of its knees in on itself, and then engaged in full.

Chapter Fifty-Seven

Borgolas watched the dead guards attack while he moved silently through the shadows toward the battle, only making a sound when he came into view of the travelers. He cackled with maniacal glee as his puppets slammed against them again and again.

The bard's large friend blocked another wild swing from the undead woman, and countered with his shield, slamming hard against her chest, causing her to stumble unsteadily backwards away from him.

"There's no escape this time," announced Borgolas and then uttered something barely intelligible, then jutted his hand toward the undead woman.

"YOU," Branick spat vehemently when he recognized Borgolas!

The sound of bone grinding against bone beneath flesh followed, as the guard renewed her attack on Branick, swinging repeatedly with immense speed, and power. She regained her ground and pushed him back. He parried and blocked blow after blow.

Corlag feinted to the side and jumped back out of Syndara's way as she struck at the second undead guard. She buried one of her axes in its neck with a crunch, lodging it between two vertebrae. Before she could rip it free, it backhanded her hard in the chest, winding her. She lost her grip on the axe, and it remained wedged in the dead man's neck. She managed to roll with the impact, back out of further harm's way.

Corlag heard Branick yell. He looked over his shoulder and saw the robed figure on the seawall. Surprise shot across his face as he too, recognized the man from the path near the Upper Fel'Thain forest.

"You've got to be kidding me," he shouted and jabbed the guardsman in the back of the neck, at the base of the skull, just below the rim of his helmet. His blade sunk in deep, and he yanked it free quickly with a sucking sound that made him shiver. The undead husk crumpled lifeless to the planks.

Borgolas pushed back his hood, firelight from the now blazing Dock Master's hut illuminated his menacing features. His eyes flared with a green glow, and he glared up at Corlag venomously.

"You have something of mine bard. Hand it over and your death will be quick," commanded Borgolas.

Syndara got to her feet, retrieved her axe and a few arrows from the corpse in front of her. Taking no chances that it would get up again, she brought both axe blades down repeatedly, severing its limbs and then rolled the torso into the water with a splash.

"Who is that," asked Syndara as she finished her grim task.

"That's the old man we met on the path coming out of Fel'Thain forest on our way to the Crossroads. He said his name was Borgolas," answered Corlag as they ran to help Branick.

The undead woman continued pounding relentlessly with her sword, the stub of her severed arm flailing about oozing thick congealed blood, her jaw constantly opening and shutting mechanically; clattering her teeth as her head jiggled and lilted to the side. Her eyes were foggy now; it was all Branick could do to keep her at bay. One of her wild swings glanced off the top of his shield, and bit into his shoulder. He yelped, and yelled.

"ENOUGH OF THIS!"

He kicked out hard and threw his weight against his shield and plowed into her with the momentum, the kick connected with her right thigh and he felt the bone shatter. Coupled with the backwards momentum of her next sword swing, the force knocked her to the ground. Branick landed the forward kick in a crouch, hunkered behind his shield.

"NO! Branick, don't," bellowed Corlag, knowing full well what would come next.

Branick began to yell, low at first, but quickly rising to an ear piercing cry of rage. He planted his feet and his armor rippled, a wave of energy burst outward from him as he raised his head to the sky and flung his arms out to his sides. Syndara and Corlag covered their ears as a shock wave shot across the harbor. The undead guardswoman was pushed back further by the assailing noise, and Borgolas was caught by surprise. He stumbled about and attempted to cover his ears, the shock wave bringing him to one knee.

Branick quickly followed the wailing bellow with a roar of bestial vigor. He closed the gap between him and the walking corpse, unleashed a flurry of attacks with his sword and shield, and shredded the undead guard's torso in front of him. The guard barely managed an attempt to swing its sword before the remaining arm was severed in the flurry of blows. He lunged over the corpse as it fell to the ground again, and he brought his shield arm down on its throat, severing the head with the impact. He paused for a mere moment, took a deep breath and rose to his full menacing height and turned on Borgolas. His muscles rippled with rage as he again set eyes on the robed man.

Borgolas recovered from his daze a moment too late. He looked up just before Branick dashed forward and slammed his fist into his chin, sending him reeling back with a groan into the side of the nearest stack of crates; the force of the impact winding him.

"This ends now," panted Branick.

Borgolas coughed and tried to catch his breath.

"You... have... no idea," replied Borgolas. From where he lay among the ruined crates he chanted something quickly and flung his hand toward the warrior.

Blinded by battle rage, Branick didn't see the attack coming. An invisible force lifted him off his feet, sent him reeling back through the air, arching up and slamming through the side of the flame engulfed shack on the pier. His world became smoke, ash and fire. The flames licked at his exposed flesh, threatening to devour it.

"Branick," shouted Corlag and rushed toward the burning building. He could hear his friend groaning as he cleared the steps two by two, prepared a protective song and burst through the remains of the door, ignoring the flames entirely.

"I'm alive," Branick managed through a coughing fit, "I think."

Branick lay in a crater of ruined floorboards that were splintered up all around him. Corlag helped him out of the debris to his feet, then guided him outside away from the burning hut.

"Damn, I think I broke a rib," uttered Branick through gritted teeth, "Ahhg! Go, get that bastard."

"I warned you not to rage." Corlag chastised.

Branick shoved Corlag gently forward and hobbled over to a nearby barrel.

"Stay here with Syndara. Don't try anything else," said Corlag before turning to face Syndara who had come to meet them.

"Get Bran on the Tabitha. I'll distract Borgolas long enough for the captain to get here and unmoor the ship."

Syndara put Branick's uninjured side against hers and wrapped his arm over her shoulders, supporting his massive bulk as best as she could and helped him limp down the pier toward the ship.

Borgolas had gotten to his feet and was dusting debris from his robe absentmindedly when Corlag returned his attention to him.

"Now, before I change my mind, hand over the artifact and you and your friends can be on your merry way," cooed Borgolas, his face serious.

"Why would I do that," asked Corlag?

"Because you know not what you are trifling with. That which you carry is the key to a thousand year old lost soul, imprisoned within its own body, and I will stop at nothing to free it. You have a weakness; you care what happens to those you do not know," he paused momentarily as he muttered something quickly and waved his hand around behind him at a warehouse building. The wall exploded inward, debris flying in all directions, and the roof buckled on the side facing the harbor as the supporting wall disintegrated, crumpling in on itself and partly falling out onto the seawall, "where as I lost the only thing I cared about long ago, and will do anything to retrieve what is mine."

"If what you say is true, then there is even more reason for me to oppose your acquisition of the artifact," he replied resolutely and began humming a bardic tune. He flicked his sword hand out to his side at his waist, causing it to ring with rhythmic sounds.

"You really don't want to do that," warned Borgolas, then roared and pushed both hands toward the bard, palms facing his target.

Corlag's eyes began to dance with yellowish flames, trails of light rippled from the corners of his eyes as he lowered his head and raised his sword into the air in front of him, hilt up, point facing the ground. He slammed the blade into the cobblestones and let loose a quick single-note bellow of his own that echoed over the city, a wall of golden light rose up into the night sky between him and Borgolas. His back started to itch and a bluish glow emanated from his pack.

Borgolas' assault hit the wall of light just after it shot up into the air, causing it to ripple like the surface of a pond that had a stone skipped across its surface, followed by a crackling sound similar to that of ice on a lake when it shifts.

Borgolas howled in frustration.

"NO! It can't be-" he bit off his own protest and redoubled his efforts, desperate to obtain the artifact.

Corlag reached into his pack and removed the artifact, which was now glowing with an intense blue-white light. Its surface danced and the carvings on the back of it were icy cold to the touch where he handled it. He felt immense power flow through his arms when he clasped it in both hands, and without thinking, raised it over his head into the air. His entire body and the area behind the barrier became engulfed in the blue-white light.

Borgolas raged with fury, slamming attack after attack into the bard's wall of energy.

"No, no, NOOOO!"

They Who Linger

~*~

Syndara helped Branick down on the deck of the Tabitha, propped him against the base of the center mast, and then moved to the front of the ship to retrieve her bow and watch the approach of the Captain and his crew. An explosive sound drew her attention back to where Corlag was confronting Borgolas. The warehouse building closest to Borgolas was in ruin. She heard Corlag's sharp bellow and gasped as a golden light shot up out of the ground in front of him. It illuminated the entirety of Barroville. The barrier of energy surrounded him, and his sword, planted in the ground in front of him, looked like it was fresh from the forge with how much it glowed.

The Captain and crew let out gasps of awe and surprise as they entered the harbor, and seeing the two men at an impasse near the ruined warehouse, did not stop. They doubled their speed to the boat, fearing for their lives as they sprinted the rest of the way down the length of the pier.

Captain Barthus yelled commands at his men as they gained the deck of the ship. He saw Branick, injured and bleeding where he slumped against the mast, and then looked back toward Corlag.

"Is that the bard down there? What is going on here," he asked?

"Aye, that's him," Branick coughed in reply, "make ready to sail Captain. He won't be long."

"Remove the moorings, ready the anchor," Barthus shouted to the deck hands. He eyed Branick with a confused look.

"Corlag, the captain is here and ready to go," yelled Syndara from the bow. He pulled the artifact from his pack, and was engulfed in a blue-white light as she beckoned for him.

"NO! Corlag, don't let that thing near him," she shouted. She nocked one of the arrows she had retrieved and fired.

Syndara's arrow left a trail of stardust in its wake as it passed through the golden barrier and slammed into Borgolas' chest.

Shocked, Borgolas took a gasping breath, a confused look on his face. He gasped again, then collapsed to one knee, then fell to his back on the ground.

Corlag snapped his attention toward Borgolas, wrapped his right hand around the hilt of his sword; rending it free of the ground with ease. The glow that engulfed him swirled down over the sword, igniting the blade with swirling blue and yellow flames. Still clutching the artifact, he lowered his left hand to his side and jabbed his sword through the golden barrier in front of him, aiming the upturned blade at Borgolas.

"You have not yet learned your lesson old friend, and this bard will be my vessel in your undoing once and for all," Corlag uttered in a voice not his own, "There is no hiding this time. Remember me now, I am Kiran'Thas. We, the watchers of old, have been waiting for your resurgence. Your freedom shall not come to fruition. You escaped death once, as our lord was compassionate with you for your hundreds of years of service, but I shall not be so kind in his wake. He used the last of his energies to banish you to a life without memory of your deeds, in hopes that you would learn anew how to live in this world, and find redemption. Alas it is clear that shall not come to pass. Your thirst for revenge, a vengeance you deem is heralded and earned by your suffering has corrupted your mind. You hunger for power even still, long after you wrought destruction on your own people, killing the one you loved. We became nothing more than Myths and Legends to the history of this world, but we have not dissipated, nor have we forgotten. We are they who linger, beneath the ruins of our own society never to die. Your judgment is at hand."

Lightning arced out from Corlag's sword in a narrow, jagged, interwoven mesh at Borgolas. The energy surrounded Borgolas. He shrieked and wailed and his robes burst into flames.

"Why," he managed between his screams, "you all forsook me because I sought only to enhance all our lives forever!"

Borgolas moaned and flailed around on the ground, trying to wriggle free of his electric bonds.

"Do... Not... think that this is my end. Your banishing me has not made me weak. My powers reside, and return in full even now... I will find another willing body before this one dies... I shall have—-"

"We shall see," replied the voice from within Corlag and thrust the artifact out towards Borgolas, ending the last of his rebuttal before it could be spoken.

The electric bonds wrapped around Borgolas' torso held him in place where he writhed naked and scorched on the ground. The bonds spread out to cover Borgolas' entire body, then flashed and a single bolt of energy shot back toward the relic as if summoned.

"NO! Not again-" cried Borgolas, the last of his words drowned out by the crackling of energy.

"I'm sorry brother, but there's no other way," replied the voice mournfully.

The old man's charred body shook once more and then fell still, the glow dissipated from Corlag, and he slumped to the ground.

They Who Linger

The husk of Borgolas lay burned and smoldering on the cobbles, empty of any signs of life.

Chapter Fifty-Eight

Syndara watched the events unfold, helpless. She saw Corlag crumple to the ground, Borgolas' remains smoldering not far away from him, and yelled to Barthus to hold anchor as she bolted down the gangplank to the pier. She ran down its length and cleared the few steps down to the seawall with a single bound, making her way to his side. She bent down and checked his pulse. To her relief she found one, and tapped him gently on the face with her hand repeatedly.

"Corlag, can you hear me," she asked without response, "c'mon, don't die on us now."

She spotted the artifact grasped in his hand, and retrieved it, returning it to Corlag's pack. She noticed it had a new sheen to it, and the etchings on its surface were glowing faintly blue. After securing the artifact, she grabbed his sword and lifted him up, one arm about her shoulders, and began to drag him toward the ship.

Branick, having seen her bolt off the ship, met her on the pier and threw Corlag's other arm over his own shoulders with a grunt of pain. He limped along, favoring one side of his body as he helped Syndara drag Corlag the rest of the way to the Tabitha.

"Raise anchor," Branick said when they stepped past Barthus and onto the ship.

Barthus nodded and yelled the command to his crew.

Syndara and Branick moved Corlag to some nearby netting and laid him down, then slumped on either side of him, completely exhausted.

"What on earth happened down there," Branick asked Syndara.

"I'm not even sure I know what I saw was real," she replied and rested her head in her hands.

"In the morning perhaps. We need to rest."

"You need a healer"

"Corlag can deal with it when he comes around."

They lay there on the netting, giving in to their exhaustion one by one.

~*~

Barthus looked out across the deck of the Tabitha from the helm, confused as to how he got aboard the ship, with no recollection as to why they were no longer in Barroville. All he knew was that he had a compelling sense of urgency to cross the Everdeep to the port city of Karamd'Var on the eastern coast of Thayrium.

"To Karamd'Var then. I wonder what awaits us on Thayrium this time," he conferred with himself, shivered and looked back toward Barroville, now barely visible.

As he looked back across the water, he was struck with fear at the blurry memories of his rush through the town to his ship. The devastation at the dock, burning buildings and giant plumes of smoke filling the sky above the town. He was sure he had seen the twisted and burned remains of people but couldn't focus the images in his mind enough to tell if the memories were real or imagined.

"What demon has been unleashed that could do such a thing," he gasped? He felt a renewed need to put as much distance between them and Barroville as possible and shouted to his men on the deck. "Unfurl the main sails men, we need more distance at our backs. Get those three to the barracks below deck," he commanded and pointed at the travelers lying in the pile of netting near mid-ship.

The crew acknowledged the captain and set to their tasks. The Tabitha sailed off into the western horizon of the Everdeep.

Chapter Fifty-Nine

Aileesha reached a knoll overlooking the southern end of the lake just before dusk. It angled out into a point, towering above the trees further down the mountain side, the jagged stalactites hanging from the underside of the arch making it look like it used to be part of the inside of a cave. There was a perfect grove of trees recessed from the edge a fair distance, right in the middle of the knoll. She decided it would be the perfect place to shelter and camp for the night. She stepped off the path, moved into the center of the grove and began looking for dry wood. Much of the ground in the grove was free of snow fall, and though chilled, was dry. The last remnants of daylight glowed fiery orange off the eastern peaks across the valley. Before long, she had gathered up the wood and dried brush she needed to start a fire, and pulled the flint from her bag that Owain had given her. The fire started quickly to her relief. She then set about gathering clean snow to melt in the cooking pot, and once it was at a boil, dropped in some frost sage, followed by a few drops of her medicine. She ate some of the dried meat and bread while the tea steeped. Once it was ready, she dipped her cup into the liquid, filling it to the brim, and walked out on the ledge to take in the view while she watched the sun set. Most of the pain that had remained worked its way out while she walked during the day, but she was sure she would have fresh pain to work through in the morning. She leaned on the stick she had made into a crutch and sipped at the tea. It was hard to imagine that such foulness could rear its head in such a beautiful place in the world. The sun finished its descent behind the mountains as she drained the last of the tea in her cup, and returned to the campfire. She added a few more logs, curled up a safe distance away, but close enough for warmth, and made a makeshift pillow out of some leaves and pine needles to rest her hooded head on. She would need an early start if she was to make good progress toward Barroville the next day. The ground cover, coupled with the heat of the fire and shelter of the trees kept the cold at bay nicely, and she dozed off quickly.

Chapter Sixty

A light wind blew through the trees around Aileesha as she began her journey towards the Weeping Falls from the mountain path the next morning. The sun was trying its best to poke through the clouds that had formed overnight, piercing through the dark sky here and there making the valley to the south look like the stars were falling from the heavens. Rays of light lit numerous patches of the forest below the falls. There was little else in the way of activity, save for the odd rabbit hopping across the path to disappear beneath some underbrush out of sight, or a bird flying overhead to perch in a tree and chirp away its warning of an outsider to any that would hear its call.

She passed by a small stream trickling down the side of the mountain towards the lake and stopped to fill a water skin from her pack. She drank some of the cold, crisp mountain water from her cupped hands before continuing on her way. She did not stop again until she had descended to the top of the falls. The sound billowed up through the trees, bouncing off the hillsides all around, drowning out any thoughts other than those of the sheer height and beauty of the falls, and the path leading down the face of the bluff into Fel'Thain Forest. Everything was touched by the misty cloud given off by the falls near the bottom of the path. Small icicles hung from the needles on the tree limbs, and the bit of snow that remained, crunched beneath her feet where she walked. The thin icy layer that had formed cracked and popped beneath her footsteps.

She cleared the tree line as the sun bored a hole in the clouds above, shining down on the peak of the falls and her path ahead. The booming of the falls beat at her chest, and she searched for the beginning of the descent along the top of the bluff to the west of the cascading water. The solid stream broke apart into a torrent of droplets as it fell to a swirling pool below, where the water raged into a funnel at the center of a whirlpool. It drained beneath the surface to trace its way under the forest and out the other side, spewing forth from Thain's Maw. It boomed in the distance, loud enough to be distinguished from the Weeping Falls. The water cascaded into Thain's Reach far below the Upper Fel'Thain Forest, and snaked along the valley out to sea.

She found the path without much delay, and before continuing, surveyed the path that led out of the forest far below to the east. She guesstimated that she would make it as far as that by midday or just before dusk. With that goal set in her mind, she began traversing down the bluff. She took care to watch for ice that clung to the rocks that had formed from the spray given off by the falls.

The first half of the descent was precarious at best, and she had to grasp for a rock or a tree root more than once to keep from losing her footing and slipping over the edge to the rocks below. Her heart sank into her stomach a few times from close calls. She started using her walking stick to crack the ice in spots then kicked it away before continuing. As she got further and further down the path, there was less ice to worry about, and by the time she was two thirds of the way down, the remaining remnants of snow were gone and the ice gave way to dew and muddy patches. She had journeyed out of winter and into the beginnings of spring all in one morning. A smile crossed her face as she picked up her pace, feeling confident that there were no more hidden slick patches to worry about.

The rocky dirt path that traversed the bluff gave way to a mossy, grass covered, worn trail with narrow patches of soil showing from years of semi constant use. Wild flowers, bushes and ferns littered the forest floor. Giant firs and cedars formed the bulk of the trees. Mushrooms grew in shadowy patches here and there, and there seemed to be an abundance of wildlife flitting about on the fringes of her periphery. The trail wound southeast through the forest, towards the road, away from the base of the bluff.

She made it to the road that wound through the forest towards the Cross Roads just after noon she guesstimated, as she couldn't check the sun's location in the sky to verify due to the cloud cover. She stopped long enough to have a bit of food and water, taking the medicine with her meal again. Feeling re-energized, she continued on.

The gloomy sky grew ever darker the nearer to her destination she got and she could sense a storm brewing in the hills. She would need to make shelter from the storm before dark. The old ruins came into view a short while later, so she started gathering tree bows to make a lean-to under the trees near the ruins. She hacked at the low hanging branches with her axe, wound them together with some wild grass, and carried them with her into the ruins. She spotted a copse that would serve as shelter from the coming rain. Soon she had her shelter made and a small crackling fire blazing away under the cover of the largest tree in the copse. The rain started lightly, turning into a torrent by the time she had finished her dinner. The rain beat on the tree bows and leaves of the bushes around her, and she could hear small streams trickling away as the rain continued throughout the night. She managed to keep the fire going near the front of the lean-to, staving off the cold, damp night air. The heat from the fire pit billowed into her shelter and remained trapped there, keeping her dry. The sound of the downpour made her drowsy. Satisfied that her shelter would keep the storm at bay, she soon gave into sleep.

Chapter Sixty-One

Aileesha was startled awake by a thundering boom from down in the valley towards Barroville in the early hours of the morning. At first she thought it was the storm, and then realized that the rain had stopped. The clouds had dissipated, revealing the stars and the moon. It was soon followed by a golden flash of light that lit the sky above the distant town to the southeast.

A horrible feeling knotted in her stomach, and she couldn't shake the thought that Syndara had made it to the town, but was in grave danger. Confident that there was enough moonlight to travel by, she gathered her things, quickly put the fire out and set off south east from the ruins at a hurried pace. She needed to reach Barroville as soon as possible. A nervous tension had gripped the air, silencing all of the critters and animals of the night. She kept checking over her shoulder for any sign of danger, fearing that the shadows themselves would spring to life at any moment to assault her.

She could see the faint flicker of firelight in the distance as she began descending the bluff from the Upper Fel'Thain to the valley below. She knew then that at least part of the town was burning. A dark column of smoke rose steadily against the night, an orange glow illuminating the underside of the growing cloud. Warning bells echoed off the mountains up the valley a little while later, hastening her step.

Aileesha nearly lost her footing halfway down the bluff, giving her pause as she caught herself before going over the edge; rocks crashed and banged off the cliff side. Some of the rocks shattered against the boulders at the bottom, causing her heart to skip a beat. She caught her breath and stared at what could have been her own demise. Then with a little more caution, she continued to race down the path as fast as she safely could in the moonlight. When she reached the bottom of the path and started racing towards the road ahead through the trees, a series of screeches ripped through the night. Immediate recognition dawned on her.

"No no no," she said aloud. Images of the shadowy beasts filled her mind.

She burst from the trees onto the rutted road, quickly gained her bearings, then headed south at a full run. Wildlife scurried in and out of the trees all along the road as she ran, as if running from a forest fire. Another thunderous boom sounded up through the valley and another flash of light lit the sky above Barroville. The trees on either side of the road gave way to farmland as she rounded a bend in the road, the town walls now in sight.

There were people everywhere on the road here, running away from the city gates. Men, women and children, farmers with their livestock, merchants and their carts, all trying to get away from the town as fast as they could. A sea of torches and lanterns flooded out from the village. Shouts and screams echoed over the walls regularly now that she was in earshot, and she noticed that most of the people fleeing had not even paused to change from their night garments. She shouldered her way through the throngs of people as quickly as she could without pushing them out of the way, working against the flow toward the gates. She scanned every face along the way, looking for Syndara in the crowd. There were no guards to be seen to keep things orderly. The air was thick with acrid smoke and she could see the flicker of light from many fires within the walls now. An elderly merchant grabbed her arm and spoke to her as if she was mad.

"Are you crazy, lass? Turn about, save yourself. The shadows are alive and lightning strikes from the bare heavens. Barroville burns for unknown transgressions," he cried out at her, shook her arm and gestured northward, urging her to heed his warning.

"I do not doubt you, good sir, but I must find my friend. She may be in there," she replied pointing at the town, "I won't leave her in harm's way like this. If she's in there, I must help."

The man looked at her blankly and did not respond. He knew there was nothing left to say, bowed his head, and then began running away from the village again himself.

Aileesha pushed through the final clumps of people and into the town. Chaos was everywhere. Fire had spread to at least a third of the buildings within the city walls, guards and citizens worked frantically bucket chaining water to buildings not yet aflame, attempting to stop the spread of the blaze. She inquired about Syndara to anyone not involved in the attempt to hold back the fire, to no avail. Another guard rushed out of an alleyway not far from her, and caught her eye as he was rushing onto the street.

"Miss, you can't stay in the street if'n yer not aiding the bucket lines. Are you from Barroville? Do you have somewhere you can go," asked the guard?

"No sir, I just arrived, and am looking for a friend that may have been staying at one of the inns," she replied.

"Describe her to me, mayhap I've seen her pass by," he said, mustering as much patients as he could, but clearly eager to get back to dealing with the fire.

Aileesha described Syndara and the guard pondered for a moment and rubbed his chin, anxiously looking at the burning buildings down the street; his brow furrowed.

"Come to think of it, yes I do believe I saw a woman fitting that description, two days ago, entering the town with two others," he answered finally.

"Two others," asked Aileesha with some surprise?

"Aye, two men. One was a bard, and the other I would assume, was a retired warrior by the looks of him. I seem to recall the captain inquired after the bard at the Hog's Head due to an incident he had witnessed yesterday in the market."

"Thank you so much," she said hurriedly, "I must find her quickly. Where can I find the Hog's Head?"

"It's that large building against the east wall with a giant hole in its upper level and burning to cinders," replied the guard as he frowned and pointed at the fully engulfed building down the street past the town square.

"Oh no," she gasped and started forward.

The guard placed an arm in front of her, barring the way, and his other hand on her shoulder.

"You can't go there, miss. Not until we fight back the blaze."

"But I have to find her, she's like family. I—"

"We'll do what we can to aid you, but not now."

"Do you at least know if anyone got out of the building?"

"Aye. As far as I know, it was evacuated before the fire spread to it. That would be the owner of the Hog's Head at the front of the bucket chain. I'll bring him to see you once we get things under control. Wait outside the gates until then."

She thanked the guard, turned back toward the gates, and seeing there was nothing more she could do in her current state, retreated through the city gates to wait.

Dawn had arrived by the time she had found a place to sit and wait away from the retreating crowd of citizens and travelers. She picked at the grass anxiously, tearing each blade into tiny pieces. She wished she could help, but she knew nothing about fighting fires, nor would her injuries allow it, and so she prayed for her friend's safety.

Chapter Sixty-Two

A soot covered woman flopped down next to Aileesha as she picked the petals from a wildflower. Her garments were so covered in ash that their original brown tones were barely noticeable and she reeked of smoke. The woman began to weep and shake uncontrollably. Tears carved trenches in the ash that covered her skin as they streamed down her face.

Not knowing what to say, Aileesha stood and moved away, leaving the woman to her silent sorrow. Thick columns of smoke still rose from beyond the interior of the walls and she assumed that the woman had come from fighting the fires. A few guards had returned to their posts at the gates, so Aileesha decided to inquire about the state of things inside the walls. They blocked the road in front of the gates as she approached. One of the guards warded her off with an outstretched hand and she came to a halt a few feet away.

"No admittance at this time Miss, we are fighting a fire," he said.

"Aye, I've been informed. I was curious how it's going in there," she asked?

"Not too good. We've managed to stop the advance of the flames, but we lost nearly half the buildings to the blaze."

"And the Harbor," she inquired, "Did the ships burn?"

"There was only one ship at port that survived that I am aware of, and word of its departure came from the dock master himself. It seems most of the trouble took place there."

"What trouble?"

"I've said enough as is. It's under investigation. All I can say is, there were some attacks and the fires were no accident."

"Where can I find this Harbormaster?"

"I have no idea, last anyone saw, he was running towards the gates heading east out of town, scared to death. I would check towards Old Strandton, especially if you're looking for a boat. The docks burned in the blaze, and as I said, the only ship that made it out of port left before dawn, during the commotion."

"Thank you kindly," she replied and excused herself.

There was no doubt in her mind that Syndara was either on the boat or she had fled east. She could feel it in her gut. She needed to find the dock master and find out what he knew about the boat that had left, and whether he had seen Syndara. Wasting no time, she headed east, skirting around the city wall through some trees that formed a large thicket. She was halfway between the north and east gates when she spotted movement out of the corner of her left eye. She looked through the trees but saw nothing. The rustling of dried leaves on the ground made her aware that there was something or someone in that direction for sure, so she cautiously advanced towards the sound to make sure it wasn't a person in need of aid. Axe in hand, she rounded the trunk of a giant pine, and pulled back in astonishment as she saw one of the shadowy creatures dragging the charred body of a man by the arm through the shade of the underbrush. It wrinkled its dark lips, revealing black, razor like fangs, but uttered no sound. She slowly backed away, tensed and ready to defend herself if she had to. The creature watched her recede into the trees until she was far enough away that she posed no threat, and then resumed dragging the body away from the town. She thought she heard it whimper once or twice as she watched it disappear into the trees.

Once it was out of sight, she doubled her speed through the trees toward the east road leading away from Barroville, all the while puzzling over why it had not attacked her immediately, and why it was dragging the man's body away from the town. It did not appear to be feeding on the body, but rather guarding it protectively. The scenario reminded her of a dog trying to protect or save its master.

As she cleared the trees, and neared the east road, she passed by another farm. A young man was working the field, periodically looking up to stare at the smoke billowing up from Barroville. A number of horses roamed the field grazing. Hope rose in her as she thought about buying a horse from the lad. She climbed over the fence and approached him.

"Excuse me," she started, "Might I inquire about purchasing a horse? I am passing through to Old Strandton, and am in need of quicker travel than what my feet can provide."

The young man spun about, startled. He had not heard her approach.

"Where did you come from," he asked surprised?

"Sorry, I did not mean to startle you. I came from the west gate. I am trying to find a friend that may have passed through, and need to travel south east to Old Strandton as quickly as I can. Are you able to part with one of your horses?"

"You'll have to speak with my father," replied the young man as he relaxed, "But he's helping fight the fires in town."

"I see," she sighed, "Are you sure you can't just sell one? I'll pay a fair price. Time is of the utmost importance."

The lad thought about it for a moment, glanced at the smoke plume again, then leaned on the shovel he had been using to dig out a rock.

"My father will be right furious with me if I sell one of them for too little. We'll need to replace the horse before summer harvest."

"Name your price then," she replied and thought about the small amount of coins in the pouch on her belt.

He thought about the value of the horses for a moment before offering his price.

"Two gold coins."

She was wary to part with half the gold she had to her name, but knew that it would leave her with enough for any supplies she may need for a while, and she may be able to resell the horse when she reached Old Strandton.

"That's a lot for a horse lad, are you sure that's your price," she countered?

He hesitated, fidgeting with his hands and looking at his feet.

"Fine then, one gold and five silver bits, and that's my final offer."

"How about one gold piece even? You know that's more than you could make in a month," she replied, pushing her luck as she reached into the pouch at her belt with two fingers and pulled out the gold coin; holding it up for the lad to see.

He reached for it hungrily, nodding his agreement, a toothy grin growing from ear to ear. She set the coin in his right palm and waited for him to pocket it.

"Deal. We have no saddles though."

"No need, but I get to pick the horse."

"Any of them but Applesauce there," he said, pointing out a sandy brown stallion grazing near the far end of the field. "That's pa's favorite."

She inspected the five horses that remained to choose from, taking note of their muscled bodies, and checking for unsoundness and blemishes of their feet and legs. A white and brown speckled mare nuzzled up to her as she approached. She extended her hand in front of its nose, and once the mare had sniffed and nuzzled her palm, she rubbed its neck and spoke softly to her. Once Aileesha had determined that the horse had accepted her, she turned to the lad and offered her hand to seal the deal.

"I'll take this one," she said. "Does she have a name?"

"Aye, her name is Clover. That's her favorite thing to eat," replied the young man.

"She's gorgeous. How old is she?"

"About three I think."

"Thank you very much for your help," said Aileesha. She rubbed Clover's side, then hoisted herself up onto her back.

"Thank you Miss," the boy replied bowing slightly. "Safe travels. Take good care of her."

"I shall, and a good day to you."

The lad opened a gate leading out of the field and closed it when she passed.

With that she guided Clover down the road toward Old Strandton.

Chapter Sixty-Three

There was something noticeably different about Maddi. It had been three days since she had started taking the tincture that Zev had made for her, and her energy levels were definitely up, but she had dark bags under her eyes, like she hadn't slept in days.

When he asked her about it, Maddi said she had been sleeping great. Better, in fact, than she ever had. Festus was unsure what to make of this. She hadn't been in any fights with the other stewards, and she was sharper than ever with her lessons. They had covered a large portion of the first volume of the Fourth Age over the last three days.

He made a note of it to check with Zev, and if it got any worse he would have to consider taking Maddi along with him.

~*~

The next day, things were definitely worse. Elania had come to find Festus early in the morning, waking him from a deep sleep, which he lamented as he rolled out from under his covers. He had been dreaming about his time spent with the adventurers that he had chronicled at the end of the Fourth Age. He missed those times dearly.

When he opened the door to his room, Elania pushed past him all in a flutter of animated worry.

"She's got something wrong with her Fes. I don't know what to do. She's chalk full of energy, but she's got darkness in her veins near her eyes, going in all directions, and the whites of her eyes are-" she paused as if truly noticing for the first time that he was in his night robe. "Oh dear, forgive me for waking you. I just, I don't know what to do. She's not acting sick, but I can't have her tending things looking like she's touched by plague."

Festus put a hand on one of Elania's shoulders. "It's quite alright Ela. Let me get dressed quickly and then we can go have a look."

As soon as he had changed they were off down the Residence halls to Maddi's room in the Stewards wing.

~*~

It was as Elania said. The whites of Maddi's eyes had a dark hue to them and the blood vessels around her eyes were dark under the skin. They made her look like she had wiped charcoal around her eyes and drawn a spider web pattern in all directions.

At first glance, Festus gasped. He had rushed over and cupped her chin in his hands, tilting her head to first one side and then the other, inspecting her face. Not wanting to worry her, he did his best to keep the worry from his face and his voice. She had no fever, wasn't sick to her stomach, had no cough or any other symptom of an illness other than what they could see around her eyes. He was at a complete loss as to what could possibly be wrong.

"Hmm, we shall have to make a journey to see Zev today," said Festus.

"Zev the Crazy," blurted Maddi? She was full of excitement. "I've heard so much about him. Does he really have a cat made of wicker?"

"He does, and his name is Wick. Speaking of which, don't ask or joke about his cat when we are there."

"Why can't I ask about Wick?"

"Well," Festus was at a loss for words, "because he doesn't know it isn't a real cat. He's quite sensitive about the subject. Actually, it's best that you don't ask any questions really. He's a very private person and doesn't much like company. He won't be expecting us. It was supposed to be a month, at least, before I visited again."

"Oh. How come?"

"Dear child," Elania said exasperatedly. "Enough questions. Get ready to leave, would you please?" Elania directed her toward her clothes chest with one hand while turning to dismiss Festus with the other. "Meet us in the kitchen shortly, you can take her out the back."

Festus agreed and left to collect a few books from the Library for Zev. He would surely need a great assortment in trade for his old friend's time.

~*~

It was overcast and wet on their walk along the path through the woods. Rain dribbled off the hoods of their cloaks, falling from the hardened brims around the edges in small, steady streams. It wasn't a quick walk by any means, as the path was slick with rain and mud. What rocks there were to stabilize the soil, merely became tripping hazards. More than once they both had almost landed in a puddle of mud and leaves.

"Do we have to go today Mr. Festus," Maddi had asked shortly after they were into the trees from the Library.

"Yes Maddi, we definitely need to go today. It's just a bit of rain. It may take a bit longer, but the day is young," Festus replied. And it had. Despite it being late spring, it was cold and miserable out. It took them all morning just to make it to Maerin and the rain had only gotten worse. Festus didn't want to risk worrying the villagers with Maddi's appearance, so they skirted around the village towards Zev's place.

They could see smoke billowing from the chimney when they crested the hill and rang the bell. Zev appeared in the window and then quickly at the door.

"What the blazing depths are you doing here in this weather. Are you trying to catch a chill?" shouted Zev before the door even finished opening.

"Zev, sorry to visit again so soon, but I need your help figuring out what is wrong with Maddi here," replied Festus. He waved his right hand, opened, palm up, towards Maddi in a way of introduction.

"If she's ill I don't want to catch nothin'."

"She doesn't appear to be ill, at least not with anything I'm knowledgeable on. No cough, no malady that I know. Maddi, can you lower your hood for Zev please," asked Festus?

Maddi did as she was asked.

Zev gasped and quickly waved his arms, beckoning them both to come inside. "Oh. That's different. Come, come. Get inside out of the rain and let's see what we're dealing with."

Festus suspected that Zev already had an idea of what could be wrong, but said nothing.

Once inside, Zev focused wholly on Maddi, seeming to forget Festus was even present. Zev directed Maddi to his work table, grabbed a log of wood big enough for her use as a seat and bade her sit there, where his hanging candelabra could illuminate her face.

Zev tilted her head from side to side, lifted her chin toward the ceiling, and there he held her chin in his right hand while he prodded around her eyes lightly with his left index finger. At first he merely muttered under his breath and nodded to himself, but the more he inspected Maddi's ailment, the further his brow creased in concern. At last, he recoiled his left hand and squealed, as if he had just held it to a flame.

Zev made a holy sign across his chest and whispered an oath of protection under his breath while cradling his left hand with his right.

Festus jumped when this occurred.

"Zev, what is it?"

"This child-" Zev halted, eyes blazing, mouth agape and just stared at Maddi.

"Zev," Festus called to his friend and snapped his fingers in front of him to break his gaze!

Zev blinked rapidly and turned his gaze to Festus before continuing his previous sentence. "She's no child at all Fes, she's-" He choked on the last words.

"What? What are you saying, Zev," Festus asked urgently? He placed his hands on Zev's shoulders and forced him to focus his attention on him instead of Maddi.

Zev recoiled away from both of them, further into the light of his candles.

Maddi began to weep, cupping her face in her hands.

Festus moved to console her.

Zev shrieked anew and reached out toward Festus. "Fes, DON'T. Don't touch her."

Festus was becoming outraged at this point. "Zev, I love you like a brother, but sort yourself and explain. You are disturbing the child beyond measure, and in turn my patience is waning."

"SHE'S A SHADOW VESSEL," shouted Zev!

Festus' hands fell to his side without him really thinking about it and a confused look spread across his face as he stared blankly at Zev, speechless.

"How..." Festus couldn't finish his question. A lump had formed in his throat and a pain filled his chest. His mind reeled to comprehend what Zev had just said. How hadn't he noticed?

Maddi's weeping turned to soft laughter, with a tinge of gurgling. Her hair dangled in front of her face, and her hands fell to her sides, shaking slightly.

Festus, backed away slowly, watching her slide backwards off the upturned log to stand with her head bowed still, and her shoulders slumped in front of her.

"Maddi... how did this happen," asked Festus, more to Zev than Maddi?

Maddi merely continued backing away from the candlelight towards the shadows that clung to the back wall of the little log cabin. Her shoulders rose and fell slightly now, in rhythm with her shaking hands and low laughter.

"Stay in the light Fes," said Zev. He had stepped around the edge of the table into the center of the lit room, minimizing his shadow.

Festus followed his que, moving to stand next to him.

Zev scooped up a rather solid looking glass rod from his work table and brandished it in front of himself.

"I'll not ask you more than once, fiend, what are your intentions with the child?" Commanded Festus.

Maddi lunged backwards the remainder of the distance, into the shadow along the wall, and a whispered reply seemed to come from everywhere in the room at once. "She is to me as dust to the end of this age."

Zev and Festus looked at each other questioningly, then Festus turned his attention back in Maddi's direction.

"Does Maddi remain, or-" he choked momentarily, "Or has she passed?"

Zev chuckled unexpectedly. "You and all your books and you know nothing of the world. This is why I don't bother with the Order."

"What do you mean," asked Festus?

"A Shadow Vessel is merely the husk of a person, fully controlled by a Shadow Spirit. It inhabits the body and puppets the being towards its own goals."

Festus felt weak in the knees, his eyes grew moist. "Oh dear child..."

"Weep not for the lost. They yet serve a purpose," whispered Maddi.

Festus didn't know what else to refer to her as, so the name stuck in his mind despite the revelation. All at once, a burning rage filled him and he burst forth with his verbal inquisition.

"What are your intentions, *fiend*?"

"Consumption."

"Of what, or should I ask, of whom?"

"Knowledge."

"Explain!"

"I will devour all knowledge, written, and unwritten within the realms of men, beginning with the historical ledgers, manuscripts, books and scrolls of the Great Library."

Festus balled his hands into fists.

Zev took a step toward the shadowy wall, his glass rod held out like a rapier. "Who gave you these instructions?"

"Shem."

"Skyfather above," gasped Zev!

Festus made a holy sign across his chest and forehead in reaction to the name.

"Shem is defeated, locked away millennia ago," replied Festus reflexively.

"Are you so sure," Maddi asked in a gravelly voice. The creak of wood being stressed followed.

"He returns," asked Zev?

"Wait, why is it responding so freely Zev," asked Festus, suddenly aware of just how easily they had been able to acquire information from the Shadow Vessel?

"I-" Zev shrugged, "honestly don't know."

Just then, the wall where Maddi had slithered into the shadows exploded outward, the cracking and splintering of wood deafened them. An unnatural gust of wind accompanied it, like an invisible wall of energy, and they were thrown across the room, landing against the opposite wall where they slumped to the floor in a heap.

Ears ringing something fierce, Festus slowly got to his feet, brushing debris from his robe. He glanced at where the back wall of Zev's home had been. It was nothing but a giant, jagged hole leading out into the clearing behind the cabin. Everything beyond it in the direction of the clearing had been flattened to the ground. Maddi was gone.

Zev coughed and cursed behind him.

Festus turned to help Zev, and jumped in surprise as a giant black cat whisked its tail back and forth, standing protectively between him and Zev. It growled low, its eyes an orange glow, and a name tag jingled from a collar. Wick's collar. Realization forced him to look to where the wicker cat had been, and sure enough, it was no longer in its place. Festus, having had quite enough adventure for one day, slumped to the floor and the light faded to darkness as he fainted.

They Who Linger

"Well, that's not quite how I hoped you two would meet," said Zev offhandedly, scratching behind Wick's left ear as he fumbled to his feet, "What a day."

Chapter Sixty-Four

The Shadow Spirit pumped Maddi's little legs as fast as it dared, gathering shadows to her body as they sprinted back through the forest and up the path to the Library. Time was limited and it had a task to complete. It couldn't fail its master, he would never allow this failure to pass without the severest of consequences. He would be ripped from his host, torn apart, and erased from existence.

It was rare to find a host so young, with an unguarded mind. He was lucky and he knew it, but inhabiting such a host was not without risk. A young host, even with an unguarded mind, would fight against possession like no other. Older hosts tended to give up more easily, seeming to accept their lot in life as doomed. The young however, were ever hopeful, dreamers of a better tomorrow, and they clung to that hope with a vice like grip.

Even luckier still was the fact that his host was to become a Steward at the very Library he was tasked with consuming. What luck indeed.

Ixxith thought the task was going so well, until that meddling Chronicler interfered. And that crazy old Alchemist with the Changeling! Bad luck that.

It was a risk to use his powers the way he did with such a young host, and it almost drained her completely. Drawing off the shadows in the forest was helping, but he needed to hurry, before the Chronicler and his friend could warn the Library. The minds of the historians and the archives containing any information about his kind needed to be erased by any means possible now. He could no longer devour them one by one, slowly over time as they slept or studied.

Ixxith had taken a great risk by allowing his host to pursue her studies with the Chronicler, but it was a risk worth taking, as it turned out the Chronicler was quite involved with the very subject matter to which he was tasked with erasing from existence for his master.

The rain had not let up since their arrival at the Alchemist's shack, and Ixxith had to use the shadows to keep Maddi from slipping and falling on her face more than once by solidifying tendrils of darkness to prop her up when she stumbled over a root or a jutting stone in the path. He could feel her mind reeling, attempting to make sense of what was happening to her, wrestling for control. This made the risk to her young body that much greater. There was nothing she could do while he had shadows to draw upon however. Faster and faster he pushed her little legs. He just had to keep feeding off the shadows a little longer. Soon it would be dusk and he would have all the energy he needed to finish his task.

Chapter Sixty-Five

Festus came too with a stinging pain across his left
cheek from where Zev had slapped. His mind reeled,
struggling to come to grips with what had just occurred.
All his travels, all the things he had seen and recorded
seemed to fall flat in his memory. It wasn't that he never
believed the stories he had listened to and copied to the
pages of his greatest works, but to see it in the flesh was
something entirely different. 'In the flesh' didn't seem to be
the right term for it even. So lost in his own thoughts was
Festus that he didn't really hear Zev's frantic explanation
of what had just happened and that Wick was in fact real.

The memories of the stories Festus had chronicled so
many years ago flooded into the front of his mind as Zev
went on yelling about his home being in shambles and that
they needed to do something about the situation. There
was no doubt. Maddi was a Shadow Touched, inhabited by
a dark spirit that was clearly at the Library for a purpose.

"What could a Shadow Touched possibly want from a
library?" Festus thought aloud, absent minded to the fact
that Zev was trying to get his attention.

Festus didn't hear Zev's questions or see his wild
gestures as he stood staring at the blown out wall. A

sudden thought caused Festus's mouth to drop open, his eyes to bulge wide, and his skin to crawl.

"It must want to consume the Archives!" Blurted Festus with sudden realization.

"What," asked Zev, in mid hand waving at the chunks of wood strewn about the room?

"It's after the Archives," Festus repeated. He turned to look at Zev and seeing the man standing on one foot, left hand outstretched and beard dangling caused him to do a double take. "What are you doing?"

Zev closed his mouth and straightened up. "Clearly not getting your attention. What are you on about?"

"We have to stop it, Zev. It's after the Archives for some reason. It's the only thing that makes sense. We'll rally the guards on the way through town."

"Stop what? Who, us? You're making no sense," replied Zev, waving his hands agitatedly. "How do WE stop THAT?" Zev pointed at the giant hole in the back wall of his home. "And they think I'm the crazy one around here."

Festus didn't respond or bother to explain at that time. He stepped toward the door, but before he could open it, Wick pounced in front of him and shook his head. Festus just looked at the cat, confused.

Wick sat and looked at Zev.

Festus also looked at Zev.

"Can you deal with this please? I have to go." Said Festus with urgency in his voice.

"I can do no such thing, Wick does what Wick wants. End of story. Just go that way," replied Zev, pointing at the hole at the back of his home.

Festus shrugged and made to leave through the hole.

Wick padded ahead of him, flicking his tail and sniffing the air. With a glance back at Zev, Wick jumped through the hole.

They Who Linger

"Well that settles that I guess," said Zev, slapping his hands against his thighs, "Wick says we're coming with you."

Chapter Sixty-Six

Wick led the way back to Maerin, seeming to follow Maddi's scent like a tracking hound. When they reached the village, Wick disappeared into the trees continuing toward the Library while Festus and Zev roused the guards.

Festus bellowed for help at the top of his lungs as they quickly walked into the center of the market square. Dusk was fast upon them, and torches approached, held high by half a dozen guards dressed in yellow and blue heraldry with the markings of the local Baron, a serpent headed stag. Their armor jingled as they ran toward the call, shields in hand. One of the soldiers had a fancier helmet than the rest, crested with a yellow plume. He stepped ahead of the rest as they arrived and called out to Festus.

"Fes, what is the meaning of this?" Inquired Captain Sparnik.

"Captain Sparnik, there is trouble at the Library. Come, there's little time to explain. We must make with all haste and I'll explain what I can along the way."

Without hesitation the Captain nodded to his men and he led the way to the path that would take them up the hill to the Library.

Festus explained what he could, all the bits that would make sense at least. Simply put, he told the Captain that a steward meant harm to the Library's Historians and Archives and that he feared for the safety of everyone and everything inside the library.

Captain Sparnik alerted his men to the potential threat and warned them to be on their guard. They were instructed to protect the citizens of the Library and to avoid harm to the Steward if possible.

Festus pondered all he had learned over the years about the tales of old, searching his memory for any hint of instruction on how to deal with a Shadow Touched, but he could not recall any such knowledge. This would be a challenge indeed.

Chapter Sixty-Seven

Ixxith burst through another study chamber door, using Maddi's young demeanor to strike panic into the heart and mind of the Scholar going about his studies inside.

"Dear child what is the matter," stammered the man with a look of concern and surprise as he moved toward Maddi, "It's alright, tell me how I can-"

Ixxith called forth the shadows to wrap themselves around the man's neck and head, and began to search for any trace of knowledge regarding his kind and the past histories that he may have studied or chronicled that could reveal any weakness the Shadow Touched may have.

The man twitched, his voice muffled. He gasped for air that would not come. Ixxith sighed in frustration, having found nothing of note, released the now limp body and turned to probe the room for books and scrolls of note as the body thumped to the floor behind them.

With unnatural speed, Ixxith repeated this process until he was satisfied that the Study Halls were scoured, and then moved on to the Archives. Scroll after scroll, book after book turned to blank parchment as he consumed the written knowledge contained in them. Organized rows of shelves became a strewn mess on the floor. Unconscious

Scholars and Lore Keepers littered the floor all through the Archives.

Ixxith harnessed the shadows to vault Maddi's little body over shelves onto unsuspecting victims and sprinted with unearthly speed toward walls and jumping off of them to land suddenly around a corner in the fleeing path of a terrified Lore Keeper who was attempting to flee into a dark corridor. None of their victims had time to scream or alert others of the danger.

Despite the aid of the shadows, it didn't seem to be fast enough. Ixxith still hadn't found what he was meant to erase above all else, the record of his master, the war that came before this age and how they had imprisoned the Shadow Touched away from the world of men.

Ixxith had found many other potentially threatening bits scribed within the consumed pages, but without that most important piece removed from existence, it would be in vain.

The sound of armored feet reverberated up the stone steps at the front of the Library, echoing off the cold, dark walls, alerting Ixxith to the approach of the Chronicler and no doubt some guards from Maerin. He let out a bestial growl in frustration, gathered a solid cloak of shadows about Maddi's body and whisked them into the shadows of a corner above the archive row he had been devouring.

There was nothing left to do but torch the place and retreat into the night to make his way to his master and report what he had discovered and destroyed.

A guardsman, trailed by the Chronicler and his Alchemist friend, led the way into the darkened interior where Ixxith had extinguished all of the wall and rafter mounted lanterns. There was no sign of the Changeling, but Ixxith was sure it was not far. It was the Changeling he feared most. He had no idea what its abilities were, but he knew that his kind feared them for good reason.

Slowly, Ixxith used the shadows to crawl into the rafters, and used the shadows to make his way towards the back of the Archives where Maddi's memory provided that there was an exit out the back of the Study Halls into the Kitchen and then outside where he could vault them over the stone wall around the cloistered garden and into the night.

Ixxith had managed to guide Maddi's small frame most of the way across the archives, balancing on the rafters in the darkness, when a low hiss and glinting yellow eyes alerted him to the Changeling's presence ahead of them on the rafter beam they were traversing. He felt the shelter of the shadows being drawn away from Maddi as the Changeling advanced, one paw in front of the other along the beam towards them.

Without the shadow melding, Maddi would be revealed to the searching torch light from below, and Ixxith would not be able to keep her from injury if she fell.

It was frustrating to know that his powers could easily lay waste to the entire place and everyone within it, but not be able to use that power because his host was too weak to survive it. The act would be suicide.

Before the Changeling could strip away the full shadow meld, Ixxith made a snap decision to jump from the rafters to the the top of one of the archive shelves, then leapt along them the rest of the way. As soon as Maddi's weight hit the first shelf, shouts alerted each other of the noise and the torch light rushed in their direction. He had to escape now or risk Maddi being taken.

"I know what you are!" Called out the Chronicler, not far behind them now.

Ixxith paused momentarily, listening for any sound ahead. He couldn't see the Changeling, but he could sense that it had gotten in front of them again. There was no other way out but past it. Foot falls grew louder and came faster, the torch light illuminating the walls quickly as the guardsmen approached. Ixxith heard a few of them draw their swords. The shadow meld once again began to weaken, and he saw the piercing yellow eyes approaching from the darkened hallway leading to the Study Halls.

A guard rounded the corner of the last row of shelves behind them. As soon as the guard saw them he shouted "HERE!"

Ixxith lashed out with a shadowy tendril at the guard's hand that held a torch aloft, knocking it into the shelving behind him. The dry parchment of scrolls and books ignited almost immediately. The guard shrieked and lunged to tamp out the flames before they could spread. Two more guards rounded the corner and rushed forward with their shields raised as a fourth came in behind them illuminating the way with his torch held high.

Ixxith gathered the remaining energy from the shadow meld at Maddi's feet and pushed up and backward, thrusting them down the hall in a burst of speed and flight, over the stalking Changeling, and with just enough distance to be able to draw on the shadows once more to soften their landing before turning to run as fast as Ixxith could force Maddi's legs to move.

The Changeling lunged after them, growling menacingly. Its ability to drain Ixxith's powers from Maddi threatened to end their escape. In a desperate act, Ixxith drew as much from the darkness as he could without exhausting Maddi and threw them at the stone wall to his right. The stones cracked and exploded outward. Before Maddi's feet could touch the ground, Ixxith flung a shadow tendril out to grasp the top of the courtyard wall and flung them over its top, far into the trees beyond.

The Changeling roared in the distance, but Ixxith could no longer sense it closing in on them. Free of the Changeling's draining presence, Ixxith drew more easily on the shadows. There was no time for rest right now, they needed distance between those he knew would pursue them. It was time to make the journey across the sea to meet his master and deliver his collected knowledge which he had consumed from the Archive records and the minds of the Scholars.

Chapter Sixty-Eight

Festus helped another of the Lore Keepers to her feet and guided her to her living quarters to lay down. It would take months to reorganize the Library's Archives and determine all that had been lost to the Shadow Spirit inhabiting Maddi.

What books and scrolls lay open on the floor of the stacks were blank, as if ink had never stained their parchment. The Scholars and Lore Keepers Festus and Zev had helped could not recall any of their studies of the past, and a genuine air of panic was setting in amongst the staff. Few had escaped the surprise attack of the Shadow Spirit, save the young Stewards and the Kitchen staff.

It was evident that the only thing the Shadow Spirit was after, was the collected knowledge they had gathered of the past. There must be something dangerous within the records, and Festus felt that whatever it was, the Shadow Spirit had not found it. His mind was reeling, trying to recall all of the things he may have learned about Shadow Touched and their kind over the years, but his head was full of fog with everything that had transpired in the past few weeks. He needed a good rest and some help from Zev to clear his mind.

Wick had not shown himself since he had left Festus and Zev to gather the town guardsmen, but Festus knew he had been after the Shadow Touched. He heard the growls and hisses of the Changeling sure as he was standing on his own two feet. He supposed it made sense that Wick would be cautious of the guardsmen, after all, most people thought Changelings only existed in stories.

Festus felt like his world had turned upside down and inside out at the same time. He couldn't help wondering what other tales were true. So many myths, legends and folklore tales erupted in his mind, begging to be investigated for their merits.

After what seemed like hours, the Library staff were all in their rooms and being tended to, worst cases first, and the lanterns had all been replaced and lit. The guardsmen, led by Captain Sparnik, were doing what they could to patch up the hole in the stone wall to keep the cold out until a mason could be sourced for proper repairs. A patrol had been sent into the woods beyond the Library in search of a trail or an sign of the the Shadow Touched, although they did not know what it was they were searching for other than a little girl, as Festus had kept the truth of the situation to the barest of explanations until he could sort out how to explain things properly to Captain Sparnik.

Zev had retreated to the kitchen and was jovially conversing with Elania and shoving the remnants of a sandwich into his face. Ela had been distraught at the sight of Maddi rampaging through the library, but luckily, she had not been spotted, and had hidden in the kitchen until Festus and a guardsman had found her huddled behind some vegetable crates. After much convincing that the threat was past, Festus managed to get Ela to come out from her hiding place. Zev remained with her while Festus had gone to aid the guardsmen with his fellow Scholars.

"We're done with the immediate needs, Fes, but we'll remain here until the morning. I'll post a permanent guard post and patrol on the Library grounds once I get back to the Barracks in town tomorrow," said Captain Sparnik, approaching Festus from the hall with the hole in its wall, "Anything to eat around here for me and my men?"

"I'm sure we can get something together. And a warm drink too. It's a cold night out there," replied Festus and turned to enter the kitchen, Sparnik right behind him. "Ela, can we fix some food and warm drinks for the good Captain and his men?"

"Certainly," replied Elania with a small curtsy, "I'll round up some of the stewards and get to it straight away. Thank you for your help, good sir." She added with a smile in Sparnik's direction, then excused herself.

"The pleasure of duty is ours." Said Sparnik with a bow.

"Zev, can you join me in my study for a chat please?" asked Festus.

Zev gave a roll of his shoulders and wrinkled his nose while he looked around the kitchen, as though he hadn't heard the question. Just before Festus was about to repeat himself, Zev shouted gleefully, lunged forward and scooped up an apple, turned to Festus and said "Lead the way!"

Sparnik had already headed back to his men when they turned to leave the kitchen. Zev and Festus passed the few guardsmen still working on patching the hole in the hallway wall as best they could with mud and spare wooden planks from the woodshop, Festus leading the way with his lantern held out to the side. He lit the extinguished lanterns in their sconces along the way once more. It was eerie in the dark halls and he wished to see things returned to a sense of normalcy before he departed for what he must do. This was the topic of conversation he needed to cover with Zev, and he wasn't sure his old friend would join him.

"Is it always so dark in here?" asked Zev as Festus lit another lantern.

"No, in fact, this is probably the first time the lanterns have been extinguished in all the years I've been with the Library." Replied Festus.

"Could just have some windows put in to cut down on the oil costs during the day." Stated Zev.

Festus chuckled. "I suppose you're right, Zev. Best not to bring that up with anyone else right now though, what with the looming cost of an exterior wall repair to the stone work and all."

"What about my wall?"

"Right, that. We'll get that taken care of as well. I'll leave instructions with Captain Sparnik to speak with the carpenter in town."

Zev paused and looked flabbergasted.

"What?" asked Festus.

"You mean the Library will pay for it?"

"Aye, it seems only fair, what with Maddi being trained as a steward here and all. I feel responsible for it all. I should have seen it sooner, I should have recalled the writings-"

"Nonsense! There's thousands of years of history archived here Fes. You could no more blame yourself than I could. Poor Maddi. There's got to be a way we can help her."

"Actually, that's what I want to talk to you about," said Festus. He turned and continued a short distance before stopping in front of the door to his study and fished out his key. He opened the door, and to his surprise the lanterns were already lit. He ushered Zev inside, had a last look down the hall and ducked inside and closed the door.

"Why the cloak and dagger?" asked Zev.

"Well, you see, I don't think there are many that would understand my leaving in the dead of night after events like this have transpired, but that is exactly what I mean to do. I need to. I have to find Maddi, and I think I can find a way to release the Shadow Spirit from her without hurting her."

Zev sat in the chair Maddi had been using for her studies and wrung his hands together, "And you want Wick and I to join you," he stated.

Festus sat in his own chair and nodded.

A long silence drew out between them, Zev itched his chin and looked at Festus.

"ABSOLUTELY!" Zev shouted suddenly.

Festus jumped in his seat in surprise at the outburst.

"Really? I honestly didn't think you would leave your-"

"And just why not?"

"Well, you ARE known to be a hermit Zev."

"Hey, we hermits like to have adventures as well, besides, Wick would be upset if I turned down an opportunity like this. He's had cabin fever like you wouldn't believe lately. Just a few weeks ago, I woke to all of my ingredients shuffled about in the wrong place on my shelves, and Wick sitting mischievously in my chair. He's that bored with the quiet life."

Festus blinked and laughed at Zev's description of the Changeling's mood.

"Well then, I think it best that we leave tonight. Can Wick track Maddi do you think?"

"Certainly."

Festus sighed with relief. "Alright then, let me gather my things and we'll stop by your place on the way."

They Who Linger

Zev pounced out of his chair and gleefully danced about. "A proper adventure we shall have, even if it is coddiwomple!"

Festus rolled his eyes and began gathering his things.

Chapter Sixty-Nine

"I can't believe I didn't check the books when Maddi brought them back. The Shadow Spirit was devouring the contents for weeks, right under my nose." Fumed Festus. They had left word with Captain Sparnik to conscript the carpenter in Maerin to repair Zev's wall while they were away, and gave him permission to oversee the stonemason work for the Library. He was not certain how long they would be gone.

"You couldn't have known to suspect anything amiss Fes. At least your personal archives are intact." Replied Zev while fumbling about his shelves for various ingredients which he stuffed into his pack.

Wick paced about the room, swishing his tail back and forth.

"Yes, I suppose so. I think the volume on the Shadow Fall and the wars will come in handy."

"Wick, grab your ball. I don't know where you hid it. We may not be back for a while." Zev gestured about his rubble strewn home.

Wick meowed deeply and bounded off outside through the hole in the wall.

"Figures he hid it outside. Sneaky bugger!" said Zev with a grin.

Wick returned quickly, a medium sized ball of red yarn gingerly gripped between his jaws.

"Good boy!" said Zev and scratched behind Wick's right ear.

The Changeling purred loudly and dropped the ball of yarn into Zev's pack which was at his feet.

"All set," Said Zev, turning to Festus who was waiting patiently near the door.

"Are you sure? No coming back once we leave Zev," replied Festus.

Zev looked around and nodded. "Sure as I can be."

Wick padded over to the hearth and nose bunted an ornately carved walking stick with his snout.

"Oh! Right. Thanks Wick. That would not have done, to forget my staff." Zev thanked the Changeling and retrieved the staff, "NOW I'm ready."

Festus rolled his eyes, opened the door and stepped outside.

Wick ran through the hole at the back of the room and sprinted around the front and on up the path to the road.

Zev looked at each exit available and laughed, then followed Festus out the door.

~*~

Wick sniffed the air and padded about on the road, searching for Maddi's scent. Festus and Zev sat on a large tree root that jutted above the soil on the north side of the wide dirt path, catching their breath. They had traveled through the night and into the morning, trying to catch the trail of the Shadow Touched child.

"Did you ever think you would be out on the road again Fes," asked Zev curiously? He looked about, taking in the serenity of the morning dew glistening on the sunlit vegetation.

"Honestly? No. I thought my most exciting days were behind me, but something about this has me rethinking that entirely." Replied Festus. He rolled his shoulders and arched his back to stretch out his aching muscles.

"Why's that?"

"I mean, why is a Shadow Touched appearing now? What is so important about the past that a Shadow Spirit risked inhabiting a young child to devour our history, if it didn't pertain to something of critical importance to keep us from realizing?"

"A fair point. Any thoughts as to what that might be?"

"I think, based on some of the volumes that were consumed, that not only does it fear something pertaining to the chronicles of the Shadow Fall, but the imprisonment that took place after the war that followed."

"You think there's something written about how it was done? I mean, assuming you believe it to be real even."

"I have no reason to believe otherwise at this point. After all, we just bore witness to the existence of a Shadow Touched."

"Another fair point. Should we be keeping a tally or something?"

Festus chuckled. "It's not a game Zev, just answering your questions."

"Where do you think it's headed?" asked Zev with a smirk.

"Well, if the tales are indeed true, the imprisonment was said to have taken place across the sea, in a lost land known as the Kingdom of O'Marah."

"O'Marah? Wait, you mean the land of giants and demi-gods and such from the myths of the Old World?"

"One and the same, yes. Only, I don't think it's as mythical as it was chronicled to be. I think there's a lost history that maybe the events we just witnessed could explain. I mean, if the written word is as threatening in its current version as tall tales, what's to say Shadow Touched wouldn't have done worse in the past to eradicate anything that threatened the return of their kind to our world?"

"You think that is what this is all about?"

"I don't know that I believe it fully yet, but yes, I do think that it's possible."

"End of the world as we know it type stuff. Oh, is that all? Sounds simple enough." Said Zev sarcastically with raised eyebrows. He leaned forward, his hands on his staff, and raised himself to his feet from the root. "Well then, we best get a move on. Wick!"

The Changeling bounded out of a patch of tall grass nearby and lazily ran over to Zev's side and rubbed against his leg, purring audibly. The Changeling stood facing into the trees to the north west after Zev gave him a chin scratch and whispered into his ear.

"He's got the scent. Shall we?" asked Zev, reaching down to scratch the side of Wick's neck.

Festus stood and stretched again and then waved for Wick to lead the way.

The Changeling licked its snout and sprinted off down the path, his movements more like a dog than a giant cat. Festus and Zev walked side by side after him.

"He really is a marvelous beast Zev." Said Festus.

"Shh, don't let him hear you call him a beast, you may end up missing a shoe while you sleep. He's a bit sensitive about improper monikers."

"Oh, sorry. You'll have to educate me in the ways of conversing with him."

"All in good time. If you're lucky, maybe Wick will explain it all himself."

"He can do that? Communicate I mean?" asked Festus.

"Don't be daft, of course he can. I mean, he doesn't speak like us, but you'll hear thoughts that are not your own. It can make you a little crazy at first if you don't know what it is." Replied Zev with a look of amusement over at Festus.

"That explains a lot actually," Festus laughed then added, "I mean the whole crazy label the towns folk gave you."

"Tish-posh! What do they know!" blurted Zev through a large toothy grin.

Up ahead, Wick stopped and turned to look back at them before he darted off the road into the trees to the north. There was a trail leading through the underbrush, clearly traveled regularly by wildlife.

"I guess this is where we see if we've still got that young energy hiding deep in our bones." Said Festus.

"You should get yourself a trusty walking stick like me." Replied Zev, thumping it against the ground twice. Before Festus could retort, Zev ducked a branch and started off into the woods after Wick.

Festus could have sworn he saw the deep, knotted veins of the ornate carving of the staff glow a faint blue momentarily. He shook his head and rolled his eyes at Zev's back again and followed him into the trees.

Chapter Seventy

They crested a hill in the middle of what looked like an old lumber clearing a few hours later. The sun was high in the western sky, and the clouds had dissipated earlier in the day. The warmth of the sun was welcome. From the hilltop, they could see down into a calmly sloping valley that led out toward the farmlands which Festus knew to be part of the eastern plains that spread out for over a hundred miles near Strandton.

"The Shadow Spirit must be leading Maddi to Stranton." Said Festus as soon as he recognized the farmlands. "I guess that makes sense if the stories are true. It will probably try to find passage on a boat across the Everdeep."

"I don't like boats." Spat Zev.

"What about Wick?"

"Oddly enough, he loves the water, but he probably won't like having to be a decorative furnishing in a confined space. I'll have to stock up on some dried meat for him."

"Fair enough, I don't like being cooped up either." Sympathized Festus.

They paused long enough to have a drink from their water skins and a quick snack from their rations and then continued on down the hill toward the farmlands.

Wick had hunted down a large rabbit down near the bottom of the hill and had devoured it by the time they reached him. Zev cupped his hand and whistled for Wick to come and lap up some water from it, pouring slowly from his water skin. Wick purred and licked his lips clean after he was sated, then bunted Zev with his nose and bounded off playfully, sniffing out Maddi's scent once more.

"I swear he should take the form of a dog Zev." Said Festus with amusement in his voice.

"Wick does what Wick wants." Replied Zev, while reaching into his bag and retrieving Wick's red ball of yarn and threw it towards the Changeling.

Wick pretended not to see the yarn bouncing off ahead of him, feigning intense focus on sniffing the path and looking all about. Zev took a breath to ask if the Changeling had lost the scent, but laughed instead as Wick chose that exact moment to pounce the distance between himself and the ball of yarn and rolled across the ground biting and pawing at it.

The stump strewn hillside gave way to long grassy meadows a short while later, and soon after that, fenced pastures and a dirt cart path with a healthy swath of green running down the middle of the two wheel ruts cut into the hardened soil.

They followed the path for the remainder of the day, past dozens of farmsteads, before coming upon a small village with a small four bedroom inn and tavern. Wick disappeared into the countryside before they entered the village, and Zev assured Festus he would be alright and that he would find them once they were back on the road in the morning.

Festus paid for a room with two beds and a meal for each of them. There wasn't a single other traveler in the establishment, and nothing to do once they had finished their dinner, so they turned in early.

The next morning was just as quiet. A quick breakfast and they were off again. Wick found them a short while after they had left the outskirts of the village, plodding out of the long grass of a field onto the road in front of them like he had been following them all along.

"Catch," called Zev and threw a whole dried trout in Wick's direction. The Changeling casually turned his head back toward them and caught the fish in his teeth effortlessly without skipping a step.

They journeyed on in much the same fashion for a few more days before coming to a fork in the road that led to Strandton. The large city's wall loomed in the distance, about a quarter day's journey, and traffic was picking up on the road. Wick became scarce. Shortly before approaching the gate to the city, Zev steered them behind a farmer's barn where Wick met them. Wick looked at Zev with slightly flattened ears, licking his lips and flicking his tail back and forth.

"I know, boy. It's just until we get a room and figure out where the Shadow Touched is. Has the scent diminished?"

Wick shook his head back and forth in answer and pawed the dirt.

"Inside the city?" asked Zev.

Wick meowed once, short and high, sounding a lot like *yeah*.

"Good. I hope so. Alright boy, do your thing." Said Zev, comforting the Changeling with chin and neck scratches.

Wick raised a paw over Zev's wrists and slowly licked his hand, and in an instant turned back into the wicker cat statue Festus was used to seeing in Zev's window, or next to the door, or in his chair.

Festus blinked a few times rapidly, hardly believing his own vision at how quickly Wick had changed form. He was awestruck.

"Fascinating!" gasped Festus.

The statue emitted a soft growl in protest and Zev lifted it into his arms, cradling it like a newborn babe.

"It's alright boy, we'll be quick." Consoled Zev. He turned his head to Festus, "Alright, let's go."

They returned to the road leading to the city gate, and soon were inside the city, asking a guard for directions to a decent Inn.

The guard pointed them down the main street, instructing them on where they could find a good deal on a clean room toward the harbor. Newer buildings gave way to old as they got closer to the harbor, and the old city wall that used to serve as the defense of the old city marked the border between Strandton and Old Strandton. Most travelers avoided the old parts of the city, its dirty, run down buildings carried an ominous feeling that attracted undesirables and more disreputable sorts.

After locating the Inn and deciding it was acceptable, Festus left Zev and Wick in the room and made his way down to the harbor to find a dock master to speak with about boats that would be sailing to Thayrium. By the end of the afternoon he had sourced out a ship Captain of a large trading vessel, the only one that was bound for Thayrium within the next few weeks, and had paid for a small passenger room. They would be ready to set sail in three days' time.

Festus thanked the Captain for his time and turned to walk back to the Inn. He bumped into a young woman with long hair, fair features, and northern clothing. He bowed low and apologized, stepping aside to let her pass, spotting an axe hanging from a hoop on her belt as she assured him it was alright and stepped over to the Captain and greeted him.

Festus couldn't help but overhear the beginning of their conversation as he once again set out for the Inn. The woman was also seeking transportation. This reassured him that indeed this would be the ship Maddi would be on if at all. They wouldn't know until departure day.

Chapter Seventy-One

Maddi found herself in the middle of a city she had never seen before without any recollection of how she had gotten there, just blurry images in her mind of running through a forest, in the dark, at unnatural speed. She knew bad things had happened, and that somehow she was responsible for them happening, but she knew she would never do the things she remembered doing. The thought of harming one of the Scholars in the Library made her sick to her stomach, doubling over with dry heaves. She couldn't recall how long it had been since she ate, or even how long it had been since she was at the Alchemist's home. That was where her memory blurred.

An overwhelming sense of dread urged her on. She stumbled down side streets, feeling like a criminal that needed to hide, but had no idea why. Thoughts of boats and a harbor kept replaying in her mind, and before she realized it, she found herself walking dockside in a busy harbor, lanterns flickering on posts all along the waterfront.

A small shack with a few people standing in line awaiting their turn to speak with someone sat at the counter, wooden window shutters ajar, was three quarters of the way up the dockside. Something forced her to walk up and join that line. All of the other people waiting were rugged looking, wore musty, patchy clothing, and stunk of fish. Maddi felt entirely out of place, but she couldn't step out of line, no matter how much she felt like it.

One by one the men in front of her completed whatever their business entailed, and suddenly she was standing before a middle aged man with a well trimmed beard and a smoking pipe dangling from between his lips. He tilted his head down, looking over the brim of his nose at her, reached up with one hand and cupped the pipe in his palm. Two long puffs later, he asked her in a deep scratchy voice through a rolling cloud of smoke, "Are you lost little one?"

Maddi stared back at the man, her voice failing to escape her throat and tears welled up in her eyes. Suddenly she burst into a fit of uncontrollable sobbing. Her emotions got the better of her. Try as she might, she couldn't stop herself. Exhausted, she sat down on the cool wooden planks and cupped her face in her hands.

The man in the booth sighed and stood from his stool. He held his pipe in his left hand and stepped out of the booth to console the child.

"There now, it's alright child. Where are your parents," asked the man?

A voice that sounded like hers, but was not her own answered the man through sobs, "I- I don't know. They- We, we were supposed to-" Maddi sniffled and sobbed momentarily again, "We were supposed to travel by boat together. They left without ME!" she shouted the last of the words and broke down entirely.

The man placed his right hand on her shoulder. "I'm so sorry my dear. That's horrible. Where were they-" he caught himself, "you headed?"

"Th- Tha- Thayrium," she stammered, fighting to control her shaking as she wept!

"By the merciful gods," stammered the man with a look of anger on his face. "How long ago was this little one?"

"Two or three days ago I think- maybe?"

"Heavens above, I wasn't here that day. I'm so sorry this happened, little one. I remember the boat and I know it had passengers. I'm sorry this happened little one."

"I was hoping, maybe, somehow I could find them."

The man stood and scratched his beard, puffed on his pipe, and then cleared his throat. "I'll see what I can do, child. There is a ship leaving port in a few days bound for Thayrium. I will speak with the Captain and see what we can do."

Maddi's sobbing ceased abruptly and she sprung to her feet, smiling from ear to ear, her face alight with hope. "Really? You mean it sir?"

The man cupped his left elbow in the palm of his right hand while he puffed away on the pipe held in his left hand.

"Certainly, little one," he said around the stem of the pipe.

"Oh thank you mister," said Maddi excitedly and threw her arms around the man in an attempt to give him a hug! Her arms barely made it around his ribs.

The man chuckled and patted her head. "Aye, come now. Let's take you to see the Captain and get you cleaned up. Have you eaten today?"

Maddi shook her head no and wiped dribbling snot from her upper lip onto the back of her hand which she then wiped on her leg.

"Come, let's get you some food," said the man. He turned and closed the door to his booth, put a key in the lock and turned it. He then did the same to the wooden shutters, then offered his hand to her clean hand, which she took, and they walked down the dock toward the warm glow of a tavern not far up one of the streets.

~*~

Ixxith was pleased with the outcome of his use of Maddi to pull at the heartstrings of the Harbormaster on the docks and the ship captain at the tavern. The Captain had fallen for the sad tale of a daughter left behind just as easily as the dock master had, and not only had he felt sorry for the girl, he offered to take her under his own care for the duration of the trip to Thayrium, and he vowed to see that she found her parents once they had arrived. They would be severely reprimanded by the authorities he had assured her, and they would return her to their loving embrace.

When they had eaten their fill and the two men had conversed a little more over a drink, the Captain led Maddi back to the ship and set up an extra hammock in his own room on his ship. He had one of his deck hands hang a curtain from some hooks that were fastened to the wooden beams around her hammock area for privacy as well.

This was more luck than Ixxith could have hoped for. He would be able to hear anything the Captain spoke about regarding ship passengers or warnings of searches. He would figure out how to slip away once the ship reached the port in Karamd'Var on Thayrium.

Chapter Seventy-Two

The Fair Tides set sail a few days later with four extra passengers and a full cargo hold and crew of thirty seven men and women, including the ship's Captain. The sun was high, the sky blue, and the waters calm with a westerly breeze that filled the sails. It was a perfect day to begin an ocean journey.

They Who Linger

End of Book One of The Everlight Saga

They Who Linger

Acknowledgements

No book gets completed without some help and support from others. There is certainly no shortage of people that I owe endless gratitude and thanks to while completing this novel. I dare not try to name them all for fear of unintentionally leaving someone out.

With that said, there are a few people that I DO need to mention here. Without their encouragement, I would have fallen prey to self doubt long ago.

My parents. Your support and example of how to live a good life over the years have been invaluable to me. Thank you for allowing me to keep dreaming (even if it didn't always make sense) and to make my own mistakes. I love you both with all my heart.

Jaime, my firefly, my wife. You have the kindest heart and provide me with endless support, especially when I am at my lowest. You are my light and my heart.

Marcus, never stop writing. You have endless talent inside of you, and you amaze me everyday with your creativity and appetite for adventure. Write until it is done, young word slayer.

My brother, Jason, this is the first of hopefully many books that will need awesome covers. It was a process, but worth it.

Mr. Keith Chambers, thank you for always encouraging me to write more and to embrace my creative gifts. I feel I would not be where I am now in my creative life without your early encouragement. You scribbled a little note on one of my short story assignments once that said 'Just keep writing, don't stop.' I took it to heart.

Mr. Cameron Bastedo, thank you for letting me run free with my creative writing in highschool and not punishing me when I failed to focus on all the grammar stuff. You led by example with your own fantasy novel writing. I always appreciated your ability to teach with humor and kindness.

And to you, dear readers, I humbly thank you for deeming this bundle of paper and spilled ink worth your time. Without you, this would be much less fulfilling. I hope, even if only for a moment, this world provides you with an escape from the real world.

Ever onward!

Robert W Ling is a Game Designer by trade with a focus on Narrative and Quality Assurance. He has worked in the video games and software/tech industries for over a decade and a half, on more than two dozen projects.

By night, he flings words and spills ink in the hopes that his own worlds will reach voracious readers across the globe.

They Who Linger is his first self published book, but he has many more in the pipeline.

To learn more about his work and new upcoming releases, visit his author page at robertlingauthor.wordpress.com

They Who Linger

Extras

Turn the page for a sneak peak at what comes next in Book Two of the Everlight Saga.

They Who Linger

In The Shadows

Book Two: The Everlight Saga

By Robert W Ling

They Who Linger

Chapter One

Corlag woke to the booming sound of thunder and lightning flashing across the sky. It took him a moment to gain his bearings and remember where he was. The rain was already blanketing the deck of the ship making it slippery underfoot.

Voices yelling back and forth, the squeak of pulleys as sails were reeled in and the clomping of boots on the deck all made his head pound.

He grasped his head in his hands and gritted his teeth, forcing his eyes shut as he tried to clear the fog from his head. His ears were ringing and every muscle in his body felt like they were on fire.

A very muffled voice to his right brought him back to the present.

"-storm is bad. Corlag, COR! Branick I think he's gone deaf or something can you-"

"He's fine- from the battle- he'll recover soon just-"

"-cover, out of the storm-"

"Bloody hells, would you two stop already? My head is ringing worse than the warning bells on War Watch."

"Cor, you alright brother," asked Branick?

Corlag simply nodded in response then pushed himself off the pile of rigging rope he had been sleeping on. That might explain some of the aching muscles he thought when he realized what it was.

The ship captain was in full command mode, pointing and shouting at every crew member in sight. His gaze fell upon the three travelers on his deck and he quickly made his way to them, gripping the railing of the stairs as he descended from the helm and crossed the deck. The ship began swaying and dipping heavily as the waves became increasingly more violent and the winds matched them.

The look on the captain's face said everything they needed to know before he even spoke, but he pointed toward the entrance to the passenger deck and in not so kind wording asked them to find a place to be other than in the middle of his crew deck.

With one hand still against his head, Corlag flashed him a thumbs up with the other and waved his friends toward the door indicated.

They almost lost their footing a few times crossing the sea drenched planks, but managed to keep upright. A few crew members that had been off shift burst through the door as they approached and bowled past them in a practiced manner that only a proper Seadog could in such rough waters.

Something in the back of Corlag's mind was telling him that the storm wasn't natural. The way the clouds were swirling, more than rumbling, and the sharp claps of thunder with bright blue lightning streaking down to kiss the ocean's surface.

They had made it halfway down the narrow wooden staircase before it dawned on him what was wrong with the storm. The wind was circling with the clouds and the water felt like it was periodically trying to suck the ship down beneath the waves forcefully. A smaller vessel would have already been pulled under. The Tabitha's size had been their saving grace thus far.

"Ship Eater," said Corlag, pausing mid-step, "It has to be."

Branick and Syndara bumped into each other as they came to an abrupt halt on the stairs.

"Come again," asked Branick? A troubled look crossed his face as he waited to hear Corlag repeat his sentence.

Corlag turned to face him on the stairs and started ushering them back up quickly without response, the serious look on his face response enough.

Branick drew his sword as he turned back up the stairs and waved Syndara up to the deck.

Syndara, not quite sure what was happening but seeing the serious shift in tone rushed back up and out into the storm. Seeing Branick brandish his sword, she followed suit with her axes.

"What is it," asked Syndara looking around the deck.

"Pretty sure he said something about a Ship Eater," replied Branick.

Syndara's face flushed of color and her eyes grew wide. While she had never spent time at sea before, she had heard enough tales in her lifetime to know that a Ship Eater encounter was never joked about.

Corlag brushed past them and made his way across the water slick deck as quickly as he could toward Captain Barthus, shouting to get his attention. The captain was all but oblivious, engrossed in spurring his crew to task against the gale that battered against his ship.

Upon reaching the captain, Corlag gripped him by the shoulders and spun him to look him dead in the eyes and shouted through gritted teeth, "It's a damn Ship Eater, not a stormfront!"

The blood drained from the captain's face, his jaw falling open. Even as he started glancing to his right at the guard rail of the ship's starboard side, the water beneath the ship began to dip aggressively.

"Ship Eater," yelled Barthus! He melted out of Corlag's grip and bolted toward the Captain's Cabin. For what, Corlag could only assume, was probably a weapon bigger than the steel sword on his belt.

Ignoring that unknown, Corlag gripped the nearest object to keep from sliding with the ship's lilting and shouted to Branick and Syndara to find a place to secure themselves. A few of the crew in the masts overhead, caught unaware due to the noise of the storm overhead, lost their footing and fell screaming into the thrashing waters, one cracked against the starboard railing awkwardly and went silent on his descent.

The crew of the Tabitha became organized chaos. Men and women running for battle stations and securing themselves to whatever they could.

Lightning lit the sky, thunder boomed and a deep, gurgling roar deafened everyone as the ship suddenly fell into a chasm of water, teeth, and tentacles. The walls of the Ship Eater's gaping maw lit up blue-green, energy crackling from tooth to tooth all around them.

The fear and horror was palpable on the air, men and women screaming and looking on in disbelief.

Branick, planted his feet firmly against the wall leading to the stairwell that led below deck and the base of the guard rail, gripped his sword in front of him, bowed his head, muttered something then turned his head to the sky and bellowed with all his might. A shock wave of sound washed over the crew of the ship, their hearts and minds steadying.

They Who Linger

Corlag brought a song to his lips to follow the calming battle cry, tendrils of blue and yellow encompassing him and his blade, the musical notes of the song coming to life and reaching out to the crew and enveloping them all in turn. He ended the song once each crew member was aglow and quickly began another, aiming free hand toward Syndara. This song emitted an orange hue and formed itself into the shape of an arrow, then another, and another until there was a full quiver worth of them. The arrows quickly drifted across the open space between them and filled Syndara's mostly empty quiver. The orange hue spread from the quiver to her arms and bow.

"Shoot the soft part of its mouth," shouted Corlag.

Syndara, axes in hand, was examining her now glowing arms in awe. She almost didn't hear Corlag's words in time, but connected the dots when she looked to him to ensure that what she was seeing and feeling was real. She sheathed her axes and drew her bow, nocked a glowing arrow and took aim.

Syndara had never felt so sure of herself or her aim as she did in that moment. Her vision felt sharper than it had ever been and she could see the veins throbbing beneath the wet flesh of the Ship Eater's mouth.

Syndara let the arrow loose and nocked another, aimed at a new spot of soft tissue, loosed and repeated until the quiver was empty. What seemed like minutes was less than a few seconds, giving the monster of the deep no time to react before the glowing projectiles had hit their mark in a half circle around its gigantic mouth.

Corlag knew there was a fifty-fifty chance this would work but also knew there would be no other option before the creature could swallow the Tabitha and her denizens whole.

The arrows erupted in a chain reaction of explosions and bright, searing white light all at once, which caused the Ship Eater to shudder violently. The water in its throat dipped further, forcing stomachs into throats and a feeling of weightlessness to wash over them all as the ship lilted further toward the creature's gaping maw.

The Ship Eater flailed its tentacles against the ship in a furious flurry. Smashing rigging and sections of railing. Some wrapped around crew members and ripped them into the darkness or simply squeezed them into pulp before whipping off toward another target.

Everything happened seemingly at once. Screams, death, defiance.

Then, just when it seemed Corlag's plan had failed, the Ship Eater let out a gurgling roar and the water rose quicker than it had descended, forcing the ship up into the air off the surface of the sea.

Everyone scrambled for something to hold fast to as the ship slammed back down toward a now closing mouth full of jagged mountains made of teeth.

The gravity shift pushed everyone on board to the deck, those still caught in the netting of the masts gripping on for dear life.

Corlag had not noticed Barthus' return to the deck, but spotted him then, held fast to the Captain's Wheel, holding one hand aloft. What he saw in Barthus' grip gave understanding to his mad dash for his cabin. There in his hand was a dwarven mining charge.

Barthus had already lit the fuse before the ship had been thrust into the air, and with all the strength he could muster, he flung the charge out towards the middle of the Ship Eater's maw.

They Who Linger

There was no time to shout for cover, nor was there any way for the crew to react as the Tabitha crashed back against the water.

A deep *whumph* sounded a moment later, a small sun visible beneath the water, lighting the Ship Eater's mouth in full to the horror of all that got a glimpse.

The explosion sent a geyser filled with giant shards of teeth, flesh and brine into the sky and over the ship.

More screams as bits of tooth acted like shrapnel, slicing through whatever was in their path.

The Ship Eater let out a deafening moan of pain and screeched as it recoiled back down into the depths, its tentacles retracting beneath the surface.

As the moaning seeped into the depths below and away from the Tabitha, the tumultuous waters began to calm.

It took a long moment for the surviving crew to begin moving again. Slowly, it became clear that the immediate threat was over. It was time to assess the damage and losses.

~*~

It had been days since the encounter with the Ship Eater and they were no closer to seeing an end to their stalemate with the sea. The waters were like glass, not a cloud in the sky and not even a whisper of wind in the air.

The ship was afloat at least, broken as it was.

Dead winds, water like glass and a battered ship that was barely held together by patch-work was the least of the problems Corlag and his friends faced.

A ship with no sails, dwindling supplies and nightmares from the deep fresh in the minds of the survivors made for a dangerous combination while being stuck at sea. Most pressing of all, there was only two days worth of drinkable water remaining in the barrels and not a storm cloud in sight. Fish they could maybe catch, but water, there was nothing they could do about that problem short of a miracle.

A bit of irony, considering what the crew and ship had just been through.

If they did not spot land soon, the crew would start to lose what little sanity they had left and probably begin a chaos spiral into madness as they fought their weakening minds and bodies while trying to survive.

~*~

Two days passed with dwindling hope and crew. A few had suffered life threatening wounds during the Ship Eater's attack against the Tabitha and had not fared well in the aftermath.

Most unfortunate of all, the most knowledgeable ship crew member in medicine and healing had fallen overboard during the attack and was swept beneath the ocean and into the maw of the beast as the Ship Eater had tried to swallow the Tabitha and her crew. The rest of the crew did what they could, but without proper supplies to treat infection or to keep the wounds clean, it had been a losing battle day by day.

This only added to the gloomy mood among the remaining crew.

Syndara sat on an empty barrel near the nose of the ship, looking out across the still calm waters, hopeful to spot anything that would provide some hope. Hours passed with nothing but the slow slosh of lazy undulations against the hull of the ship. She sighed heavily, swiveled on her perch and stood to walk back to mid-ship and the company of her friends.

It was then that the first sign of hope appeared.

A flapping sound overhead, followed by a piercing call as a gull landed on the end of a broken part of one of the ship's sails and fluttered its wings.

The gull was soon followed by more. A whole flock of them. Zipping about overhead looking for anything they could grab from the semi successful morning fishing endeavors of the deck crew.

A few of the birds landed on the deck near the ship's starboard rail and began fighting over remnants of entrails from the few fish that had been caught and gutted before being taken below to the kitchen crew.

Syndara couldn't help but let out a hearty laugh. She jogged the rest of the way to mid-ship, and shouted "Land birds on deck."

Corlag and Branick looked her way from their quiet conversation and up to the gulls overhead with grins on their faces.

Within moments, the deck was a flurry of activity. Captain Barthus was barking orders to his crew, ordering them to find anything and everything that could be used as an ore and commanding the port holes cleared for rowing crew below deck. A plan quickly formed.

Once the gulls began their return flight to land, the Tabitha and her crew would follow.

They Who Linger

They Who Linger

They Who Linger